HIDING FROM
THE PAST

PRAISE FOR *THE GODS HELP THOSE*
BY ALBERT A. BELL, JR.

The Gods Help Those: A Seventh Case from the Notebooks of Pliny the Younger by college history professor and author Albert Bell is a deftly scripted historical mystery that is certain to be an immediate and enduringly popular addition to community library mystery and suspense collections. An intriguing case set in ancient Rome, this historical mystery is fast-paced and hard to put down."

—*Midwest Book Review*

"The mystery of who and why unfolds very well. I enjoyed the walks through Rome's streets and the palpable religious tension bubbling under the surface. Pliny and Tacitus are an enjoyable team to lead readers through the case. The author has a good mix of characters representing the various classes of Roman society. ...[A] good mystery with enjoyable setting details."

—*Historical Novels Review*

"At one level, this novel is an entertaining mystery with all the misdirection, intriguing characters, and bracing plot for which a reader could wish. At a deeper level, it is a meditation on the nature of power—of conquerors over the conquered, of owners over slaves, of men over women, of parents over children. The intertwined threads of the story create an easy-to-swallow, bitter pill. The novel should leave a careful reader still thinking about the nature of the Roman Empire and its society long after the covers are closed."

—KG Whitehurst

MYSTERIES BY ALBERT A. BELL, JR.

HIDING FROM THE PAST

AN EIGHTH CASE FROM THE NOTEBOOKS OF PLINY THE YOUNGER

ALBERT A. BELL, JR.

[MMXX]

PERSEVERANCE PRESS · JOHN DANIEL & COMPANY

PALO ALTO / MCKINLEYVILLE, CALIFORNIA

A Perseverance Press Book
Published by John Daniel & Company
A division of Daniel & Daniel, Publishers, Inc.
Post Office Box 2790
McKinleyville, California 95519
www.danielpublishing.com/perseverance

Distributed by SCB Distributors (800) 729-6423

Book design: Eric Larson, Studio E Books, Santa Barbara
www.studio-e-books.com

Cover painting: "Hiding from the Past" © by Chi Meredith
Egg tempera on panel
www.sites.google.com/site/meredithchiartist

10 9 8 7 6 5 4 3 2 1

LIBRARY OF CONGRESS CATALOGING-IN-PUBLICATION DATA
Names: Bell, Albert A., Jr., [date] author.
Title: Hiding from the past : an eighth case from the notebooks of
Pliny the younger / by Albert A. Bell, Jr..
Description: McKinleyville, California : John Daniel & Company, [2020] |
Series: Pliny the younger ; 8
Identifiers: LCCN 2019029463 | ISBN 9781564746108 (paperback)
Subjects: LCSH: Murder—Investigation—Fiction. | GSAFD: Mystery fiction.
Classification: LCC PS3552.E485 H53 2020 | DDC 813/.54—dc23
LC record available at https://lccn.loc.gov/2019029463

AUTHOR'S NOTE

THIS BOOK has been more of a challenge than others in this series because it contains several flashbacks. Writing those sections hasn't been the challenge as much as deciding how to distinguish them from the sections that take place at the narrative date of the book. I already use italics to set off sections written from Aurora's point of view. I didn't want to use another font for the flashbacks—and my editor wouldn't want me to. I finally decided to accept the suggestion of my writers' group and put (A.D. 77) at the head of the flashbacks and (A.D. 87) at the head of the sections that take place in the narrative date. I find that a bit jarring, because it would have meant nothing to Pliny, but they said it made things much clearer for them. Having been in the group since 2001, I've learned to respect their collective judgment on most things. I have put those dates at any place where I felt there was a possibility of confusion about when a section is set. My editor, of course, has had the final say. If a section doesn't have a date at the beginning, it takes place in A.D. 87.

Another option, I guess, would have been to give the dates in the Roman fashion, either A.U.C. (*Ab Urbe Condita*, from the founding of the city; 753 B.C. was the legendary date) or in terms of regnal dates of the emperors. But A.D. 77 was in the reign of Vespasian, while A.D. 87 was in Domitian's reign. Figuring out all of that would be like dating things today in "the eighth year of Franklin Roosevelt" and "the third year of Dwight Eisenhower." Perhaps readers can visualize the book as a movie, with a fade-in to the flashbacks, perhaps even a change to black-and-white.

While this hasn't been an easy book to write, I've enjoyed seeing Pliny the Elder and Monica, Aurora's mother, as living characters

7

instead of memories and Pliny and Aurora as teenagers still uncertain about their relationship. On the other hand, I've missed Pliny's mother, her servant and friend Naomi, and other characters in Pliny's household who have populated the earlier books. If the series continues, they will return.

I say "if" because I am getting on in years and I have several other projects on my bucket list. One of those projects I accomplished when my cozy mystery, *Death by Armoire*, won the Genre Fiction category in the 2018 *Writer's Digest* contest for self-published books. My wife wants me to retire, but I don't want to. I like having a schedule and some discipline in my life.

As far as the Pliny series goes, I also face a dilemma in that after H comes I, but in Latin I and J are used interchangeably before vowels. Julius Caesar was just as easily Iulius Caesar. Given the alphabetical sequence that I have established for the titles, what would I do for a next book? Would it be *I, Julia*? (Hmm, I actually sort of like that possibility.) And then what about K? Aside from Kalends, the K section of a Latin dictionary is non-existent.

For the meanings of unfamiliar Latin words, please see the Glossary at the end of this book. It also contains the modern names of the cities that Pliny's party visits on their travels. For information about me or any of my books, go to my website: www.albertbell.wixsite.com/writer.

HIDING FROM
THE PAST

PROLOGUE

[*A.D. 77, JULY*]

WHO'S THERE?" Junius peered into the darkness of his mill in the little Alpine town of Collis Niveosus, trying to see by the flickering light of a small oil lamp. "Snowy Hill" was anything but what its name suggested at the moment. The summer had been unusually hot and dry. At least melting snow from higher up in the mountains had watered fields when rain had been scarce. Junius and his two workers—his son-in-law and a slave—would soon be grinding that grain.

"I know you're in here," he said. "And I know what you're after." He hung the lamp from the lamp tree just inside the door. "You'll never find it, you know."

A hand shot out of the darkness and clamped around Junius' throat. "Then maybe I'll have to beat it out of you," a voice snarled.

Junius' head slammed into the stone wall. His face contorted in fright.

"What do you have to say now?"

Junius could only groan as his head hit the wall again.

"Just tell me where it is and I'll stop."

Junius said nothing and his head hit the wall again.

"Last chance."

Junius said nothing. His head slammed into the wall one more time. The hand released its grasp as he slumped to the floor, leaving a bloody streak down the wall.

I

GAIUS, WHY ARE YOU doing this?" my mother pleaded as my servants and I mounted our horses outside the walls of my villa on Lake Comum. I had come up here to supervise the final stages of the work we began last summer to add some much-needed space to the house. I'm planning to move some servants here from my other estates in hopes of making this one more productive. A cold, snowy winter had prevented the workmen from making as much progress as I had hoped. March was now offering a chilly start to spring, but the work needed to be finished.

I gathered the reins of my horse. "I'm doing it because Tacitus is my friend. He would do as much or more for me."

"But all the way to Lugdunum? The trip there and back will take you...months."

"Probably two, so we'd better get going."

"But there are rumors of bands of Gauls coming out of the mountains and raiding in our territory. The winter was hard up there, I hear, and they're desperate." Mother grabbed the reins of my horse and wouldn't let go. She has always been small and frail, but today her grip was firm, drawing strength from desperation. "Gaius, please. Anything could happen to you. You could be attacked and killed on the road. I might never know about it. And I would never see you again."

"Domitian could have me arrested tomorrow, Mother, and you would never see me again. Anything can happen at any time, whether

I'm here or somewhere else. We can't just sit idle and hope nothing ever happens to us."

"Tacitus' message didn't ask you to do anything, Gaius. He was just telling you that his poor brother is ill and he's going to Gaul to see about him."

"He didn't have to *ask* me to do anything. This is what friends do." She stumbled as I jerked the reins away from her harder than I intended and turned my horse to look over my travel party. Her slave and confidante, Naomi, helped her regain her balance.

I was taking four of my male freedmen—not slaves because freedmen, unlike slaves, can legally carry weapons—and two extra horses to carry some supplies. Tacitus' servant who had brought the message, a man named Charinus, would also ride with us. With the help of my stablemaster, Barbatus, I had picked out the strongest horses I owned. I needed animals that were capable of speed but also had stamina.

This might be a fool's errand, I knew. I had a general sense of where Tacitus would be traveling, but the chances of crossing his path were remote. I only knew I had to get started if I was to have any chance of meeting up with him. My hope was to cover forty miles a day. I can make the seventeen-mile trip from Rome to my estate at Laurentum in an afternoon at a leisurely pace. Even cavalrymen carrying their equipment can do sixty miles in a day.

"At least take one *raeda*," Mother said.

"That would only slow us down."

"But if you can't find an inn each night, what will you do?"

"We'll sleep on the ground. We can manage that for a night or two."

The last person waiting to mount was my servant Aurora. She is not just my slave. I can admit it to myself, if not to everyone else—she is my lover. Fortunately, my wife, Livia, prefers to stay on her estate near Perusia and tolerates my relationship with Aurora as long as I don't flaunt it. My mother has come to accept the situation. I don't dare say "approve of," but…

Mother surprised me when she took Aurora's hand. "If I can't stop

him, please watch out for him, dear. Are you prepared to protect him?"
She patted her own thigh at the spot where Aurora carries a knife in
a sheath strapped under her stola. I believed the weapon was a secret,
but perhaps not as much of one as I thought.

"Always, my lady." Aurora winked.

"Well, don't let him do anything foolish," Mother said, fighting back
tears. Naomi put an arm around her shoulder.

"I'll do my best, my lady," Aurora said with a soft smile, "but you
know your son." She rolled her eyes, making my mother chuckle. A
head taller than Mother, Aurora bent down to give her a kiss on the
cheek, a gesture my mother returned. "Take good care of yourself, my
lady. We'll see you as soon as we can, I promise."

Much to my surprise, Mother embraced Aurora. "I hope so, dear.
I truly hope so."

I knew what Mother was hinting at. While she was bathing a year
or so ago, she discovered a *kanker* in one of her breasts. Women know
that such a lump presages death. The only question is how long it will
take. Tacitus' mother died two years after she found a lump. As much
as I felt the need to make this trip, I was afraid my mother might die
before I returned. She had yet to tell me about the disease—I learned
of it from Naomi—but I had no doubt now that she had confided in
Aurora as well.

"We need to get started," I said, adjusting the strap on my traveler's
hat and fighting down a different kind of lump that was forming in
my throat.

But there was one more unavoidable delay. Aurora had to say
good-bye to Joshua, a baby who came under my protection seven
months ago, shortly after he was born. I know how much Aurora wants
a baby—and what a huge complication of our lives it would be if she
had one. We have a nurse for Joshua whom we trust implicitly. Aurora
hugged the boy and kissed him on his forehead.

"Aurora," I said in my best master's voice, "we need to go. Now."

She handed Joshua back to the nurse and stepped away. "Yes, my
lord." The boy fretted and reached out for her. Aurora hesitated, and I
was afraid she might decide to stay here.

I had been surprised that she consented to my request to make this trip. I think she figured that I would need her more than Joshua would. He had the nurse, my mother, and Naomi to take care of him. I held the reins of her horse while Barbatus helped her mount.

"I think we're ready," I said.

"My lord, excuse me," one of my freedmen, Albinus, said from the back of the group. "Would it be possible for us to take one more person along?"

"Whom do you have in mind?" I was reluctant to add anyone else to the group. Even one more person—and one more horse—could introduce any number of possible problems and delays along the way.

"Sophronia, my lord."

I patted my horse's neck, the way Aurora has taught me, to calm him. "Why take another woman on the trip? And why Sophronia?"

Albinus, whose skin is as white as his name implies, has never been reluctant to speak for himself, though never disrespectful. "She would provide company for Aurora, my lord. And make things appear a bit more...proper, if I may say so."

"'More proper'? In whose eyes?" I knew exactly what he meant, of course, and he was right. A second woman in the group would divert attention from Aurora. "So again I ask, why Sophronia?"

"Well, she's good with horses, my lord. And a good cook."

"And she is your lover, isn't she?"

Albinus blushed and looked down.

"I'm not blind, you know. I am aware of what goes on in my household." It was actually just a guess, albeit a reasonable one from the way I had seen the two of them together. "But you make a good point. Barbatus, get her a horse. Albinus, get her ready to travel. Or is she already packed?"

"Yes, my lord, she is."

"Remind me never to play *latrunculus* with you," I said.

Albinus' brow furrowed. "Forgive me, my lord?"

"You've boxed me in very nicely." For a moment I considered telling Albinus to stay here, but he had been the first to volunteer. I'd always known him to be sturdy and dependable. I thought I might make him steward on the estate someday. "Well, there's no time to argue about it. We've got to get moving."

I pulled my broad-brimmed hat down securely and wrapped my cloak more tightly around me. I hoped the day would warm up as the sun got higher.

———⊶⦿⊷———

Gaius and I were riding at the rear of our party, to let us maintain a little distance that would give us some privacy. This whole trip seemed unreal. With no serious planning and no idea exactly where Tacitus might be, we were setting out to travel several hundred miles and hope that our path crossed his at some point.

"Why doesn't Tacitus just sell this estate," I asked, "and move his brother to Rome?"

"He's afraid Lucius would be very upset if he were moved from the place where he's lived all his life. The young man, I gather, has never really grown up. His mind doesn't grasp the passage of time. Tacitus says, no matter how long he goes between visits to the estate, Lucius always thinks he was there yesterday. The servants take good care of him, but he cannot live without them to tend to him. Besides, the estate is quite profitable."

"I know it's important to you to show your friendship for Tacitus, but it's not as though you can actually do anything for his brother."

"It's a question of what I can do for Tacitus, not for his brother."

"Wouldn't it make more sense for us to go to Lugdunum and meet Tacitus there? As much as I love horses, I'm not looking forward to living on one for a couple of months." The biggest problem facing me—one I could never discuss with any man, not even Gaius—was that I would probably start my monthly in a few weeks. Roman women usually put on a loincloth and retire to their rooms for a few days at that time of the month. Men don't want to be around us then, any more than we want them around. Female servants can be assigned work away from any men. But now I was going to be sitting on a horse, surrounded by men, with no way to disguise what was happening. I'd have to see if Sophronia had thought about this problem. Maybe I should have said no when Gaius asked me if I would

go on this trip. I wondered if I had enough material to make a couple of loincloths when they became necessary.

Perhaps I should have stayed with Joshua. I was going to miss him for the entire time. He would grow up so much. Would he even remember me by the time I got back?

Gaius took a moment to reply to my question. "Charinus says he'll be somewhere near Genua about the time we get there."

"I think that's as likely as two archers, who can't even see one another, shooting arrows into the air and hoping they'll collide. While we're looking for Tacitus and his party, he could get another message saying his brother has recovered. He might go on to the estate or he could turn back to Rome and send you a message to that effect. We might never cross paths with that messenger. We could get all the way to Lugdunum with no idea of where Tacitus is or we could end up roaming all over Gaul."

Gaius' only response was "I have to do this." I knew that was the end of the conversation.

This trip, pointless or not, at least offers a chance for Gaius and me to spend time together away from any possible interference from Livia. She has, at times, arrived unannounced at one or another of Gaius' estates— and always at the one where we are. Obviously someone in our household is keeping her informed of our movements. And of what else, I hate to think. We have tried to keep track of which servants leave the house and how long they're gone, but we haven't identified anyone yet. Regulus isn't the only one with spies in our house, it seems.

"I don't know Sophronia," I said to Gaius, trying to restart our conversation.

"No, you wouldn't. She was one of several slaves my uncle acquired when you and I were still children. She's perhaps five years older than we are, as is Albinus."

"Do you know where she came from?"

Gaius shook his head. "Does it matter?"

"I guess not." But somehow I felt like it did.

"All I know is that she works in the kitchen and is Albinus' lover."

"Are you sure about that?" I jerked my head in their direction. "Have you seen any signs of affection between them?"

"Not a great deal today. But they're riding together, aren't they? Do you expect them to couple on horseback?"

"You don't have to ridicule me," I said.

For a moment Gaius and I watched the pair in silence. Sophronia's dark hair contrasted sharply with what showed of Albinus' white hair under his broad-brimmed hat. She must have been quite a striking woman in her youth, a bit taller than most women. But now, nearing her thirties, she was carrying extra weight. Seeing her from the back, I was aware of her bottom. Remember, I told myself, she is sitting on a horse—not the most flattering pose for any woman. Her skin was not as fair as Albinus', of course, but was much lighter than what my Punic ancestors had passed down to me. Lighter skin is the ideal in Rome. I'm glad Gaius doesn't seem to care.

"They hardly seem aware of one another," I finally said. "He's paying more attention to the scenery than to her."

"Well, it is lovely scenery," Gaius said. "Look, all I know is that Albinus admitted they are lovers, even blushed when I asked him." He prodded his horse with his heels and guided him toward the front of our group. "I need to get us moving faster."

I knew he was just tired of talking about this particular topic. But I couldn't let it go. Something about Sophronia's presence didn't feel right. Why did she want to go on this difficult trip when no one was making her and she had no pressing reason to do so? If it was just to be with her "lover," why wasn't she taking more advantage of that opportunity?

I meant what I said to Aurora. The scenery on either side of us was extraordinary. My estate at Laurentum is, and always will be, my favorite, both for its accommodations and its location on a bluff over the sea and the private suite of rooms I've added to it. But, on a day like this, if I could move it up here, I would gladly do so. We Romans call this area Cisalpine Gaul, "Gaul on this side of the Alps." It begins at the point where the peninsula of Italy joins the mainland. Lugdunum and Tacitus' estate are in Transalpine Gaul, "Gaul across the Alps." Of course, if you live in Lugdunum, I suppose those terms would be reversed. But we Romans decide what is "this side" or "across." What we really mean is "our side" or "the other side." Not that it matters anymore. Since Julius Caesar's day, both sides have been ours.

My mind was wandering, and I was willing to let it. Lake Comum, on my right, glistening in the late morning sun, was so calm and still you would think you could walk across it. The lake is deceptively deep and cold, especially at this time of year, when the melting snow on the slopes on the other side runs down into it. The water gets so cold that it takes extra time and wood to heat the bath at my estate, which draws water from the lake, thanks to a device for raising water from a lower to a higher level built by my father on a design by Archimedes.

The leaves were opening on the trees on either side of the lake, but at a distance they looked more like the fuzz one sees on a baby's head when he's a few months old...like Joshua's head. I never would have drawn that comparison until a few months ago. I have to admit I've grown attached to the boy, much more attached than I would have thought possible. For a moment I had the sensation that I could hear him laugh, feel him snuggled up against me.

The circumstances of his arrival in my household are complex, to put it mildly. I've kept as careful a record of the events as I can, in case I ever have to explain it to him, or to anyone else, possibly in a law court. It's already hard to remember my house—my family—without him in it. Babies, as tiny and vulnerable as they are, have a natural ability to dominate everything around them. Livia has made it clear she will never bear me a child. She won't even couple with me—not that I regret that—so Joshua may be as close to having a son as I'll ever get. Aurora has considered him her child from the day we first encountered him. It's not beyond the realm of possibility that I might adopt him someday, as my uncle adopted me.

I shook my head in bemusement. I think of myself as a typical member of the equestrian class, a rather traditional Roman. Crusty old Cato the Censor would have approved of me, I believe. I look askance at men who deliberately flout the standards of our society, like those old Cynic philosophers urinating in temples. But I'm married to a woman who despises me. The woman I love—and who loves me—is my Punic slave. We are the "parents," if you will, of a boy whose name betrays his origins even before one becomes aware of his circumcision. How did I get to this point in my life?

More to the point, would I change any of it, even if I could?

<hr />

Traffic on the road was light. We passed through Comum in late morning. The break gave us the opportunity to relieve ourselves in a proper *latrina*, instead of behind a bush, and to rest the horses for half an hour or so. I have business investments in the town, but this was not the time to check on them. We got something to eat and bought supplies for a couple of more meals. Then we were ready to get back on the road.

"If we push the horses," I told everyone as we remounted, "I think we can make it to Mediolanum about dark, or not long after that. It's only another thirty miles. We'll be tired, and so will the horses, but we will have all night to rest."

For the next few hours we talked very little and concentrated on getting the most we could out of our horses. I silently expressed my thanks to the engineers who created such straight, level roads. In ordinary circumstances we take them for granted because they're always there. When we need to get somewhere in a hurry, though, they're like a gift from the gods. No obstacle—other than an occasional slow-moving wagon—stands in our way, although I guess our roads don't quite compare to the Royal Road of the Persians that Herodotus describes. The king's messengers, he claims, with fresh horses every fifteen miles or so and changing riders periodically, could cover over 1,600 miles in seven days on that road. "Neither snow nor rain nor heat nor gloom of night," he says, "stays these couriers from the swift completion of their appointed rounds." They made our forty miles a day seem positively leisurely.

The sun was going down, but the full "gloom of night" had not yet settled in when we arrived on the northern outskirts of Mediolanum. We stopped at the first inn we came to. Albinus, Sophronia, and two other of my servants went in with me and Aurora while the others held the horses. There was only one room available, we were told by the surly, heavyset innkeeper, whose left eye refused to look in the same direction as his right.

"Then I guess we'd better look somewhere else," I said.

The innkeeper spat on the floor. "You won't find nothin' else, sir. Not at this time of day."

Another pair of travelers entered the inn. One was pulling money out of a pouch. "All right," I said quickly, "I'll take the room."

"Well," Albinus said, patting Sophronia's bottom, "I guess that means a night in the barn for us."

"Will that be all right?" I asked the innkeeper.

He jerked his head in what passed for a nod. "Just don't you go pissin' in the hay. The horses have to eat it."

The two women could have had the room, but my servants correctly assumed that I wasn't going to sleep in the barn. Aurora would share the room with me. Without any instructions being given, Aurora and I unpacked what we needed and headed upstairs while the others led the horses to the barn, which was across the street from the inn. I was actually glad to have someone watching our horses and gear for the night.

The room was clean enough. We massaged one another to relieve some of the soreness from a long day on horseback. That led to greater intimacy and a night of deep sleep.

The next morning I was awakened by the sound of Aurora closing the door. Sunlight was barely visible through the shutters over the one window. By the time Aurora returned with a bowl of water, which she put down beside the bed, I was reasonably awake and finished with the chamber pot.

"I roused the others," she said. "I think we can be ready to go in half an hour or so." She set a vial of olive oil on the table next to the bed. "Shall we get cleaned up?"

We couldn't bathe properly, but we helped one another wash off. When she ran her hands over my face, Aurora said, "You need a shave. You were scratching me last night. Neither of us likes that."

"Do we have time?"

"I'll be quick. There's no telling where we'll be tonight, so we'd better take advantage of this opportunity."

Men of my class usually have male servants who play the role that Aurora does in my house, tending to the master's clothes, keeping up with his appointments, and shaving him. The last is no small task. It's difficult to shave yourself when the only reflection you can see is in a bowl of water or on a piece of polished metal. In large households like mine one servant is designated as the *tonsor*, the barber. For poorer men, every other street corner in any city is occupied by a barber. He has a stool and the equipment to trim hair and shave anyone for a small fee.

The *tonsor* in my house is a servant named Laelius. I require that all of my male servants be shaved at least every other day. Like most Romans, I leave the beards and mustaches to the German barbarians one sees fighting in the arena. A couple of years ago, though, Laelius was ill for several days. On the second day Aurora ran her hand over my cheek and said, "I could shave you." She has done so ever since. I own a razor with a blade that folds into the handle, but Aurora prefers to use her knife.

A stool with my tunic draped over it stood in one corner of the room. I tossed the garment on the bed and pulled the stool into the middle of the floor. As I sat down Aurora removed her stola to keep it clean and steadied my head against her breasts, rubbing olive oil on my cheeks and chin. Some men shave only every couple of days. If they had Aurora, they would probably shave twice a day. I make sure to start every day that I possibly can this way. One of the worst effects of a visit from my wife is that I have to go back to having Laelius shave me for a few days.

"Didn't one of our tutors tell us a story," Aurora asked, "about a man who didn't trust anyone but his daughter to shave him?"

I couldn't nod, but I said, "That's from Cicero—the *Tusculan Disputations*. Dionysius, tyrant of Syracuse, didn't trust anyone to put a blade at his throat."

"You mean like this?" Aurora tightened her grip on my head, wedging it between her breasts, and pressed the knife ever so slightly against my throat.

"Yes, just like that." I swallowed as she relaxed the pressure. Even though I knew she was joking, the sensation was as unsettling as it was thrilling. "So he made his three daughters trim his beard and his hair," I managed to choke out, "starting when they were children. When they grew up, he made them use a hot coal to singe the hair rather than a razor to trim it." I patted her hand. "I'm glad I can trust you."

"I'm glad you believe that." She kissed the top of my head.

<hr />

The sun was high when one of the men asked if we could stop. There was no other traffic in sight at the moment, so Gaius gave his permission and urged everyone to be as quick as possible.

"The women claim that old wall," Sophronia called out before anyone else could say anything. We dismounted and I joined her as she stepped to the other side of a stone wall that was about chest high, probably the remains of some shepherd's hut. The men clustered around a large milestone—ten feet tall, at least—on the other side of the road.

"Watch the emperor's name," one of them said with a laugh.

"You have to watch it," Charinus said, "if you're going to hit it."

"Well," Sophronia said as we squatted behind the wall, "you've done an impressive job of screwing your way to the top of the household." She used one of the most vulgar Latin terms for coupling. "You even get to sleep in a proper bed in a proper room while the rest of us have to fight off bugs in the straw and listen to horses neighing and farting all night."

The crudity of her language offended me, and I'm sure it would offend Gaius if he heard it. "I'm sorry there wasn't enough room in the inn. Gaius Pliny did the best he could."

"As long as you're happy, that's all that matters to him. We all know that."

"There's more to our relationship than that. Gaius Pliny and I have been friends since we were seven years old."

Sophronia snorted. "Just wait. I was once my former owner's favorite. His wife acted like she could accept it, as long as we were discreet. But she finally told him to get rid of me, so he sold me, just like Gaius Pliny's wife will eventually make him get rid of you."

I knew Gaius would never sell me, no matter what Livia said, but I wasn't going to argue the point. Sophronia had brought up the subject of her former owner. I saw my chance to learn something important without appearing nosy. I tried to remain casual. "What made the wife change her mind?"

"I was being a better mother to her daughter than she was. She got jealous, said I was drawing the girl's affection away from her. I wasn't trying to, but the poor child had no one else to turn to. Her mother openly showed that she didn't like the girl. Can you believe it? Her own daughter!"

This all sounded too familiar. "Who was your former owner, before you came to Comum?"

"Not that it's any of your business, but it was Livius."

"Livia's father? That Livius?"

II

I KNEW WE WOULDN'T make it from Mediolanum to Genua
in one day. It's ninety miles between the two towns. When we passed
the fortieth milestone I began looking for a likely place to spend the
night. The clouds on the horizon—bringing on early darkness—and
the wind that was picking up injected some urgency into the search.

"We could get some rain tonight, my lord," Albinus said, slowing
his horse to drop back beside mine. He seemed to have become the
leader and the spokesman of the group of servants traveling with me.

"That looks very likely. I hope we can find some sort of shelter." We
had passed a village in the early afternoon, but it had been much too
soon to stop. Now we were in the middle of an uninhabited wilderness
and had not passed any other travelers in an hour or so. "I wish I could
make the end of the day longer, by just another hour."

Albinus scratched his head. "How could you do that, my lord? Take
an hour from some other part of the day? That would be like cutting
a piece off one end of a blanket and sewing it on to the other end. The
blanket wouldn't be any longer."

"I'm just saying that I'd like to have an extra hour right now."

"The day is the day, my lord. Maybe you can seize it, as I've heard
people say, but you can't change how long it is, can you?"

"Each hour is longer in the summer and shorter in the winter."

"Well, yes, my lord, but there are still only twelve in a day."

"You're right." I was in no mood for a philosophical or horological
discussion.

We entered a copse of tall trees that grew right up to the edge of

26

the road, which had been cut through them to keep it straight. A small river ran across our path, with a bridge over it. The density of the trees made it much darker here, as if another hour had suddenly elapsed. Everything about the place felt sinister. I was opening my mouth to warn everyone to keep a hand on their swords when barbaric yells erupted from the woods on each side of us. Rough-looking men, three on horseback and four more on foot, rushed at us, surrounding us and grabbing at the reins of our horses. The bridge made it difficult to maneuver our mounts.

We drew our weapons and tried to defend ourselves. Fighting from horseback against men on foot is difficult, especially if the horse becomes agitated. Mine reared and I fell off him. Out of the corner of my eye I could see that a couple of my men had also been pulled off their mounts. I heard a woman scream but it wasn't Aurora's voice. Dodging a blow from one man who was swinging a club, I thrust my sword into his midsection.

When I turned to face another man, I saw one pull Aurora off her horse and try to wrap his arms around her, as though to carry her into the woods. In his eagerness to assault her, he pulled her stola up, making it easy for her to get to her knife. His face showed a mixture of confusion and surprise when, in one smooth motion, she slipped her knife out of its sheath and reached over her shoulder to stab him in the throat. His blood gushed over her. I heard another groan from across the road and saw another bandit crumble to the ground. My band of household servants was acquitting themselves well.

I could see three horses approaching from the south, speeding up when they saw what was happening. The barbarians must have noticed them, too. One of them, a heavy, older bearded man, pointed at Aurora and shouted something in a language I didn't understand. Charinus held up his sword and yelled back at him in what seemed to be the same language. The man sat back on his horse, his facial expression changing as though he was listening. Charinus' tone became somehow magisterial as he pointed his sword at Aurora and then at himself. The Gaul sheathed his sword and he and his band withdrew into the woods, carrying their dead.

I held up a hand to stop my people from following them. "If we go into the woods, we'll be on ground where they have the advantage. We might never come out of there."

Charinus sheathed his sword. "We won't need to pursue them, my lord. I don't think they'll bother us again."

Breathing hard, I looked at him in amazement. "How did you understand him?"

"My mother and I came from the same area they did, my lord. Our village was destroyed and she and I were captured when I was ten. We learned Latin, of course, but she always clung to her native speech and insisted that we use it between us."

"Well, what did he say? What did you say? Why were you pointing at Aurora and at yourself?"

Reluctance showed on Charinus' face. "He was telling you that his name is Orgetorix, my lord. He said the man that Aurora killed was his son, and he vowed revenge on her and on you." My eyes widened. "I told him that if he did manage to kill her, or you, he would end up either dead in the arena or a slave, as I am." His voice turned bitter. "And that is worse than death."

His resentment surprised me. I know that Tacitus does not treat his slaves badly, any more than I do. "Cornelius Tacitus is a humane master, isn't he?"

"I'm sure he thinks he is, my lord. But we are slaves."

"No, you're a freedman, aren't you?" He was carrying a weapon.

"Technically, yes. But what are *liberti* except a different type of slave?"

"We could have a long conversation about that, but we don't have time to dwell on it. We've got to get out of here."

"I don't think we're in any further danger, my lord. Orgetorix seemed to understand the situation."

I studied Charinus as he returned to his horse. I had met him a few times when he was at Tacitus' house in Rome, but he lived on the estate in Gaul. Tacitus seemed to have great respect—one might almost say affection—for the man.

The riders we had seen in the distance came up to us and drew to a halt. There were only three of them, but they offered reassurance in case the Gauls did come back. Their leader looked down at us with genuine concern. "Are you all right?"

"Yes," I said, "thanks to your timely arrival. I'm not sure we could have held them off much longer."

The man pointed to Aurora, and I turned to see why. "Is she all right?" he asked.

"It's not my blood," Aurora said, concealing her knife behind her leg.

"I'm glad we came along," the man said. He was no more than thirty and fair-haired. "My name is Lucius Valerius Catulus. My father owns land a few miles down this road." He pointed behind him. "My men and I are on our way to…tend to some business in the village up ahead." One of the other men chuckled. "You must have passed it a while ago."

"Yes, we did. I'm Gaius Plinius Secundus. I'm very grateful for your arrival."

"I guess you could say the gods provided good fortune."

"I suppose some people would say that." I touched the Tyche ring I was wearing on a leather strap around my neck. Aurora and I had found the object, depicting the goddess of fortune, when we were twelve. We took turns wearing it, although neither of us professed any belief in such a thing as Fortune. But once in a while something happens that casts doubt on my doubt.

"Would you like us to stand guard while you get ready to travel again?"

"That would be most appreciated."

I walked among my party, patting shoulders and offering words of praise and encouragement. I hoped that would create a distraction and allow Aurora time to slip her knife—which she isn't supposed to have—back in its hiding place. "Is everyone all right?"

All of my people were still standing or still on their horses, except for one. Albinus' mount had been hamstrung and now lay on his side, struggling to get up. Albinus lay dead beside him. His leg had been pinned under the animal when it collapsed and he had fallen easy prey to a bandit. His throat had been slashed. The blood seemed particularly garish against his white skin. Sophronia knelt over him, weeping, kissing him, and smoothing his hair. Perhaps she really did love him, I thought.

"We need to get out of here as quickly as possible," I said. "They may gather reinforcements and come back."

"You can't leave him!" Sophronia wailed.

"We'll take Albinus with us, of course," I said. I did not need Sophronia's tears to remind me of my duty, as a human being and as a patron to these people.

"You can put him on my horse, my lord," Aurora said. "I'll ride with someone else."

"My horse is strong enough to carry two," I quickly offered.

Aurora knelt beside the injured horse and patted his neck. She grew up loving these animals. Her father raised them on a farm in North Africa before he sold her and her mother to pay his debts. She was riding, she has told me, by the time she was three.

"We need to do something about this poor horse, my lord," Aurora said, her eyes almost as tear-filled as Sophronia's. "We can't leave him here to suffer."

"I'll take care of it, my lord," one of my men offered. He was a burly fellow named Macronius. "I've had to do it before."

"All right," I said. "Thank you."

We laid Albinus across the back of Aurora's horse, covered him with a blanket, and tied him as securely as we could. The smell of death seemed to disturb the animal. Aurora had to soothe him before she turned to comfort the injured horse. Macronius drew his sword and plunged it into the animal's neck. It gave a brief whinny and was dead. Macronius apparently knew exactly what he was doing. He must have had experience butchering animals or assisting at sacrifices. Like so many of my people at Comum, he was little known to me.

"I need to clean myself up, my lord," Aurora said.

"Certainly. Just be quick about it."

She got a clean stola out of her pack and went down to the water under the bridge.

"Let's move this animal to the side of the road," I said to the others. "Then we *must* get out of here." My men grabbed the horse's legs and dragged him off the road into the edge of the woods. At least he wasn't blocking anyone's passage now. The scavengers would eat well for the next few days.

Aurora came back up the riverbank, wearing clean clothing and with her hair wet. Her bloody stola was folded to conceal as much blood as possible. It would never come clean and would be fit only for rags.

"Let's go," I said.

"We'll escort you until you're in sight of my father's house," Valerius Catulus offered. "I'm sure he'll be glad to give you shelter for the night."

"That's very generous of you."

Once I was mounted I extended my hand and pulled Aurora up on the horse behind me. She wrapped her arms around my waist, just the way I hoped she would, and rested her chin on my shoulder so we could talk easily. I could feel some water dripping off her, or maybe just a few last tears for the horse. I felt the muscles in her long, slender legs tighten against my horse's sides and the backs of my own legs. When it comes to horses, she is the most adept woman I have ever known—better with them even than most men—and the animals seem to recognize her and become comfortable with her right away.

"I hope that's the worst danger we face on this trip," I said. "My mother would have been right. We might have disappeared into those woods and no one would ever have heard of us again."

"I don't even want to imagine what they would have done to Sophronia and me before they killed us," Aurora said. Her arms tightened around me.

"Well, they didn't, did they?" I kicked my heels into my horse's sides to pick up some speed. We could not get away from this place fast enough to suit me. "So let's put it out of our minds as best we can."

Especially the leader's threat that we hadn't seen the last of him.

———✦———

But I couldn't put it out of my mind, and I didn't think Gaius could either. We had each just killed a man. It wasn't the first time for either of us, but that didn't make it any easier to forget. When a blade goes into another person's body, at first it feels like you're hitting him. Then you pull it out and he starts bleeding. That's what makes it real, for me at least.

Even though I had washed myself in the cold water of the river and changed my stola, I could still feel the warm blood of the man I had killed. He might have been able to defend himself if he hadn't been trying so hard to pull my gown up and get his hand between my legs. I knew who his father was and wondered what his name was. I wondered how Gaius would feel the next time I shaved him with my knife. I wondered how I would feel. Maybe from now on I should use his razor.

I held especially tightly to Gaius, partly because I needed the warmth of his body and partly out of fear. I had heard what Charinus said about the Gaul vowing vengeance on Gaius and me. He didn't seem worried about the threat and Gaius was ready to dismiss it, but I took it seriously. Any man who loses his son cannot help but want revenge. How far would he go to exact it?

A light rain was starting to fall. A flash of lightning frightened my horse, but the weight of two riders and soothing words from Aurora kept him from rearing. The light did let me see a structure off the road ahead of us to our right.

"That's the house," Valerius Catulus said. "A quarter mile ahead you'll see a road where you turn off. It's just after you pass the next mile marker." He and his companions turned their horses around. "And now we have business in the village."

"I wonder what sort of business they could have," I asked Aurora, "to bring the owner's son out at this time of day and in this weather."

"My lord," she chuckled, "you can be as naïve as Cornelius Tacitus says."

"What do you mean?"

"They're going to see a woman, or women, my lord. What else could it be? There's probably a brothel in the village."

"Oh" was all I could say. I really had not considered that possibility.

We turned where Valerius Catulus had indicated. A couple of more flashes of lightning let us see that it was indeed a large place, with outbuildings behind it. The road leading to it was well maintained, made of hard-packed sand, running between vineyards on each side.

"I see a few lights," Aurora said over the wind.

When we got closer to the villa I could see that it consisted of a pair of two-story wings joined by a central one-story portico surrounding a garden. The main entrance was flanked by two sets of fountains. Someone had seen us coming. An older man, gray-haired and a bit heavy, and a woman perhaps fifteen years his junior stood in the portico. The woman was small and blond and obviously the mother of the young man we had met on the road. Behind them stood two boys holding torches, slaves to judge from their clothing.

"Good evening," I said, making sure my equestrian stripe was visible. "I'm Gaius Plinius Caecilius Secundus." The four names always carry a little more weight than just the three.

"Good evening. I am Gnaeus Valerius Catulus. This is my wife, Lucretia. We bid you welcome." The man's tunic was high quality but did not bear an equestrian or senatorial stripe.

"Can we be of some assistance?" Lucretia asked.

"We've run into some trouble, I'm afraid. We were attacked back up the road." I thought about mentioning Orgetorix's threat but decided I would trust that Charinus had forestalled it. No man in his right mind would welcome strangers if he knew a band of savages was on their trail.

"Oh, dear." Lucretia brought her hand up to her mouth. "There has been a pack of brigands around lately. I'm sorry they set on you. Are you all right?"

"They killed one of my men." I pointed to the horse carrying Albinus. Lucretia gasped.

"I'm very sorry to hear that," Catulus said. "Did you get any of them?"

"We killed three of them."

"Excellent work!"

"Your son and his men came along just in time to help us run the savages off."

Catulus smiled broadly. "I'm glad they were able to help."

"Now it seems we're about to get caught in a storm. Your son suggested we might find shelter here."

"Of course. Our stable is behind the house, on your right. I'll meet you there, and you can leave your man's body in one of the stalls. We'll make arrangements for the funeral."

"I'll gladly pay the costs."

Catulus dismissed the offer with a wave of his hand. "We're clearing land to plant more vines, so we've got plenty of wood."

As they walked back into the house Catulus and his wife exchanged animated words that I could not make out. Lucretia glanced over her shoulder at us. Catulus, I noticed, walked with a limp.

The stable was large, but only a few stalls were occupied. We had just gotten our horses into it and laid Albinus in an empty stall when the rain began in earnest. Catulus came in through a door that, I assumed, would take us to the house.

"Do you have everything you need?" he asked.

"I believe we do. It's most gracious of you to take us in."

"I'm happy to do it, Gaius Pliny, in the name of simple hospitality. Besides, my wife believes in those stories about entertaining gods in disguise. That's what she was going on about." He chuckled. "You wouldn't happen to be gods, would you?"

I laughed. "Gods we most certainly are not." (Except perhaps for the living, breathing embodiment of Venus standing right behind me.) "We're just a band of beleaguered travelers who are most grateful to get out of the rain."

"Well, feed your horses and then I'm sure we have enough rooms for your party."

I stood beside him as my servants, with the help of two of Catulus' men, fed the horses and made certain none of them had been injured in the fight. "I'm afraid I don't recognize your name," I said. "Do you come to Rome often?"

He shook his head. "Very rarely. I'm not an equestrian, as you can see, and my bad hip makes travel unpleasant. Anyway, most of my business is close around here. My vineyards keep me busy. I'll let you sample what we make."

"I look forward to that. Please, if you should visit the city, you'll be welcome in my house. I live on the Esquiline Hill."

He bowed his head to acknowledge the invitation. "You're most gracious. Now, shall we get into the house? I may slow you down, I'm afraid. The pain in my joints gets worse in weather like this."

We followed him into the house. He did limp noticeably, favoring his right leg and hip. His wife was waiting for us in the kitchen, with two servant women standing behind her.

"Are you ready for us, Lucretia dear?" Catulus said.

Lucretia bowed and smiled, apparently still not convinced that we weren't gods. "Welcome, sir. I hope we can make you comfortable. I've set things up for your servants here in the kitchen. Gnaeus Catulus and I will be happy to join you in the *triclinium*."

"I would enjoy the company," I said. Actually, the last thing I wanted at the moment was to have to make meaningless conversation with people I didn't know, but it looked like I had no choice.

Moving into the *triclinium*, Catulus and I took our places on the couches. Two of his servants brought in plates of bread, cheese, dried fruit, and smoked fish. I was surprised, and relieved, to see Aurora carrying a tray with a pitcher of wine and three cups on it. She placed it on the table and took a place behind my couch while the other two women stood behind Catulus. His wife came in and reclined beside him.

"We weren't expecting company," Lucretia said, "so I'm afraid it's rather simple fare."

"It looks very good," I said. "We've had a long day and a frightening end to it. Thank you for your hospitality."

"May I ask where you're headed?" Catulus said.

"We're going to Genua."

He nodded. "You should make that easily tomorrow."

"Assuming we're not attacked again."

Catulus frowned. "That's always a risk when you're traveling, isn't it?"

"Yes, but Orgetorix threatened me. It seems one of the men we killed was his son." Even though Charinus had talked our way out of the situation, I wasn't sure a barbarian would forgo his revenge that easily. "I didn't want to alarm you, but it's better to be forewarned."

"Orgetorix, eh? I've heard that name recently. Then I'll post guards tonight and have some men escort you tomorrow at least as far as the next village."

"I would appreciate that, and I hope I haven't exposed you to danger by stopping here."

"Living out in the country like this we're always vulnerable."

I took one more bite of the smoked fish, which was very good, and washed it down with some of Catulus' wine, which did not compare to the quality of the fish. I made sure that Aurora had all she wanted, as Lucretia shared with the two women standing behind her. "Now, do you have accommodations for us tonight? I don't want to inconvenience you."

"We have plenty of room," Lucretia said. "The rooms on the top floor of the other wing are unoccupied. We hope our sons will marry and fill them with grandchildren someday, but that isn't happening yet."

"Sons?" I said. "We met Lucius. How many others do you have?"

"Only one," Lucretia said with a touch of sadness. "And no daughters. Marcus is living in Massilia right now. We're trying to convince him to come home, but he thinks we might be able to increase our wine production and begin exporting some. He wants to be our agent there. He enjoys life in the city."

"And he has a much better head for business than Lucius," Catulus said. "Lucius is the older, but he hasn't really grown up. He thinks we don't know that he's carousing with women up in the village tonight. He owns the brothel there."

After a bit more chitchat about weather and a few of my host's questions about Rome, I felt I had discharged any obligations of a guest. I sat up on the couch, and Aurora stood up behind me. "This has been a most pleasant end to a harrowing day, but I think we should get to bed so we can get an early start tomorrow."

Valerius Catulus reached for some more fish but did not get up. "As my wife said, the rooms on the second floor of the other wing are yours to choose from. I hope you'll forgive me if I don't accompany you. The stairs cause me a great deal of pain in my hip."

"That's quite all right," I said. "I'm sure we can find what we need. Aurora, would you tell the others it's time to turn in?"

In a few moments my other servants were on their way across the garden of the house toward the other wing. Aurora and I walked a few paces behind them. The rain had stopped, and the clouds were breaking up, revealing a half moon and the thousands of stars that one sees when not in a large city.

There was nothing exceptional about this house except the waist-high wall between the columns all the way around the garden. Openings had been placed at each end of the garden and in the middle on each side. Stairs to the rooms on the upper floor were located at each end of the building and a set in the middle. I assumed that three rooms opened off each set of stairs, an arrangement typical of a Roman building with an upper floor like this.

I ran my hand along the top of the short wall. "This must make it easy to control how people move."

"Especially if one of the people is a small child," Aurora said. "Maybe we could do something like this when Joshua starts walking. I'm already afraid of him drowning in the *piscina* before we have a chance to teach him how to swim."

"That's certainly worth considering," I said as noncommittally as possible. Aurora's "we" sounded...wifely. Of course, I wished she were my wife, but was I really going to start remodeling my house—possibly all of my houses—based on her suggestions and on the needs of a child who wasn't even mine, or ours?

———◦•◦———

Lucretia was right. There was no shortage of bedrooms to choose from. Gaius found one that suited him. He stood back from the door and let me look into the room. From the size of it and the lovely frescoes of a garden, I thought it must be a room planned for one of Catulus' sons, a kind of master's quarters for the upper story. I nodded my approval. Gaius told everyone else to pick a room that satisfied them.

"Be good guests," he said. "Leave everything just as you found it. I want to be on the road as the sun is coming up."

Gaius and I were both too tired, in body and mind, for lovemaking, so we just lay in one another's arms. I know I was still reacting to the attack and I imagined he was, too.

"I need to tell you something," I said, "about my conversation with Sophronia earlier today."

"What is it?" His voice sounded thick as exhaustion overcame him.

"Sophronia was in Pompeia's house before she came to Comum."

Gaius not only woke up; he sat up in the bed and grabbed my bare shoulders. "What?"

I told him what Sophronia had told me.

"Wait, she claims she was a favorite of Livius? But he—"

"Yes, I know. Given what we know of his sexual preferences, she wouldn't have much appeal for him. At first I was confused, too. But she meant the second Livius, your wife's stepfather, not her father. And she claims she was a kind of second mother to Livia, so close to her that Pompeia got jealous and made Livius get rid of her."

Gaius rubbed his chin and I could hear the stubble scratching. I would just have to make time to shave him in the morning. "If Sophronia was so important to Livia, I wonder why she hasn't asked to have the woman turned over to her. She's never said a word about her."

"Probably because Pompeia would never stand for it."

"But Livia has her own estate at Perusia. Her mother can't control who lives there."

"Maybe Livia wants her as a spy in your household."

Gaius reacted as I thought he would, with his eyes rolling and his shoulders slumping. "Not that again. I'm hardly ever at Comum. And it's a long way from there to Perusia. What good is a spy who's so far away and has nothing to report?"

"What if she were to be moved to Rome? Has Sophronia said anything about wanting to go to Rome?"

"Not to me. I'm hardly aware of the woman when I'm in Comum. Her duties keep her in the kitchen. Livia has said that she doesn't think my cook in Rome is very good, but she hasn't suggested anyone else."

"I'll bet she's just biding her time. You've only been married a year. Maybe she's gathering information she can use against you, to divorce you."

"She can divorce me any time she wants. She knows I won't try to stop her."

"But what if she wants to humiliate you? Everything we do on this trip is going to be reported to her. I'd bet on it."

"Including this?" Gaius kissed me, long and hard.

"Especially that," I said, taking a breath. I rubbed my hand over his chest. "You should send her back to Livia as soon as possible."

"Just because she was once a slave in that household? Livia hasn't said anything about even knowing or caring about Sophronia. Aren't you being overly suspicious?"

"That's what you've taught me."

Gaius lay down and turned his back to me. "We'll just have to keep a close eye on her during this trip," he said over his shoulder.

I couldn't do anything but stay quiet as he went to sleep. But I couldn't stop thinking about Sophronia. What bothered me, the more I thought about it, was that we had started packing for this trip as soon as Tacitus' message arrived, that same afternoon. Albinus volunteered to go. He said nothing at that time about Sophronia going with us or being in love with her. But the next morning they asked, at the very last moment, making it awkward, if not impossible, for Gaius to refuse. And she already had a bag packed. She did seem to be genuinely grieving when Albinus was killed, though.

What does she want? And why am I so worried about her?

III

W E WERE UP the next morning before dawn and made our way to the stable. Sophronia stopped in the stall where Albinus' corpse was lying to say her final good-bye to him. She knelt beside his body, stroked his hair, and kissed him one more time. Aurora stood behind her, then took her arm and encouraged her to get up. Sophronia jerked away from her. Was she moved by her love of Albinus, I wondered, or dislike of Aurora?

I took hold of Albinus' arm and tried to bend it but could not. In some of his notes my uncle had recorded that a dead body begins to stiffen a few hours after death, then relaxes after about a day. Whenever I have a chance, I check to see if that always holds true, and I've never found a case where it didn't. Superstitious people say it's because the dead person is frightened by the horrific sights and sounds of the underworld, and then relaxes as he grows accustomed to them. That's ludicrous, of course, but I have no other explanation, just observations. I placed a blanket over Albinus.

"It looks like you're ready," the elder Valerius Catulus said, leading three of his men into the stable. Each man was carrying a bag. "Lucretia has packed something for you to eat. These fellows will ride along with you for a while."

"We give you our thanks," I said.

The eastern horizon was just beginning to lighten when we reached the main road and turned south. No one had much to say. Sophronia let out an occasional muffled sob. I was sorry that Aurora and I no longer had any reason to share a horse.

A couple of miles down the road from Catulus' villa we passed another large house that appeared to be abandoned. It looked as though someone had set fire to it and left the ruins. Most of the roof had fallen in. "What happened to that place?" Aurora asked, turning to one of Catulus' men, a tall, gloomy fellow named Syrus.

"Ghouls," he said.

"Did you say ghouls?"

"Yes. Creatures that would eat humans or animals and take on the shape of whoever or whatever they ate." He sounded utterly serious. Some people are able to make their jokes more believable that way.

From the other side of Aurora I couldn't help but laugh. "That's preposterous."

"All I know is what I'm told, my lord. It happened some time ago, when I was a boy."

"What happened?"

"The couple that lived there—Leander and Chloe was their names—they had no children. When they got old they hired some people to help them run the place. Turns out, though, the people they hired was a pack of these flesh-eating ghouls."

I shook my head in disbelief. "People around here actually believe this nonsense?"

Syrus looked a bit offended. "Call it that if you will, my lord. When animals began disappearing and, finally, a couple of villagers disappeared, folks started suspecting something. They traced it all to that house."

"Traced what?" I asked.

"Strange noises, glimpses of beasts, occasional bones. They attacked the place and set fire to it. We don't know if they killed the ghouls. They could have changed their shapes and got away."

"What happened to Leander and Chloe?" Aurora asked.

"Never seen again. Some around here think they was ghouls themselves. Or maybe eaten by the ghouls."

"Did you ever see one of these ghouls?" I asked Syrus.

"No, my lord, but I know lots of folks who did."

There was no conversation during the rest of that leg of the trip. My rational mind simply refuses to acknowledge the existence—even the *possibility* of the existence—of creatures such as Syrus described. My uncle, in his *Natural History*, gave accounts of fantastic creatures such as the Dog-headed people, the Cynocephali, who supposedly live in the mountains of India, but he had never seen them. He simply reported what he had found in his reading. I doubt that he had ever seen the Umbrella-foot tribe either. They supposedly lie on their backs in hot weather and shade themselves with their huge feet. He describes the Choromandae, a forest tribe with hairy bodies, gray eyes, and teeth like a dog's. They don't speak but give off a horrible scream.

But, even amidst those monstrosities and others, he never mentions creatures that could change their form.

Earlier writers pass on all sorts of improbable things. It's a rule, I think, that the farther away—in distance or time—the writer is from what he's describing, the more fantastic his descriptions become. Plato's accounts of Atlantis come to mind. Stories get garbled as they are passed from place to place, or from one generation to the next, and translated. Herodotus claims there are ants as big as dogs in India. Like my uncle, he had never been that far east and likely had no idea what he was talking about. But, like Syrus, they "know lots of folks." But "lots of folks" can be completely wrong.

———————

Half an hour later we rode into a little village. Villages are, by definition, small, but this one had almost outgrown the designation. Two buildings on one side of the road held at least half a dozen shops. The other side of the road was taken up by an inn, a small bath, and several more shops. We stopped but, seeing no convenient mounting stone, did not bother to get off our horses.

"This is where we'll leave you, my lord," Syrus said. The men with him handed their bags of provisions over to my servants.

"Thank you for coming with us," I said. "And for an entertaining story."

"If only it were just a story, my lord. I'm glad our services weren't needed in any other way. I wish you well on the rest of your journey. It appears you may have some company." He pointed to a party preparing to leave the inn and helping one another mount. "They may be your best protection."

As we resumed our ride, Aurora drew her horse close to mine and said softly, "Gaius, I've been watching to see if we're being followed."

"What makes you think we would be? Charinus seemed to warn them off rather emphatically."

"I killed the man's son, Gaius. I'm not sure a few harsh words from a servant would suffice to settle that score. Would you let yourself be 'warned off' if someone killed Joshua?"

She was right, of course, even if Joshua wasn't my son. "Have you seen anyone?" I knew she would be quicker than I would to pick up signs of someone following us, no matter how subtle.

"I haven't seen anything obvious, and that's what worries me. I don't think those men could be that unobtrusive in their movements."

"Then whatever Charinus said seems to have been effective."

Aurora looked at each side of the road. "Or maybe we don't know what he actually said. All you know is what he told you that he said."

I laughed. "By the gods! I have made an utter skeptic of you, haven't I? What could he possibly have said other than to point out to Orgetorix the possible punishments for an attack? You ought to be grateful to the man for stepping in like he did."

"But did you notice that, as soon as Charinus started to speak, Orgetorix lowered his sword and the other men turned to listen?"

"I'm sure they were surprised to hear one of us speaking their language."

Aurora shook her head. "They weren't just surprised. It looked more like gestures of respect...almost awe."

I lowered my voice and glanced at Charinus. "Darling, you have very keen instincts, I admit, but why would a Gallic chieftain be in awe of a Roman slave?"

"He wasn't always a Roman slave. And I've been trying to remember just what I saw. Everything happened so fast, but I think I saw him knock a man down but not kill him."

"Some people don't like killing."

"You and I don't like it, but we've done it when it was necessary."

"Maybe Charinus felt it wasn't necessary in that situation." This discussion was feeling more like an argument and was beginning to annoy me. "He's a household slave, not a warrior. He was taken as a slave when he was ten years old. He wasn't some defeated chieftain."

Aurora's mouth twitched. "I just think we ought to be alert. A couple of times he used a word that ended in -ix. That's a person's name in their language, I believe."

"What's so important about that?"

"He put his hand on his chest both times he used it. What if it's his name? What if they recognized it? What if he was giving them some kind of command?"

I looked over my shoulder but could not see anything that concerned me. Unplowed fields and bits of woods on either side of the road did not look like easy terrain to travel with any speed. "I think you're overreacting," I said. "If we keep within sight of other travelers we should be safe. And we can move faster on the road than anyone who's following us would be able to if they have to cross fields and encounter other obstacles. Thank the gods and the engineers for straight roads."

Traffic on the road struck me as heavy, but I was glad of it. We rode along with various groups of people at different times, passing some and catching up with others, always checking the sides of the road. Aurora drew attention, especially from the men we passed, as her stola fluttered up around her knees.

We arrived on the outskirts of Genua shortly before dark. "Now begins the difficult part of this trip," I said to Aurora, "the part that will depend entirely on luck. As you said, Tacitus and I are like two arrows fired by archers who cannot see one another. The likelihood that we will connect is infinitesimal."

"The odds are probably no worse, my lord, than the odds against you and me, starting from where we did, ending up in the same house, even in the same bed."

How could I argue against that?

We stopped at the first inn we came to and I asked if anyone had seen a party of travelers that could have been Tacitus'. The color scheme of his *raedas* is distinctive and bold—gold and green—though nothing as audacious and tasteless as my mother-in-law's bright red-and-yellow wagons.

When I came back with a negative answer, Aurora said, "That's good news, isn't it, my lord? They're a large party, according to what Charinus says, hard to miss. If no one has seen them, they must not have gotten here yet."

"But how long should we wait?" I countered. "What if they came through and no one did notice them? That would mean they're farther up the road and getting farther and farther away from us by the hour."

"My lord," Charinus said, "I made this trip with my lord Cornelius Tacitus once before. We stopped at an inn just inside the south gate of the city. He knew the innkeeper because he had stayed there before. That seemed to be his habit. If I'm not presuming too much, I would suggest that we at least check to see if he's been there, maybe get rooms there. It's a nice place."

I consider myself logical, and I hate making wild guesses. Charinus' suggestion made sense and gave me some basis for making a decision. "All right, let's go." We fell in line behind him.

Aurora rode close beside me and lowered her voice but still used the honorific in case anyone overheard her. "My lord, is it wise to trust him so implicitly?"

"Damn it, Aurora," I whispered, "we're in a big city. Do you think there will be a band of Gauls waiting around the next corner to attack us?"

"No. I just—"

"This decision is mine to make, and I've made it. I'm tired. All I want right now is to get settled for the night." I kicked my horse with my heels.

We followed Charinus to a large inn on a side street. I had just paid the innkeeper when I heard women's excited voices behind me. I turned to see Aurora and Julia embracing.

———— ⋙•⋘ ————

It took an hour or so to get everyone settled, the horses stabled, and guards posted on the *raedas*. Then, with Julia and Aurora joining Tacitus and me, the innkeeper let us have a private room off the main dining room. We could finally sit down to eat and talk. Despite the difference in their social status, Julia and Aurora have become as close as sisters in the last few years. They are similar in age and have shared personal tragedies that have brought them even closer. They bear no physical resemblance, so I guess they're more like sisters from different fathers. Julia, like her mother, is small—a good hand shorter than Aurora—with fair skin and light brown hair. She is quick to laugh.

"Gaius Pliny," Tacitus said, "I wish I believed in the gods so I could give them thanks for finding you here. At least I can thank you. You didn't have to do this. I didn't send my messenger to suggest anything of the sort."

I was somewhat embarrassed by his effusiveness. He had hugged me longer than I thought necessary—given his attraction to men as well as women—and clapped me on the back until I was afraid he was going to leave bruises. "What else would a friend do?" I said, drawing back before he could hug me again. "Have you had any further word about your brother? Another messenger perhaps?"

Tacitus shook his head. "All I know to do is to forge ahead. I don't know what I'll find when I get there. But it takes so damn long."

"When you're impatient, it can seem to add to the time or difficulty of a trip." I knew I sounded like my mother.

"Gaius, I'm not just impatient. My brother is sick." Tacitus' voice was plaintive. "The message I received said he might not live much longer. Considering how long it takes for news to travel this distance and how long it's taken me to get this far, he could already be dead. I'm willing to take risks to get there sooner, even if all I can do when I get there is bury his ashes."

It had already been a long trip, especially for Tacitus coming from Rome, and he still had about two hundred fifty miles to go. With a wagon in tow, it would take another seven days or more, but I could see he needed encouragement. "Let's not think like that," I said. "Let's accept the risks and hope for the best." Where was this maternal voice coming from?

Tacitus reached over and patted my shoulder. "You're a true friend to come with me. I just want to get there as fast as I can."

"The *raeda*s do slow you down. We made excellent time with just the horses."

"I've been thinking about that, and about the route we should take. When I've made this trip before I've followed the Via Julia, the coast road, west from here down to Nemausus, where I get on the Via Agrippa and take that road north to Lugdunum."

"That's the most logical route," I said, "and the best roads."

"And it takes *forever*. But, if we were to take the Via Postumia north out of Genua, then turn toward Augusta Taurinorum on this side of the Padus River, there are decent roads on that route, just not so many places to eat or sleep. Once we get to Augusta Taurinorum, there's a fine road across the mountains that passes not far from my estate before it goes into Lugdunum."

"That would be faster, but we still have a large party. The size alone will slow us down."

Tacitus took a long drink of wine. "I know. That's why I'm going to propose splitting us up. Let's send the women west and we'll just ride horses on the northern route, with half a dozen men. No wagons."

I tore off a piece of bread, which was a lot better than one usually gets in such a place. "We could do that. We managed without a wagon on our way down here, but that was just for a couple of days. We were fortunate to find lodging both nights."

Julia shook her head vigorously. "I won't hear of it. You are my husband. Your brother is my brother. I intend to be there when you find out how he's doing. 'Where you are Gaius, I am Gaia.' I promised you that when we married."

"I made the same promise to you," Aurora said, taking my hand. We had held our own private ceremony, just the two of us, a few days before I married Livia. It meant nothing legally, but we regarded it as the ultimate bond between us. Tacitus and Julia were the only people we told after we did it. "And your mother told me to watch out for you," Aurora continued. "I can't do that if I'm not with you. I can ride all the way as well as you can, if that's what it takes, but I *am* going with you."

It wasn't just what she said but the tone she used. I took a deep breath. "Have you completely forgotten who is the master here and who is the slave?" I regretted the words even as I heard them tumbling out of my mouth like rocks down the side of a mountain. There was nothing I could do to stop them before they crushed her.

Aurora looked at me with as much pain in her eyes as if I had slapped her. "No, my lord," she whispered. "I have not forgotten. How could I ever forget?" She stood and bowed her head, with her hands clasped in front of her like an obedient slave. "Will you excuse me, my lord?" She turned and walked away. Her shoulders trembled slightly; one hand went to her face. I suspected she was crying.

Julia got up and leaned across the table, shaking a finger at me. "Be thinking *very* hard about how you're going to apologize for that," she said as she started after Aurora.

After a moment and another sip of wine Tacitus sighed loudly and said, "Well, we obviously are going to have the women with us. They may not be speaking to us—at least not to you—but they're going to be with us. That means we'll be taking at least one *raeda*, and that will slow us down."

"I'm sorry." I put my head in my hands. "I don't know why I said that. I'm tired. I've been thinking about my mother all day. Will I see her again?"

"So you took it out on Aurora."

"Is that what I did?"

"Yes. And I don't know how you're ever going to apologize enough for it." He turned to me with pity or disgust in his eyes. "Gaius Pliny, you are an ass, an absolute braying jackass. That woman loves you." He pointed toward the door through which Aurora had just left. "She has loved you—adored you, worshipped you—since you were seven years old. I've known you long enough to know that you realize that." He cocked his head. "You do realize it, don't you?"

My face contorted as I tried to hold back tears. "Of course I do.

Don't you know I feel the same way about her? You, of all people, must appreciate my dilemma. What can I *do?*"

"First you have to figure out how you can possibly make up for what you just said. Then you have to hope she'll forgive you."

I sat looking down at the table, rubbing a finger over a knot in the wood, until Tacitus said, "Do you have any idea what you might do? I can't even come up with a suggestion."

I put my hands on the table and pushed my chair back. "I know exactly what I'm going to do. It's the only thing I *can* do."

"What—"

"I'll be ready to go at dawn." I got up and walked out of the inn.

———— ·◦· ————

I turned right when I left the inn. Not that it made any difference. I didn't know anything about this town and couldn't see much through my tears. When I got to the next corner, I stopped. A hand touched my shoulder from behind. I thought it might be Gaius, the last person in the world I wanted to talk to right then and the person I most wanted to see. But when I turned around, Julia embraced me.

She let me cry until the tears slowed and I could say, "Why did he talk to me like that? He's never said anything that cruel before."

"And he regrets it from the bottom of his heart, I promise you."

"You're just saying that."

"No, I'm not." She shook her head emphatically. "You didn't see his face after you left. He is sorry, and the two of you will get past this. You just don't want to do or say anything that makes it worse."

"That's what you should tell him." I jerked my head toward the inn.

"I did, and I will again. And I'll bet Tacitus is giving him an earful right now."

I wiped my eyes and managed a crooked smile. "You are such wonderful friends."

Julia slipped her arm through mine. "Let's take a walk. It'll give Tacitus time to talk some sense into Gaius Pliny."

———— ·◦· ————

A cool evening breeze came in off the ocean as I sat on the bank of the river that runs through Genua. The city is old enough that it was built with walls for protection, but the peace that Rome has established around the inner sea, which we claim as *Mare Nostrum*, has obviated the need for such structures. Genua's gates are left open and buildings have been attached to the city's walls. If our world could change enough to make defensive walls unnecessary, I wondered if we would ever out-grow the need for slaves.

As I left, Tacitus had shouted some suggestions at my back for ways I could make up to Aurora for what I'd said. I hadn't listened because I knew what I had to do. Emancipating her was the only way I could see to atone for the verbal slap I had given her. I was as ashamed of what I said as Ovid was when he hit his mistress. "Put the chains on me!" he cried.

But, if I emancipated Aurora, it would change our relationship forever. Once done, it couldn't be undone, just like our decision to make love for the first time. If you can call that a decision. A deci-sion has to involve your mind, your rationality, and that's not located between your legs. Emancipating her had to be carefully thought through.

I'd never brought up the subject with her because I was afraid she might ask me to do it. A few of my slaves have asked, and I have usually agreed. I offered to free Naomi, my mother's servant and confidante, but she refused to accept it. She said it would do nothing to change her life, and being a slave made her feel closer to my mother. They are companions rather than mistress and slave.

I picked up a few small stones and tossed one into the river.

I guess Naomi's right. A manumitted slave, a *libertus* or *liberta*, usu-ally stays in the former owner's house, doing the same work he or she had previously done, usually for a wage. Manumission is a reward for years of service, proudly mentioned on tombstones. Its primary benefit accrues to any children born after manumission. They are free citizens, but Naomi is well past child-bearing age. I know some people who were born after their fathers were emancipated. One, Larcius Macedo, a member of the Senate, is a brute in his treatment of his own slaves.

I don't know if he's forgotten where he came from or remembers it all too well.

Liberti can work outside the house and earn some money. Macedo is an extreme example of a man who inherited what his father was able to amass after he was freed and then ruthlessly built on it. More typically, a *libertus* will work to save up money to buy the freedom of a woman he considers his wife, and any children they may have. I have several *liberti* in my various households, but only a few have gone out on their own. They're usually the ones I'm just as happy to see leaving. I don't even mind giving them some money to start out with.

A freed slave has nothing. Even the clothes on his or her back belong to the master. For a woman that means finding a place to live and some sort of work, most likely in a *taberna*. Many of them, if they don't find a husband, eventually become prostitutes because they can't survive any other way. What if I freed Aurora and she chose to leave? She would be free to marry someone of her choosing, without my consent. Or would she be reduced to prostitution? Given her skill with a blade, she might find work as an assassin.

I tossed another stone into the river. The current was slow enough that the stone made a ripple in the flowing water.

"The water is soothing, isn't it, my lord?" a man's voice said behind me. Charinus sat down next to me.

"Yes, it is," I said. "I dislike being on it or in it, but I can sit beside it for hours on end."

Charinus tossed a pebble into the water and pointed to the ripple it made. "There's a paradox for us, my lord. That pebble sank right through the water. The water could not support it, but, over time, the water will wear the pebble away."

"Are you a philosopher then?"

"No, my lord. Just a man who thinks about things."

"Is that why you didn't kill the man you were fighting back there on the road? You had him on the ground."

"Yes, I did, my lord. But we had won the fight, and other men were coming to our aid. That man's death wouldn't have changed anything, so why not let him live?"

"The Gauls have been fighting against Rome for years, since Julius Caesar's time. Thousands have died, on both sides."

"Then would one man tip the balance in that fight?" Charinus used both hands to mimic the balances in a scale going up and down.

"If you're a philosopher, you must know the *sorites* argument. One man here, another man there, then another."

"Yes, my lord. When do the individual pieces become a heap? Or, in this case, an army. Rome will not last forever. No empire ever has. Not Babylon, not Persia, not Alexander's. Just like those rocks at the bottom of the river, they will be worn away in time."

"We can—we must—do everything in our power to delay that process."

"And enslaved people believe they must do everything in their power to hasten it."

The man was advocating treason! "So you think the man whose life you spared—"

"I don't know what he will do, my lord, or what part in the heap he will become. I just didn't see any reason to kill him." He stood up. "Sleep well, my lord."

———— ◦◦◦ ————

I finally went to bed but couldn't sleep, so I knew when Aurora climbed into bed with me. I hardly dared to breathe. She kept her back turned toward me, and I didn't think I should touch her. "I didn't expect you to do this," I said as her bare back touched mine.

"All the other rooms were taken, my lord, and I didn't want to sleep in the stable. Be sure we have time to shave you tomorrow. I didn't do it this morning."

"Shave me or cut my throat?"

"I'll decide by tomorrow morning, my lord." Her voice sounded matter-of-fact.

"Maybe you should cut out my tongue."

She sighed deeply. "No, you can do such wonderful things with your tongue. I would miss it more than you would."

I raised myself on an elbow and half turned toward her. "I'm sorry, you know, so *very* sorry."

"I know, Gaius." She patted my thigh without turning over. "We don't need to talk about it now. We have a long day ahead of us."

We slept back-to-back for the entire night.

———◦∘◦———

Aurora said virtually nothing as she prepared to shave me the next morning. She placed a stool in the middle of the room and opened my razor. I went to my knees and grasped her knees, the formal pose for a suppliant, one who knows he cannot do anything but throw himself on the other person's mercy. "Please forgive me," I said.

Aurora gasped in surprise. "Gaius, I do forgive you." She ran her fingers through my hair. "Now get up and let me shave you."

I took a seat on the stool and leaned back against her.

"Tacitus is going to be in a hurry to leave," she said as she rubbed olive oil on my jaws and chin. "I had a long talk with Julia yesterday. She assured me that you are sincerely sorry. She warned me that you might do something extravagant to make up for what you said.'What, sacrifice a hecatomb to me?' I said. She said you'd be willing to do that, but she suspected you might offer to emancipate me."

I don't think I gasped audibly, but I must have tensed enough for Aurora to feel it, pressed against her the way I was.

She pushed me away from her. "That's it, isn't it?" she said, distress heavy in her voice. "You're going to emancipate me?"

I reached into my bag and pulled out the single sheet of papyrus on which I had written and sealed her emancipation notice the night before. She took it from my hand, read it, and started crying.

I took her by the shoulders. "I know it's not really enough, but it's all I could think of."

She pulled away from me. "No, Gaius, you don't understand. I'm crying because I don't want to be emancipated."

Now I was completely lost. "What? Doesn't every slave want to be freed? I know Naomi didn't, but she's an unusual case."

"I'm not every slave, Gaius. I want to be as close to you as I possibly can. As your slave I'm closer to you even than your wife."

I pursed my lips. "I could divorce her."

"Offering to emancipate me feels like you're threatening to divorce *me*. As long as I'm your slave, we have an emotional bond and a more important legal bond."

"But, if you were free, you could go wherever you want to."

"Right here is the only place I want to be. If I were free, Livia could attack me, and you know she would. As long as I'm with you—as long as I belong to you—she won't dare."

"But I thought—"

"I know you mean well, my darling, but I don't want to be emancipated." She tried to tear the piece of papyrus in half.

"It's sturdy stuff," I said. "The Egyptians build boats out of it, you know." I held her hands. "Instead of tearing it up, why not put it in a safe place? You might need it someday. As long as that document exists, you are technically free."

Aurora rolled up the piece of papyrus and put it in her bag. "I have forgiven you, Gaius. Isn't that enough? I feel as free as I want to be, and I feel safe as long as I'm with you. That's all I need."

IV

ASS WE CAME DOWN from our room, Aurora said, "This route will be the same one we followed on that trip with your uncle ten years ago, won't it?"

"When we got stranded in that little town because of a broken axle on our *raeda*? I hadn't thought about that in a long time, but I believe you're right. What was the name of the place?"

"Collis Niveosus, wasn't it?"

I nodded. "That sounds familiar. There were certainly hills, but no snow at that time of year."

"I still think, if we'd had a couple of more days back then, we could have figured out who killed that poor man."

"We were just fifteen years old. I doubt anyone there still remembers the incident."

"Whoever killed him must remember it.... He got away with murder."

"He, or she?"

Aurora shook her head. "I'm sorry, but you never did convince me that she was guilty."

"As you said, if we'd had a few more days..."

We had been fifteen when we got stuck in Collis, a small town at the entrance to a pass through the Alps. Just a few days before we arrived a man named Junius had died in what the authorities decided was an accidental fall. Since we were stuck there, Aurora and I undertook what we still consider our first investigation. In the years since, I have sometimes wondered if it was just our youth and inexperience that kept us from reaching a conclusion, or if the authorities had been right all along.

"It will be interesting to see if the town has changed," Aurora said.

"Those little places rarely do."

"So, you think whoever killed Junius is still walking around free."

"If the killer was, in fact, someone from the town. It could have been someone passing through."

When we emerged on the street I was surprised to see Sophronia standing beside the *raeda* that Aurora, Julia, and two of Julia's servants would ride in. Before I could say anything Julia approached me.

"Sophronia asked to ride with us." She glanced back over her shoulder. "She said Livia has charged her with always being available to serve you."

I snorted in derision. "She means 'to spy on me.'"

"I can tell her no, Gaius, with good reason. Having her with us would make things crowded."

"Let's do that. It will cause more tension between Livia and me. She'll wonder what I'm trying to hide from her."

"You mean what *else*, don't you?" She touched my arm and turned back to the *raeda*. She spoke briefly to Sophronia, who glared at me, picked up her bag, and joined the other party.

Tacitus picked out the men he wanted to come with us. I decided to take the three men I had brought with me, just so I wouldn't have to rely on telling someone else's slaves what to do.

Charinus seemed to be bidding farewell to Tacitus' people who were taking the coast road.

"Why don't you take Charinus with us?" I suggested.

Tacitus looked at Julia before replying.

"He seems a reliable fellow," I said. "His knowledge of the language saved us once."

"I've never had any trouble from him," Tacitus said. "I sometimes wonder about him, though. Has he mentioned that his father was some sort of priest among them?"

"No. He just talked about his mother."

"Sometimes I'm not sure how thoroughly Roman he is. But you're right. His knowledge of the language and the area could be helpful." He went over to the *raeda*, said something to an obviously unhappy Julia, and then turned to Charinus, who nodded.

We did not notice anyone following us as we set out and separated into two parties, ours going north and the larger group traveling west on the Via Julia. Traffic going into and out of a fair-sized city like Genua was constant, so we didn't worry about being attacked. Tacitus' horses were strong, and we made better time than I had expected.

My uneasiness increased in the afternoon as traffic thinned out and just before dark, when we stopped for the night in a grove of trees beside a stream. When another small caravan pulled into the grove, I gave a sigh of relief. I had no reason to think those people would fight alongside us if we were attacked, but sheer numbers might make Orgetorix hesitate.

The women closed the side panels on our *raeda* and slept in there while the men took turns standing guard and keeping a small fire burning to ward off the evening's chill and any curious animals.

When it was my turn to take a watch I kept myself awake by thinking about our visit to Collis Nivcosus a decade ago. Aurora and I had been travelling with my uncle and Aurora's mother, Monica, his slave and mistress. My uncle wanted to inspect an estate near Lugdunum that one of his agents had purchased for him. He said it would someday be mine, so I'd best get acquainted with the place. He was always encouraging me to travel, something I wasn't eager to do. My mother had turned down her brother's invitation to come with him. I accompanied him not out of any curiosity about the estate—I sold it soon after I inherited it—but primarily because Monica was taking Aurora with her.

Aurora and I had known one another since she and Monica came into our household from North Africa when she was seven, the same age I was. Her father sold her and her mother to settle some debts. We quickly became friends, a relationship that upset my mother, as did my uncle's connection with Monica. I insisted that Aurora share my tutors. My uncle agreed in order to please Monica and because he acceded to just about anything I asked for. Aurora learned to speak and read Greek and Latin with a facility that amazed everyone around her. Between the two of them she and her mother kept up their fluency in their native Punic tongue.

I added two pieces of wood to the fire and stirred it a bit.

By the time we made that trip Aurora had started her monthlies, my voice had changed, and our relationship was no longer just that of two children. But we didn't know what it was. A fifteen-year-old boy and girl don't "play" together the way they did when they were nine or ten. We became more conscious of the master–slave gulf that existed between us. If she had not been a slave, Aurora would have been married by then. Every time I looked at her, I was glad she wasn't.

That trip north had been uneventful until we were within sight of the little town of Collis Niveosus in the pass through the Alps. The *raeda* that Monica, Aurora, and two others were riding in—one of four in our little caravan—hit a bad spot in the road and the axle snapped. No one in the village had the skill or the equipment to craft another one. The closest place where we could secure a replacement was back in Augusta Taurinorum, and that trip would take several days each way, plus time to make the repairs. We settled into an inn to wait.

All anyone could talk about was the death six days earlier of one of the *duovirs*. Like many small Roman towns, this one was led by two elected magistrates who shared power for a year at a time. We Romans have always been leery of entrusting power to one man. For centuries we elected two consuls every year. Even now, when we give one man power for life, we try to hide the fact from ourselves. The Senate goes through a charade of renewing his power each year. Of course, they would never dare to *not* renew it. As Aurora and I listened to people talk about what had happened, we gathered that the *duovirs* had not been on the best of terms.

I jerked when someone tapped me on the shoulder. "Excuse me, my lord," Charinus said, "I'm here to relieve you on watch."

"Everything seems to be quiet," I said as he gave me a hand up.

"Let's hope it stays that way. Good night." He sat down, crossing his legs in an un-Roman fashion.

But it wasn't a good night. I could not find a place on the ground or a position comfortable enough to let me sleep soundly. At one point I despaired of ever getting to sleep and sat up, wrapping my blanket around me. Then I noticed that the fire was burning low and no guard—Charinus or anyone else—was anywhere to be seen.

I put another piece of wood on the fire and stirred the embers.

"I'll take care of that," Charinus said as he walked out from behind the *raeda*.

"Where have you been?"

"I had to relieve myself, my lord. I thought I should get away from the camp." The fire blazed up enough for me to see his eyes meeting mine, challenging me. "Shall I show you the place I used?"

The sun was barely streaking the eastern horizon the next morning when Tacitus began urging us to get on the road. I think he would have had the horses at a gallop the whole way if I hadn't made him slow down.

"Gaius, it's over two hundred miles from Genua to my estate. I feel like we'll never get there."

"Believe me, my friend, I understand how important this is to you," I said, "but we've got to give the horses some rest or they're going to drop under us. Four passengers and all that baggage in one *raeda* make quite a load."

"I know," he said. "I'm glad we have two horses to pull it instead of one."

I patted one of the horses on his rump. "We can ease their burden a bit by alternating them with the horses our men are riding."

"Good idea. Let's do that when we stop for lunch."

We reached Augusta Taurinorum before dark without incident. I began to hope that Orgetorix and his band had thought better of attacking us, even though I knew they were more likely just looking for a better spot.

We were able to find a decent inn that served passable food. There were only three rooms available. Tacitus and Julia took one, and we were going to put Julia's servant women in another. I would have the third room, while the male servants slept in the *raeda* or in the barn. I assumed Aurora would be with me, but she was reluctant as we talked in one corner of the dining room.

"I think I should sleep with the other servant women," she said, glancing over her shoulder at them. "There's enough room."

"But why? None of them care about your relationship with me. Sophronia's not here to report what we do to Livia."

"It could get back to her eventually, and that would be bad for both of us."

"You don't feel like you're in any physical danger, do you?"

Aurora dismissed that thought with a wave of her hand. "Not at all. But the other women… You don't realize how jealous servants can be when they see one getting special treatment from a master."

"Why should they care? I don't mistreat my other servants because of you." I took her hand and drew her to me, but she pulled away.

"Gaius, please don't make this awkward for me." I looked over her shoulder at the knot of servant women. Julia was talking to Tacitus on the other side of the dining room, with the other women grouped behind her.

"Has anyone said anything to you?"

Aurora hesitated, then said, "Well, when we stopped to relieve ourselves this afternoon, I ended up alone with one of Julia's women, Alkippe, that darker-haired one over there." She motioned with her head toward the woman. "She said she knew why we had kept Sophronia from coming with us. She had practically called me a whore, 'the master's little pet.'"

"I'll put a stop to that right now," I said.

Aurora put a hand on my arm and moved to block me. "No, don't say anything. That would just prove her point and make everyone think I run to you with every little thing. I can take care of myself."

Orgetorix's son wasn't the first man Aurora had killed to protect herself or me. But the sniping of a group of jealous women was a different kind of attack. I glanced at the woman Aurora had indicated, but she turned her head as though she couldn't be bothered with me. "Are you sure you want to spend the night in the same room with her?"

"I think I have to. I don't want to antagonize her any further."

"Do you want me to say something to Julia?"

Aurora shook her head. "From what I've seen in the wagon, Julia seems to trust Alkippe. She's ingratiated herself with Julia by being very obsequious." She fell into a mocking tone. "'Yes, my lady, this' and 'Yes, my lady, that.'"

"That's how she should address her mistress, isn't it? Respectfully?"

"It's more the tone than the actual words. 'Servile' is the best way to describe her. I can be respectful, but I could never talk to you—or your mother—like that."

I sighed. "All right. I'll be lonely, but if you think it's best..."

Aurora smiled and lowered her voice. "It's never best for you to be lonely, darling, but this is how I think I need to handle the situation. I'll be lonely, too, even with the other women in the room."

"You have your knife, don't you?"

She nodded. "It's in my bag. I don't think I need to be wearing it right now. Sophronia saw me kill that man, but I'm not sure she knows where I got the knife. Everything happened so fast. She may report back to Livia, who has her own suspicions of me because of what she once saw. Alkippe has a sharp tongue. That's her most dangerous weapon."

"Could I look forward to a visitor later tonight?"

"I don't think that's a good idea. If one of them wakes up and sees that I'm gone, it will just give them more to gossip about. Sorry."

"I understand."

We stepped away from one another as Tacitus walked across the room toward us. "We've got the sleeping arrangements worked out, I believe. Things didn't turn out quite the way we expected. That fellow"—he pointed to a well-dressed man talking to the inn's owner—"is traveling on an imperial pass. He has claimed a room. Gaius, you and I will need to share a room. We'll put the women in the largest room they have here. Our men will sleep in and around the *raeda* or in the barn."

The man Tacitus indicated turned to say something to one of his servants. That's when I saw how badly disfigured his face was. I could only guess that he had suffered a horrible beating or been attacked by an animal. On a strap tied behind his head he wore a patch to cover whatever remained of his right eye. What I could hear of his voice sounded like a croak.

————— ⚬◦⚬ —————

I was definitely not ready to get up when Tacitus shook me awake the next morning. I had to remind myself that I don't have a brother, so I can't fully appreciate his anxiety. He was bustling with energy from a good night's sleep, something I had not enjoyed. From his chatter, I gathered that he had already waked everyone else and been downstairs to settle our bill. He was trying to tell me something about what the innkeeper had said.

"You know that man who commandeered the other room last night?"

I nodded. "The one with the monstrous face?"

"The very one… He wants to travel with us."

I squinted to bring Tacitus' face into focus. "Why?"

"He was supposed to meet some people here to travel with them to Lugdunum, but he was late getting here and they didn't wait for him. He doesn't want to travel by himself."

I was sitting on the edge of the bed, feeling around for the chamber pot under it. "I can understand that, although his face might frighten off any would-be attackers."

"It was horrible, wasn't it?"

"I won't enjoy having to look at him, but I suppose we should show some sympathy. So, I don't have any objection. Does he have servants with him?"

"Two. They slept in the barn last night to guard his horses."

"My only concern is that, the more people we have with us, the more likely we are to run into delays. And I know you want to move as fast as possible."

"I do. But there is the matter of this fellow's imperial pass. He could simply have waved it under our noses and demanded that we take him along with us. At least he was polite enough to ask."

Tacitus was right. A pass bearing the *princeps*'s seal allowed the person carrying it to demand any service he required from anyone he encountered, as he did with the room last night. He could have taken our *raeda* or some of our horses, anything except our servants, and he could have made them work for him. Anyone he met on the road had to get out of his way and let him pass. On the other hand, anyone accompanying him could share those benefits.

I put the chamber pot back under the bed for a servant to empty and slipped on the clean tunic Aurora had laid out for me the previous night. "Having him and his pass in our party could work to our advantage."

"That thought had occurred to me," Tacitus said. "On the other hand, if he rides with us, we'll have to listen to his voice and look at his face. Have you ever seen such a mess? I'm not even sure how he can chew or breathe."

"I don't see how he could have survived whatever happened to him that did so much damage. Maybe he'll ride in the back." I buckled my sandals. "All right, it's settled. Let's get everyone organized and get on the road."

"Everyone *is* organized. The *raeda*'s waiting at the door. I let you sleep as long as possible."

"Then you are a true friend indeed, even though you kept me awake half the night with your snoring. I kept wishing you could live up to your name."

Tacitus nodded sheepishly. "That's what Julia says. That's why we have separate rooms."

Our party was mounted and waiting for us in front of the inn. I spoke to Julia and then asked Aurora if she had slept well.

"Yes, my lord, thank you. And I hope you did."

"Not with my husband snoring away, he didn't," Julia said. "I'll guarantee that."

Our new traveling companion joined in the laughter. Unfortunately, he seemed to have decided to ride in the front with Tacitus and me while his two servants joined our men behind the *raeda*. Trying to avoid looking at his face, I noticed that he was an older man, probably about fifty, with his hair going gray, and boasted an equestrian stripe on his tunic. I was glad to see that he appeared to have kept himself fit, with no more of a bulge around his waist than one would expect at that age. We didn't need some overweight layabout wanting to stop every few miles because he was tired from the effort that riding a horse requires.

"Good morning," he said, leaning down to shake my hand. "Are you Gaius Pliny?" His croaking voice required a listener to pay close attention to grasp everything he said.

"Yes, I am."

"I'm Lucius Nonius Torquatus. I'm sorry that my face causes you such unease."

"No, it's—"

"You don't have to pretend. I saw you wince, even if I have only one eye. I know how my appearance affects people. My own mother can't stand to look at me. She didn't recognize me the first time she saw me after this happened. Neither my face nor my voice. It doesn't bother me, of course. But then I don't have to look at it."

"I know I'm being impertinent, but may I ask what happened?"

Torquatus smiled. At least I think he smiled. His mouth was so crooked it was hard to read his expressions.

"I would be surprised if you didn't ask. Most people point and stare. They think I must have looked at Medusa." He held up a hand to forestall my objections. "Yes, I actually have heard them say that. Mothers tell their children that a monster like me will eat them during the night if they don't behave themselves." His words were turning bitter, but he took a breath and stopped himself. "Several years ago I was attacked by a gang of thugs and beaten nearly to death. I was hit hard in the throat several times."

He offered no explanation of where the attack took place or how he came to be in the company of such men. I decided it was best to let the matter rest. "I'm glad for your recovery. We'll look forward to having your company."

"Not to mention my pass," he said with a smile that was more frightening than reassuring.

The innkeeper brought my horse and Tacitus' over to a mounting stone. With his help we settled on the beasts, ready for another long day's ride. People who don't have horses look at those of us who ride—equestrians in a literal as well as social sense—as having an easy time of it, but it takes constant effort and exertion to control the animals, with both the reins and one's knees. Some men even count it as a form of exercise. I've never been comfortable on horseback, no matter how much Aurora has tried to teach me about riding. At least this one obeyed my commands most of the time. I maneuvered him until I ended up beside our new companion and we continued our conversation.

"I'm most pleased to make your acquaintance," Torquatus croaked. "I met your uncle some years ago—before this happened—and I greatly admire Cornelius Tacitus' father-in-law, Julius Agricola."

"You should be careful about saying that aloud," Tacitus said.

Torquatus looked around. "I think I'm in safe company, and I look forward to traveling with such distinguished young men."

What Tacitus calls my "damnable curiosity" wanted to know what business Torquatus had that merited an imperial pass, and how he got one if he professed admiration for Agricola, whom Domitian despises. But I thought that wasn't the best question with which to continue a conversation, so I said, "I've heard the name Nonius Torquatus. Would I know any of your family?"

"My family is large," Torquatus said, "and widespread and not very imaginative when it comes to names. I have several uncles and cousins with the same name. But more handsome faces, or at least less repulsive ones."

"When did you meet my uncle?"

"We were at a dinner given by Verginius Rufus."

"Oh, were you a friend of Verginius?"

"Not in the formal sense, as your uncle was. I was fortunate enough just to have known him and been at the low place at his table. He was a great man."

"Yes, he was." Verginius had been an *amicus* of my uncle, sharing a legal status that we call *amicitia*, "friendship." At a couple of points when my uncle was away on business for Vespasian for an extended

time, my mother and I had stayed with Verginius, and I had brought
Aurora along. My uncle wanted us not just with our servants but in a
house headed by an adult male who had the *auctoritas* to protect us.

"Do you ever wonder," Torquatus said, as though musing aloud,
"how different things would be if Verginius had made himself *princeps*
when Nero died? He certainly could have done it. He had the reputation and the support of a good segment of the Senate and the army."

"Yes, but he had no taste for it. I heard him say, in his later years,
how glad he was that he had stayed out of that bloody conflict and
how much confidence he had in Vespasian." I raised my voice on those
last few words. This was a dangerous conversation to be having in so
public a place. Even if we could trust one another and our servants,
there was no telling who might be listening behind a door or a shuttered window. I wanted to talk about something else. "What business
takes you to Lugdunum?"

"My cousin is the governor of Gallia Lugdunensis. When Domitian
learned that I was planning a trip there, he asked me to deliver some
documents to him." Torquatus patted the two leather bags draped over
his horse in front of him.

"Wouldn't it have been faster to use imperial couriers?" From Tacitus' expression I could see that he found the situation curious as well.

"He says there's no urgency and the documents are sensitive. You
know the *princeps* has difficulty trusting even some of what should be
his most trustworthy servants."

As our caravan swung into motion Torquatus asked, "Do we know
anything about the weather up ahead? Any reports from people coming
from that direction?"

"The innkeeper says people who've come through in the last few
days have reported very cold weather," Tacitus said.

"It's early spring," Torquatus said. "That's to be expected. It doesn't
really warm up this far north, my cousin says, until June. I just hope
we don't get caught in a late snowstorm."

"We're not carrying a lot of supplies," Tacitus said. "Our plan is to
pick up what we need as we go along." He added with a laugh, "If we
got stranded, we might have to eat one another."

"On a nice day like this," I said, "it's hard to imagine such a prospect, but the weather at the foot of the Alps can change overnight, with little or no warning. I've learned that from being at my estate on Lake Comum this time of year."

"Do you think it's advisable then," Torquatus said, "to take the route Tacitus was describing to me? I'm having second thoughts about my own decision to go this way. It's not too late. We could turn back and take the coast road and then turn north along the Rhodanus. That's the way I've gone before. It would be much safer."

"And take *much* longer," Tacitus said. "No, I need to get to Lugdunum as quickly as possible, as I told you this morning. Domitian may not feel any urgency about those documents, but I certainly do about my brother. If you think otherwise, of course you're free to choose your own route."

"There aren't many good places to stop on this route, are there?" Torquatus said. "Just Collis Niveosus."

"Do you know the place?" I asked.

"Only by reputation."

"There are worse places to stop."

"You've been there?"

I nodded. "For a few days, ten years ago."

"In the winter? I've heard the winters there can be horrible."

"No, I was there in the summer, in July."

"Well, I guess Collis it is." Torquatus did not look the least bit pleased with the prospect, from what I could tell of his expression.

The air did seem to cool quickly the farther north and west we traveled. Torquatus chattered on about various people we might have known in common and other topics of minimal interest to me. I was curious that, at his age and his rank, he had held only minor offices, all of them before his disfigurement. He was no more politically advanced than Tacitus and I were, and we were over twenty years his juniors. His appearance could account for that. Perhaps he just preferred to stay out of public life.

And yet he carried an imperial pass, which neither Tacitus nor I could ever hope to acquire as long as Domitian was *princeps*.

When we stopped for lunch on the side of the road, Aurora and I found one another. We sat on a rock and shared a cup of wine with the bread and cheese that Julia parceled out to everyone. "That Torquatus never seems to grow tired of hearing his own voice," she said.

"At least I don't have to contribute anything more than an occasional 'I see' or 'That's true.' And I try to keep my eyes straight ahead. What strikes me most strongly is the way his tone can shift. I've heard people who knew Caligula say that he could be talking about some ordinary subject and suddenly fly into a rage. Torquatus has seemed on the verge of losing his composure several times this morning."

Aurora nodded. "I can't imagine going through life with a face like that. I think it would drive me into a rage." After she swallowed a bite of bread she said, "Does it strike you as—and I hate to say it—a huge coincidence that his path crossed ours?"

I took a sip of wine as I pondered her question. "Well, people do travel, and there are only so many routes they can take. They're bound to cross now and then. Are you getting at something?"

"To put it concisely, why would Domitian use a man of equestrian rank as a messenger?"

"His cousin is governor of Gallia Lugdunensis. It seems reasonable to ask Torquatus to deliver something to him, particularly if it's something highly confidential. Using Praetorians or other high-ranking messengers would attract attention."

Aurora didn't look convinced. "Would Domitian trust someone who speaks so highly of Agricola?"

I took a long look at Torquatus, sitting next to Tacitus and Julia, both of whom were trying to look anywhere but at him. "That question has been on my mind all morning. He may not be sincere. Do you think his presence is not coincidental? Or not innocent?"

"I think we can be sure that Domitian has a spy or two in Tacitus' household."

"Tacitus himself admits that," I said. "He just doesn't know whom to suspect."

"That's not important right now. Let's say the spy reports that Tacitus is going to be making this trip, with no advance planning. One of Domitian's lackeys is, conveniently, related to the governor of the area. Domitian doesn't have time to organize a scheme, so he sends Torquatus to catch up with Tacitus and accompany him to Lugdunum, pretending to admire Agricola."

"And my uncle, for that matter. I never heard him mention anyone named Torquatus."

"The stewards in your houses would know if they were acquainted. At any rate, he carries documents—sealed documents we can't see—that could be entirely innocuous and for show."

"I doubt that they're the 'Kill the bearer of this letter' type."

"No, but they could threaten Tacitus in some way." Aurora gasped as she caught the full implication of her own reasoning. "What if Domitian sees this as an opportunity to have Tacitus arrested while he's far away from Rome—"

"Where Agricola and his veterans can't protect him."

"Exactly."

V

THE REST OF THE DAY passed without incident. Torquatus eventually ran out of things to chatter about. I welcomed the silence. We made about thirty miles and decided to stop at a small inn, where we were happily received because the place was empty. The innkeeper's shock at Torquatus' face was mitigated by his admiration for the imperial pass. He had never seen anything like either of them before.

"Do you know anything about the roads ahead?" I asked. "The weather?"

"People coming south over the last few days, sir, say the snow has been heavy, especially for this late in the winter, but the pass through the mountains is open, so far as I know."

"That's good to hear," Tacitus said. "I just hope it holds true for a few more days."

The next day we had to get out extra clothing during our lunch stop because of the cold wind coming down off the Alps. Just putting on a second tunic, though, doesn't protect one from the weather because the garments are loose and don't cover one's bare legs. I wished I had some strips of cloth to wrap around my legs, as the emperor Augustus used to do when he was cold. We were traveling so light, though, that I was unwilling to start ripping up perfectly good garments. I hoped we could find some warmer clothing when we got to Collis Niveosus.

We reached the little town just as darkness was falling, along with the temperature.

"The place looks just like it did when we were here ten years ago,"

I said as we came to a stop in front of the only inn in town. During a lull in the conversation I had explained our presence here at that time to Torquatus, without mentioning a murder. Tacitus, of course, had heard the story, at least some of it.

"Well, the *raeda* still has both axles this time," Torquatus said with an unpleasant laugh, "so we'll hope our luck holds and we can get out of here quickly tomorrow. Let's see about accommodations." He kept looking around nervously, like a soldier expecting an attack.

He, Tacitus, and I entered the inn, which was warm enough, thanks to its hypocaust. Since our previous visit had been in the summer, I hadn't been aware of the temperature in the building. Before we could ask for anything, the innkeeper, unable to take his eyes off Torquatus, said, "Sorry, gents, but I'm full up." I thought he just didn't want Torquatus in his place. For simpler folk a face as ugly as Torquatus' could be a bad omen.

Torquatus pulled his imperial pass out of the pouch he was carrying and waved it under the innkeeper's nose. "Do you know what this is?"

The innkeeper, Roscius, I recognized in spite of the weight he had gained and the hair he had lost. He was completely bald on top, with a gray fringe around his head. He showed no comprehension of the document. "Let me get my wife, sir." He scurried into the kitchen and returned with a tall, Amazonian woman whom I remembered from our previous trip. Her name was Lucina. She was wiping her hands on a cloth. About forty, she was still quite attractive. She took the pass from Torquatus and read it while her husband stretched to look over her shoulder, nodding and pretending to understand. A little girl, about four years old and blond, clung to the hem of Lucina's garment, frightened by Torquatus' face, no doubt.

Lucina took a long look at Torquatus, then turned her attention back to the pass. Her ability to read at all surprised me, as it had ten years ago—a woman in such an out-of-the-way place. What surprised me even more was with what a smooth voice she read, not stumbling at all over some of the technicalities. She was not self-taught, I guessed.

"So, you see, it's an imperial pass," she informed her husband as she finished. She pointed to the most important passages and read them to him again. "It says we're to give this gentleman and his party anything they need."

"Where's his name?" Roscius asked.

"It doesn't need a name," Lucina said. "What matters is the emperor's seal down here."

From my own experience I knew that what she was saying was true. Passes weren't always given to people by name. They could be handed out to whoever needed one. Sometimes they could be sold for a nice sum, although that was illegal. For a moment I wondered if that's how Torquatus got this one.

"And that seal," Torquatus said, "means that you have to give us lodging for the night."

"But we're full up," the innkeeper said.

"You'll have to find somewhere else to put those people," Torquatus said matter-of-factly, as though merely saying the words would make it happen.

"There's…there's no place else in town," the innkeeper spluttered.

"But he's right, Roscius," Lucina said. "We have to accommodate them. How many rooms do you need, sir?"

"How many do you have?"

"Five," Lucina said. "Well, six, but my daughter-in-law and granddaughter use one."

"We can make do with five, I suppose," Torquatus said.

Roscius started to protest. "But—"

"There's no 'but' about it, husband. Don't be so thick-headed. That's what this says. And, see, there's the emperor's seal." She pointed again to the blob of wax at the bottom of the page.

"What am I supposed to do with the people who've already paid for rooms?" Roscius asked. "Where are they supposed to go?"

The little girl looked anxiously from one adult to another as the conversation grew more intense.

"That is *not* my concern," Torquatus said. "And we need some warmer clothing or blankets. This weather isn't what we were expecting."

I cringed at the harsh, unfeeling tone that so many of my peers use when dealing with lower-class people, and I disliked Torquatus as much as the innkeeper obviously did.

"We'll take care of things right away, sir." Lucina bowed her head and handed the pass back to Torquatus.

"Oh, and we passed a bath on our way into town. Who owns it?"

"I do, sir," Roscius said. His tone showed that he knew the admission would bring on more work for him.

"Excellent. I know it's late in the day, but we'll need to have the water heated. We've had a long journey and we did not get to bathe last night."

All Roscius could do was sputter and head for the bath. Lucina introduced herself and said, "If you'd like to have some supper while you wait for us to take care of all this..." She motioned to the dining area of the large room.

Torquatus turned to me. "What do you say, Gaius Pliny? Shall we have something to eat?"

I had been standing in the shadows behind Torquatus. Lucina, who was on her way to the kitchen with the little girl still attached to her garment, stopped at the mention of my name and turned back toward us.

"Gaius Pliny? By the gods..."

I stepped forward. "I was Gaius Caecilius when I was here ten years ago. My uncle was Pliny. He adopted me in his will."

"Oh, yes. The old gentleman who had so much trouble breathing."

I nodded. "That was what caused his death in the eruption of Vesuvius."

"My condolences, sir." Lucina moved closer to me and spoke in my ear. "Are you certain someone didn't kill him, the way you kept trying to prove I killed my husband?"

I squared my shoulders. "I felt justice required that I look into his death."

"Some people still aren't sure I'm innocent."

"Frankly, neither am I."

She bent down and patted the little girl's bottom. "Run on into the kitchen, darling. Grandma needs to talk to this nice man. I'll be there in a minute. Tell your Aunt Roscia I said to give you a sweet."

We watched the little girl skip away.

"Your granddaughter?" I said.

"Yes, Junia's child, Junilla." She did not turn back to me. "Her mother died during the birth. Now my son and his wife and I are raising her."

"What about…what was his name?"

"Draco?"

"Yes. Isn't he her father?"

"He is, but he's never gotten over Junia's death. He says he can't raise a child by himself, especially a girl. She knows he's her father but this arrangement seems best. Junia lost her first child, before he was a year old. That makes this one even more precious."

"My mother lost a child at birth, before I was born. She still grieves for her."

"That's what we women do when a part of us dies." Lucina was silent for a moment, then said, "Are you going to expose me…about the rest?"

"I didn't ten years ago. Why would I now?"

"Perhaps you've had time to think it over, to regret what you did—or didn't do—then."

"No, I haven't thought it over. I hate to disappoint you, but I haven't thought about that situation, or about you, again until this day."

"You and that girl! All you did was stir up questions and trouble for me."

"You know perfectly well she did more than that for you."

Lucina took a deep breath. "There is that, yes, but I hope you're not going to be poking into that whole business again. Is she here with you?"

I nodded.

"Well, that's no surprise. I'll bet the two of you haven't been apart for more than a few days since then."

I had spent a year in Syria on the governor's staff without Aurora, but that was none of Lucina's business. As a result of that experience I had vowed to myself that I would never be away from her for any long period again, but that was also none of Lucina's business. "Listen, we are in a hurry to get to Lugdunum. All we want is lodging for the night and something to eat. We'll be on our way in the morning."

"And good riddance to you, sir, if you'll pardon my saying it with a smile."

The woman was dancing right on the edge of insubordination. "I can understand your feeling that way. Was anyone ever arrested for your husband's murder?"

"No. That's all in the past. Just leave it be, please," she said.

"I don't intend to stir up old unpleasantness. We'll just be here overnight, as I said. I am surprised, though, to hear you call Roscius your husband."

Lucina's shoulders sagged. "When Junius died, Roscius took over all his property. As you learned, Junius owed him money that I didn't know about. Roscius told me I could be his wife or his slave."

"Better the former," I said.

Lucina shook her head. "Most days, sir, I can't tell the difference. He told me he would let his wife get on top. Considering how much he weighs..."

I couldn't miss the poignancy in her voice, but that wasn't my main concern at the moment. "Doesn't it bother you to think that one of your neighbors might have killed your husband?"

Aurora and Julia had quietly come into the inn. Now Aurora moved closer to me, listening intently. I could see, from the quick lift of her head, that Lucina recognized Aurora.

"I don't think any of them would be capable of such a thing, sir," Lucina said. "It's more likely to have been someone passing through who killed him, as I told you ten years ago. We get a lot of traffic on this road. It's the easiest pass over the mountains. Junius may have gotten into an argument with someone. He did have a bit of a temper, and he liked to gamble. We'll never know, but I've made peace with it." She sighed. "Now, if you'll take a seat, I'll bring you something to serve as a *gustatio* while we fix you a proper supper."

Several of the tables were occupied, but Lucina made everyone get up and move. They glared at us as we called the rest of our party into the inn and took over the dining room. Aurora and I stood in a corner, trying to avoid looking at the people who were being forced to leave.

"This really isn't fair," she protested quietly to me. "It's cold out there. Where are those people going to go?"

"I know it's not fair," I said. "But do you want to spend the night in the *raeda*? Is that fair?"

She stuck out her lower lip. "Well, no. But can't you say something to Torquatus?"

"Say what? He's the senior man here, and he has the pass. We're traveling with him, not the other way around. He's only doing what he has every right to do."

"There's got to be something you can do."

"I'm touched by your confidence in me, but I'm afraid it's misplaced in this instance."

"Please try, Gaius." She squeezed my hand. "Think how you'd feel if we were being tossed out of our rooms."

I found Roscius, who had returned from the bath and was explaining to an angry customer that none of this was his fault. "You should blame the narrow-stripers," he sneered.

Yes, I thought, the narrow-stripers like me. I wished I could cover the mark of my rank or rip it off my tunic. "Where are these people going to go?" I asked.

"I know folks in town who'll take them for the night. We'll put some out on our farm. I imagine some of them will have to double up, but nobody's going to be sleeping on the ground." He turned his head to spit on the floor. "No thanks to you, *sir*." His emphasis on the last word was as close to sarcasm as he could make it without crossing that line.

I reached under my tunic and took out my money pouch. "You said six rooms." I counted out enough *denarii* for him to parcel out. "This should take care of everyone, shouldn't it? Share it among the people who are being displaced." I knew that, unless his rates were exorbitant, that was much more than the cost of the rooms.

Roscius' eyes widened. "Why, yes, sir. That's most generous of you."

Maybe it will keep us from being murdered in our sleep, I thought.

When I turned back to Aurora, she gave my hand another squeeze that promised more gratitude later that night. "Thank you."

As we walked into the dining room, an old dog with a gray muzzle, sleeping on a mat in one corner, raised his head. "Oh, look," Aurora said. "It's Argos."

The dog had been here ten years ago and had quickly developed an affection for Aurora. Now he struggled to his feet and walked slowly over to her. She knelt and scratched his head.

"You sweet old thing," she said. "It's wonderful to see you again." The dog followed her as we approached the table where our party was sitting and settled beside her chair.

Torquatus' eyebrow arched in its distorted way when Aurora sat down next to me at the table with him, Tacitus, and Julia.

"It's all right," Julia said, patting Aurora on the arm. "She's a dear friend of mine."

I wanted to draw attention away from the awkwardness of having a slave sitting at the table with us. "I hate to roust people out like this."

"Why?" Torquatus snorted. "It's our right. I've endured enough misfortune in my life that I'll take whatever recompense I can get, wherever I can get it." He stroked his chin as if he needed to remind himself of what had happened to him. "That's what my pass is all about."

I couldn't deny that I had thought in those very terms when I heard he wanted to travel with us. I just hadn't realized how much of an impact we would have on other, real people. I hoped I had defused the situation and ransomed us.

With the help of Roscia and Junilla, Lucina set bread, cheese, a pitcher of wine, and bowls of fruit on the table. "I hope that will be a good start for you," she said. She looked more closely at Aurora and put a hand on her shoulder. "You were here then, too, weren't you, dear, when my husband was killed? And now you're all grown up and sitting by your lord, just like your mother did then."

Aurora nodded and lowered her head. Knowing what I knew from ten years ago, it was amusing to watch the interaction between them. Lucina certainly recognized Aurora but had to act casual.

"You've naught to be ashamed of," Lucina said. "But the rest of you weren't here then, were you?"

Everyone else shook their heads. Julia broke the loaf of bread. Its warmth emanated across the table. "It really smells good."

"It's my mother-in-law's recipe," Lucina said.

Julia took the little girl in her arms. More than anything she wants a child. She has had one miscarriage that I know of. "What's your name, sweetheart?" she asked.

"Junilla," the girl replied softly.

"Her mother, my daughter, was named Junia," Lucina said. "She died at the birth, so we decided to call her daughter Junilla."

"I'm so sorry to hear that," Julia said. She stroked the child's hair. "You're a beautiful little girl. I'll bet you're a big help to your grandmother."

"She surely is," Lucina said. "Come on, sweetheart. Let's let these good folks eat." She turned back to the kitchen.

Torquatus poured us all some wine and leaned back in his chair. "Now, Gaius Pliny, it seems you didn't tell me the whole story of your previous visit here. What's this about somebody being killed?"

"I've heard only bits and pieces of it," Tacitus said, "and I don't believe Julia has heard much of it at all." Julia shook her head.

"Does it have anything to do with that innkeeper's wife?" With his one eye, Torquatus cast a long look in Lucina's direction. "As attractive as she is now, she must have been quite a prize ten years ago. Maybe even worth killing for?"

I took a deep breath. "It was nothing quite as simple as that...."

VI

[*A.D. 77*]

WELL, AT LEAST this place looks decent," my uncle said as we filed into the only inn in Collis Niveosus. "I suspect we're going to be here for a while." The short walk from our wagon into the building had left him wheezing. Monica, his slave and companion and Aurora's mother, helped him settle his bulk into the nearest chair.

"Surely there will be somebody around here who can repair the wagon," Monica said. Her voice had a haughtiness that female slaves often acquire when they know they're the master's favorite. It makes the other slaves in the household—especially other females—dislike them intensely.

"Not likely," my uncle groused. He caught the eye of a stout man who seemed to be the owner of the place. "You, sir, we've had an accident," he said. "The axle on one of our *raeda*s broke just down the road. We had to leave it with a couple of guards. Is there anyone around here who could fix it?"

The innkeeper shook his head. "No, sir. Nobody in this town has the equipment to do that big a job. You'll have to send back to Augusta Taurinorum for help."

My uncle slapped his hand on the table he was sitting beside, causing me to start. "Damn! That will take days."

"It's all right," Monica said, patting his arm. "Your new property isn't going anywhere. Whether you inspect it tomorrow or ten days from now, it won't make any difference."

"But it means just sitting here."

Nothing bothered my uncle more than inactivity. When he was eating or bathing, he had a scribe read a book to him so as not to waste the time. He traveled around Rome in a litter, with a scribe reading to him or taking dictation. I need quiet surroundings to absorb what I'm reading, but my uncle's phenomenal memory and ability to shut out distractions enabled him to retain whatever he heard.

"It won't hurt you to relax, dear," Monica said. He allowed her considerable liberty in addressing him, something that annoyed my mother—his sister—no end. "You don't have to be busy every last minute."

"No one knows when their last minute will be, love," my uncle said. "I may have a couple of days or a couple of years left, and I haven't done everything I want to do."

"But you've done so much," Monica said in her Punic-accented Greek. "What can it hurt to slow down for a few days?" I liked her soft voice, which her daughter had inherited, without the haughtiness, and her pale, round features. Aurora's angular, Punic appearance and browner skin must have come from her father, not her Greekling mother.

My uncle snorted. "It looks like I'll *have* to slow down, like it or not. At least I've got Glaucon and some books to work on."

Glaucon was my uncle's favorite scribe. His facility with Tironian notation enabled him to write as fast as my uncle could talk, and he had a mellifluous reading voice.

I had not wanted to make this trip in the first place and certainly didn't want it to be dragged out any longer than necessary, so I ventured to offer a suggestion. "Couldn't we squeeze everyone into the two *raedas* we have left and go on with the trip? We could leave a few servants here to bring the other *raeda* when it's repaired or just take it straight back to Rome."

We had started with three wagons. My uncle and I were riding in one, along with Monica and Aurora, who was fifteen, like me, and had been my friend since she and her mother came into our household eight years ago. Glaucon occupied the other seat in the wagon. Several servant women were riding in the second *raeda*, the one with the now

broken axle. The third wagon was packed with clothing and other supplies, and with my uncle's books. Six of our male servants were riding
horses along with us.

"I don't think that would do," my uncle said. "It would be far too
crowded for Glaucon and me to work. You know how uncomfortable
we all were just covering that last mile into town, jammed together in
one wagon like that. And you don't have to say that my girth makes
any place where I am…well, crowded. Monica never lets me forget that.
And it would be hard on the horses, especially going over the mountains. We're just going to have to settle in here for a few days. That is,
if there's room." He turned to the innkeeper. "What is your name, sir?"

"I'm Quintus Roscius," the man said.

"Well, Roscius, I am Gaius Plinius Secundus. I need some rooms
for my party."

"How many of you are there?"

"We left two men to guard the broken-down *raeda*, so we have
four men on horseback, four women riding in a wagon, and five of us
in the other wagon. A couple of the men will need to sleep in the barn
to look after our baggage, so we need rooms for ten or eleven people."

"I can accommodate you, sir. You'll have to decide how you share
the rooms, though."

My uncle and Monica exchanged a glance. Although they have an
intimate relationship, they don't share a room. My uncle's snoring is
legendary in our household, and probably in a couple of households
on either side of ours.

"Well, let's see," my uncle said, counting on his fingertips. "I know
Gaius doesn't want to share a room with me, and I wouldn't inflict that
on anyone. What we do with these two is what makes it awkward."
A short man, he stood between Aurora and me and patted us on our
shoulders. "What do you say, Monica? Shall we just throw them into
the same room and see what happens?"

Aurora, in spite of her beautiful olive skin, turned the brightest red
I'd ever seen on a girl's face. I could feel her warmth on my own face.

We finally sorted it out that my uncle and I would each have our
own rooms, Monica and Aurora would share a room, our servant

women would have a room, and Glaucon would share a room with the men who weren't guarding the *raeda*. The male servants, except for Glaucon, would alternate with the men sleeping in the barn so no one would have to do that every night during our stay. Three of our men would leave for Augusta Taurinorum in the morning. That would ease the congestion for the rest.

With those arrangements made, we had a light supper. An older woman, whom Roscius introduced as his mother, Aemilia, oversaw the two servants who brought it in. Afterwards, Monica suggested we take a walk, but my uncle declined. "Glaucon and I have some work to do. We've already lost a lot of time today." I glanced at the table where Glaucon was sitting. His face remained impassive. One of his primary attributes as a scribe is that you hardly know he's in the room. When you do notice him, you have no idea what he's thinking.

My uncle simply disliked physical activity. His literary work had become his excuse for avoiding it. He was getting to the point that he was incapable of strenuous exertion. When Vespasian summoned him to his home atop the Palatine, my uncle had to be carried up the hill in a chair. It was a task that made me pity the slaves required to do it.

"You two go ahead then." Monica's voice betrayed her disappointment. I think she is genuinely concerned about his health, even if it's out of her own self-interest. If my uncle died, she would lose her privileged position. My mother barely masks her disdain for Monica and would, I'm sure, insist that I, as the master, sell her or move her to one of our remote estates, and Aurora with her. "Look around the town. It seems to be a charming little place."

"'Charming' looks like another word for boring," Aurora said. "It's so small."

My uncle chuckled. "In my experience, the smaller the town, the bigger and dirtier the secrets people are hiding. When everybody knows everybody else, they have to work much harder to conceal things. Everybody has to be complicit, to some degree."

"You're not going out to gather gossip," Monica said. "Just look the town over and give us a report."

A tour of Collis didn't take long. It sat on the last wide spot on the road leading across the Alps, just before it entered the pass. The majestic mountains dominated the view, no matter which way we looked. The highest peaks we could see were snow-covered, even in July and in spite of the day's warmth at street level. Aemilia had mentioned that it was an unusually warm summer. The town, which lacked a central square because there was no room for one, was only three blocks long and two blocks wide.

We came to the eastern end of the town and sat down on the bank of a stream. Aurora slipped off her sandals and put her feet in the water. She let out a little squeal and jerked them out. "It's so *cold*! I've never felt anything nearly that cold."

"Well, it is melted snow," I said, splashing more water on her. I liked being with her in situations like this, when we could be so relaxed, playing like we did when we were younger.

"We didn't have anything this cold on the edge of the desert where I came from. I've never felt anything like it in Rome."

As the sun went behind the mountains, the air turned cool. Aurora moved closer to me and slipped her arm through mine, the way she used to do when we were children but hadn't done in a long time. "You've got something on your mind," she said. "You've been very quiet the whole time we've been walking."

I finally got up the nerve to say what had been bothering me. "I'm sorry about what my uncle said. You know he was just joking, and sometimes he's a little crude."

"Oh, I know. Usually he's funny. But…what he said…have you ever thought about it?"

"You mean…about the two of us…in a room?" This conversation felt like it could get awkward, and I wanted to be sure I knew what we were talking about.

"Yes."

"No, of course not," I lied. "Have you?"

"No," she said too quickly. "No. It wouldn't be…proper, would it?"

We both kept our eyes on the water bubbling over the rocks. "What do you think is going to happen to us?" I asked. "Will we become like my uncle and your mother?"

She brushed her hair back. She likes to wear it loose, even though a girl her age should be putting her hair up. I like it down, too. I sometimes wonder what it would be like to run my fingers through it. "Would you want that, for us to be like your uncle and my mother?"

"I don't know. I certainly don't want to marry anybody right now. I know I'll have to marry someday. My mother and my uncle are looking for a girl for me. It won't happen for a couple of years, but it's probably going to be the niece of Verginius Rufus."

At the mention of a possible marriage, Aurora moved away from me. She picked up a handful of small stones and, without looking at me, began flipping them into the water. "Do you know her well?"

I tossed a small pebble into the stream, aiming it so that it landed near one of Aurora's, and looked up at the mountains. "We've met. She's a nice girl, about fourteen. I haven't seen her in nearly a year."

"That's what your mother wants, isn't it? For you to marry a nice girl. She doesn't want you to end up like your uncle, with a woman like my mother."

"Your mother's nice. I like her."

"Your mother doesn't. She hates my mother—"

"I think 'hates' is too strong." I couldn't imagine my mother hating anyone. She was displeased about the situation with Monica, but hate?

"No, it's not. Not at all. You don't know how your mother talks to my mother—and talks *about* her—when you and your uncle aren't around. She blames her for your uncle not being married."

"I think his former wife deserves the blame for that."

Aurora drew back and looked at me quizzically. "I didn't know he was ever married."

"It was well before you came here, and only for a short time. We don't talk about it. We're specifically told *not* to talk about it. He's always been so obsessed with his books. Glaucon might as well be his wife and the books their children."

Men of our class are required to have three sons in order to hold office or inherit property. Since so few men have that many—Vespasian has two and neither of his sons has any yet—Augustus began the practice of bestowing the "privilege of three children." My uncle had to ask Vespasian for that legal fiction. My father had only one child; my uncle has none. We're not exactly providing men for the imperial service or the army. My mother worries that other people think of us as not living up to our responsibilities. She worries about it too much, in my opinion.

"I'm afraid, if something happens to your uncle," Aurora said, "your mother will insist that you sell my mother and me."

"She'd have better luck insisting that I fly to the moon."

Aurora leaned her head on my shoulder. "It's sweet of you to say that, Gaius, but—"

I took hold of the strap around her neck that held the Tyche ring and pulled it out from under her stola so I could see it. "Put your hand on this." When she clutched the ring, I put my hand over hers. "Aurora, I swear by this ring that, as long as I am alive, you will have a place in my house and in my *familia*." And in my heart, I thought, but I couldn't bring myself to say that aloud. Could I ever bring myself to say it to a slave?

We looked at one another, and I leaned toward her. I knew I was going to kiss her for the first time, and she seemed to be expecting it, inviting it.

But then a dog poked his wet nose between us. We both yelled and jerked apart. A male voice behind us said, "Argos, no!"

Aurora and I scrambled to stand up. A large brown-and-white dog looked up at us, wagging his tail, his tongue hanging out. Aurora knelt and began scratching his head and cooing to him.

A boy about our age called from down the road, where he and an older woman were pushing a handcart toward town. "He won't hurt you," he said. "I'm sorry. I didn't mean for him to bother you."

"It's all right," I said. "We were just…talking."

"Yes," Aurora put in, "just talking." Her expression told me that she knew something important had just happened, even if it only almost happened.

When the handcart drew alongside us, the boy and the woman stopped. "Are you from the broken *raeda?*" the boy asked.

"No, we're from Rome," I replied, "but we were riding in the *raeda*."

"And you're a wise-ass," the boy said with a chuckle.

"He was just trying to make a joke," Aurora said.

"He's not very good at it."

"No, he's not." Her look told me not to say any more. "My name is Aurora. This is my lord, Gaius Caecilius. What's your name?"

"I'm Junianus." He drew his shoulders back as though he needed to defend that statement. "This is my grandmother, Secunda."

I looked at the woman, uncertain what to say.

"From your expression," she said, "I suspect you've met my sister, Aemilia, at the inn."

"Yes, ma'am," I said, "just a while ago, during dinner."

"We're twins. I'm the younger, the second born, so I'm Aemilia Secunda. Everyone calls me Secunda."

"My uncle is Gaius Plinius Secundus," I said. "But he doesn't have a twin."

"We're taking some supplies from our farm to the inn," Secunda said. "Shall we continue?"

"Sure," I said. As we walked I looked at the cheeses and loaves of bread that filled the small cart.

"We supply a lot of the food for the inn," Secunda said.

"What we had tonight was very good."

"Thank you, young man."

"I guess you'll be eating more of our food for a few days," Junianus said. "That *raeda* sure isn't going anywhere any time soon."

"We're going to send someone to Augusta Taurinorum tomorrow," I said, "to bring another axle and make repairs."

"Then I reckon you will be here for a while," the boy said, eyeing Aurora.

Aurora continued to pet the dog as he walked close to her. She's always been good with horses; that gift now seemed to extend to dogs as well. My own distaste for animals keeps me from fully appreciating her talent. When I consider the places on their bodies that they lick, I do not want them touching me. "You called him Argos," she said. "Like Odysseus' dog in the *Odyssey*?"

"Yeah." Junianus took a step closer to Aurora and rubbed the dog's back. "That dog was real old. I hope this one lives that long, and still knows me when we're both old. I don't know if it's really his name, though."

"What do you mean?" Aurora asked. "Was he somebody else's dog?"

Junianus shook his head. "I think maybe a dog has what he knows is his name in dog language. You know, in his own head. But he doesn't seem to object to Argos, so that's what I call him."

Aurora laughed. "Oh, another wise-ass. You two should get along well." She jerked her head toward me.

The conversation reminded me that, when Aurora came into our house, her name wasn't Aurora. It was Shachar. Monica, for whom Greek was a second language, told us that was the Punic word for the dawn—which was when she gave birth after a long night in labor. My uncle never has liked foreign names for his slaves. He says it makes them sound like characters from one of Plautus' plays, so he changed her name to Aurora. I remember the confusion on her face, even after her mother explained it to her, when we began calling her by her new name. When we were playing by ourselves, I called her Shachar until she got used to Aurora.

I'll probably experience the same feeling someday. I know my uncle plans to adopt me in his will. I should become Gaius Plinius Secundus Minor, but I plan to keep my father's name, as Roman men often do after an adoption—as Octavian did when Julius Caesar adopted him—so I will be Gaius Plinius Caecilius Secundus. I say it over to myself now and then, just to get accustomed to the awkwardness of it.

As we walked, Junianus stayed on the other side of Aurora and kept up a stream of inane conversation, explaining who lived where and how long they had been there. He caused her to turn slightly away from me, which I realized was his intention. "What brings you this way?" he finally asked. "I'm sure this isn't your final destination. It's just a place that people pass through. They have a drink, take a piss, and they're gone."

"Now, son," Secunda said, "mind your manners."

Aurora giggled and started to answer but I cut her off. "We're on our way to Gallia Lugdunensis. My uncle wants to inspect a piece of property he has purchased there."

"Seems to me, it'd make more sense to inspect a place *before* you buy it."

Again Aurora laughed softly. I felt like she was laughing at me.

"One of his agents inspected it." Something about this boy set my teeth on edge. "My uncle is a busy man."

"He doesn't need your approval to buy it, does he?"

"Of course not, but I am his heir. It will become my property some-day, so he thought I ought to see it."

"He's your uncle, not your father, but you're his heir. Don't you have a father?"

"Everybody has a father," Secunda said. "Did something happen to yours, Gaius Caecilius, if you don't mind me asking?"

"He died a long time ago."

"Mine's dead, too," Junianus said. "But he just died six days ago."

Aurora touched the boy's arm. "Oh, no! What happened?"

———◦•◦———

[A.D. 87]

AS I listened to Gaius tell the story I was taken back in time to a moment ten years ago when I was trying to understand my feelings for him. And trying to decide whether to let them develop or to squelch them, if I could.

Even though my mother was the older Pliny's favorite, at fifteen I could not imagine myself ever having that kind of relationship with Gaius. He wouldn't admit it—or couldn't see it—but his mother disliked my mother intensely for two reasons. First, my mother acted arrogantly because of her standing in the old man's eyes. I didn't see that at the time, but I know it now because I have to guard against that attitude in myself. And, secondly, because Plinia felt—quite rightly—that their relationship kept her brother from having a "proper" family. She and I have become more understanding of one another—I can even say I love her now—but at the time I was sure she would never allow Gaius and me to be anything but master and slave. I even feared she might force Gaius or his uncle to sell me. I touched the

Tyche ring on its leather strap, remembering Gaius' promise, made here ten years ago. Could I, as a slave, hold him to it?

His mother and uncle had talked about possible marriage partners for him. As it turned out, though, Verginius' niece died unexpectedly less than a year after we were in Collis. If Gaius had married her instead of Livia, he might have been happy, at least for a time. What would that have meant for my relationship with him?

By that time in our lives Gaius and I had read Ovid's advice to young men and women and had found it amusing but not particularly valuable. We didn't have to worry about finding places to meet or passing notes or hiding from a possessive husband. One thing—in addition to his advice on positions for coupling—that did interest me, though, was what he said about making a man jealous. In Ovid's words, "The horse runs swiftly from the starting gate, when he must pass others, and knows that still others follow."

As we walked back to the inn that day, with Secunda, Junianus, and his dog, I laughed at everything Junianus said. I didn't have any interest in the boy. He knew enough about the Odyssey to name his dog Argos, but he seemed younger than his years and quite unsophisticated compared to the people I knew in Rome, even in our own household. I admit I was shameless, though. I wanted Gaius to see that another male could find me—a slave and a foreigner—attractive, even appealing. Maybe all women feel that way. Even if we like one man, we don't want him to merely assume that he is the only man who might catch our eye.

I knew Gaius' uncle was joking about putting Gaius and me in the same room for the night, but I had to admit to myself that the idea had occurred to me more than once, especially after reading Ovid's Art of Love. *Gaius and I had played together for years, but two fifteen-year-olds don't "play" the way they did when they were nine. I had started my monthlies about a year before that trip. That change to my body brought with it new feelings which I was still trying to understand. At fifteen we were young but hardly children. Only two years later, his uncle would die in the eruption of Vesuvius and Gaius would inherit his name, his vast estates, and his position in society. And me. He would make his first appearance in the courts at eighteen, opposing Marcus Aquilius Regulus and defeating him. That case* guaranteed that the long-simmering antipathy between the Pliny family and Regulus would continue into another generation.

I have long since settled my feelings about Gaius, and I know how he feels about me. He and I are as committed to one another as we can be without being able to marry. We are married in spirit, if not in the words of the law, and have sworn ourselves to each other.

But I wonder if Junianus is still around. I'd just like to talk to him and find out how he coped with his father's death. Ten years ago he expressed strong suspicions about one person. I wonder if he still feels that way.

VII

OH, NO," Aurora said. "He died? What happened to him?" She put her hand on Junianus' arm. He put his hand over hers and held it there.

"He was working in his mill when they found him. They said he fell and hit his head."

"Who is 'they'?" I asked.

Junianus took his eyes off Aurora and looked at me as though he was surprised to rediscover my presence. "Magnus found him."

"Who's Magnus?"

Secunda cut in. "He works for Junius in the mill. That's not his name, but everybody calls him Magnus because he's so big."

"And Junius was your son?" I asked.

"Yes," Secunda said. "My only child, Lucius Junius."

She seemed sad, of course, but in control of her emotions in a way that Roman matrons of my class are supposed to emulate. Leave the wailing and crying to the hired mourners. My mother had shown no more emotion than this when she learned of the death of my father.

"So this Magnus found Junius. What did he do?"

Junianus sneered. "He called Roscius, the other *duovir*, and a couple of his butt-kissers."

"Roscius? The owner of the inn where we're staying?"

Junianus nodded. "And of most everything else in town."

"He's one of the *duovirs*? Who's the other one?"

"My pa was."

"When did this happen?" Aurora asked. She took her hand off his arm and stepped back from him.

"It was six days ago," Secunda said. "He seems to have fallen at night. Magnus found him in the morning."

"What would he have been doing there at night?" I asked.

"The equipment was old. There was always something that needed repairing."

"Where is the mill?" I asked. "Can we see it?"

Junianus and Secunda both looked at me like I was crazy. Aurora knew what I was getting at, though.

"Why?" Junianus asked.

"If you see *where* something happened, it can help you understand *what* happened. At least that's what my uncle says." He has told me stories about trying to figure out how one of his soldiers or one of his slaves died when the cause wasn't obvious. Or when the cause seemed obvious but was actually something else. Just because you find a dead man at the bottom of a pond, he once said, that doesn't mean he drowned.

He makes notes about what he learns. He says he'll never publish those notes because some of his conclusions run contrary to what most people think, and he's made me promise never to publish them. Glaucon has been instructed to write in a small script and on the front and back of those scrolls, so as not to waste space and to discourage anyone else from reading them. There are over a hundred of them. I have no idea how he finds anything in those scrolls, but he doesn't really need to. His memory is phenomenal.

He has aroused in Aurora and me an interest in people's activities, particularly in their more unsavory activities. We like to listen to him and his friends discuss court cases. "Socrates would have made a good investigator," my uncle says. "It's mostly a matter of asking the right questions to the right people." That's what I was trying to train myself to do, with Aurora's help.

"The mill's at the other end of town," Junianus said.

"Oh, yes," Aurora said. "At the waterfall. We walked by there. It's a lovely spot. And that big wheel is fascinating."

"Yeah. The water turns the wheel, and that turns the grindstone. It's all gears and stuff that I don't really understand. That's all that Magnus does understand. He likes gears and wheels and knows how to make them work when they don't."

"Magnus isn't stupid," Secunda said, "though some people think he is. He's just smarter about some things than others."

When we came to the inn, Secunda said, "I need to stop here and make this delivery. Junianus, I'll see you back at the house after you've shown these nice people around."

"Yes, Gran'ma."

As we walked up the street to the mill, I said, "I can't believe how much Secunda and her sister look alike."

"Well, they are twins," Aurora reminded me.

"I know, but even for twins the resemblance is amazing."

"My pa and my uncle looked a lot alike, too. More like brothers than cousins, most folks around here said," Junianus added.

"Were they close in age?"

"Just a few months apart."

I wanted to find out something about the two men as *duovirs*. My uncle says that, when a person is murdered, the first person to see the dead body isn't the person who finds him, but the person who killed him. "Is this the first year that your father and Roscius were *duovirs*?" I asked.

"*Pssht*. Oh, no. They've been sharing it for maybe ten years. Nobody else in town wants any part of it if Roscius wants one of the places, and he always does. So the two of them just get elected every year, again and again."

"It's a good thing they like one another then," Aurora said, "if they have to work together."

"You're not listening," Junianus said. "They hate—or hated—one another. My pa was just trying to keep Roscius from taking over the whole town. His father had hated Roscius' father for years."

"Why?" Aurora asked.

"My pa never told me. I think it had something to do with money somebody borrowed and never paid back. I once heard them arguing

about it, and it sounded like there was more than money at stake. My
pa got so mad he left town and lived in Augusta Taurinorum for a few
years. That's where he met my ma and where my sister and me were
born. He came back here when his pa died, twelve years ago."

"So you have a sister?" Aurora was always interested in whether
people had brothers or sisters, I guess because she and I don't. Information was pouring out of Junianus like wine from a punctured wineskin,
so I let Aurora continue to question him. "How old is she?"

"She's eighteen, two years older than me. At least our poor father
got to see her get married. He did want a grandchild so bad, but he
didn't get to see that."

"Who's she married to?" I asked.

"One of our neighbor's boys. Name's Marcus Draco."

The dragon, I thought.

"It really hurt Magnus when she got married," Junianus said. "He's
been daft over her for years, but Pa didn't think he was all in his right
mind."

"Did that make Magnus mad?" I asked. "Did they argue about it?"

"Well, he don't get mad. He's what you'd call a gentle soul, I guess,
but he sure was hurt."

"Is Magnus as big as his name suggests?" Aurora asked.

Junianus nodded. "Even bigger. His parents moved into town before
I was born. They're Gauls. You'd be surprised how big some of those
Gauls are."

"Aren't all of the people around here Gauls?" I said. "This is Cisalpine Gaul. We could say that you're a Gaul. For that matter, my father's
home was north of the Padus River, so maybe I should call myself a
Gaul."

Junianus didn't seem to like that suggestion. "Oh, another wise-ass
comment. It's a question of what language you speak. A lot of them
have been here long enough that they think of themselves as Roman.
They don't speak anything but Latin, and they have Roman names,
like you and me, and Magnus and his family. But lately there's more
and more of them coming over the mountains and settling around
here. You hear their language in the baths and the market as much as
you do Latin."

"There are districts in Rome where you *never* hear Latin," I said. "There are so many people coming in from so many different parts of the empire."

"Like me," Aurora said.

Junianus ran his eyes over her. "Makes me wonder then how long Rome will be Roman. And maybe that's not a bad thing."

That was an uncomfortable question many of my class asked ourselves. What would we do when non-Romans outnumbered Romans? But what constituted a "Roman"? I decided to move to another topic.

"Even if they didn't like one another, did your father and Roscius manage to work together?"

Junianus made a disgusted face. "Mostly Roscius lords it over everybody. My pa tried to block him when he could. They were married to sisters. I think that made things even worse."

"So one *duovir* was your father and the other was your uncle?"

"That's the way it works out, doesn't it?"

It's a small town, I thought, but *duovir* of this place or *princeps* of Rome—power is power, on whatever scale. Senatorial families in Rome were joined by all kinds of connections, like a bigger version of Collis. Those family connections produced all kinds of twists and turns. Tiberius Gracchus had been killed by a mob led by his cousin. As my uncle said, everybody is complicit to some degree.

We had arrived at the mill and stood at the door watching as three men ground a load of grain. Argos stayed back. "He doesn't like the noise," Junianus said. I had to admit the grinding of the huge stones was difficult for me to abide. At least it kept the men working here from hearing what we were saying. For myself, I don't like bright lights or loud noises.

"That's Magnus." Junianus pointed to the man closest to us, who certainly deserved his name.

"Who are the others?"

"The one farthest away is Draco, Junia's husband. The other's Leonix, one of Pa's slaves."

"How many slaves does he have?"

"Three. We're not rich." He didn't say "like you," but his look implied such a comment.

"So this is yours now?" I waved a hand over the mill.

Junianus nodded. "At least until Roscius takes it over."

"How can he do that?" Aurora asked.

"He's got a piece of papyrus that he says my pa put his mark on when he borrowed some money. There's a magistrate coming from Augusta Taurinorum to look it over and settle some things."

"What does somebody from there have to do with this place?" I asked.

"My sister and Draco wanted somebody from outside to look over the document. They thought my pa was going to leave the mill to them and the farm to me. My sister can read, but Roscius can't. He claims he knows what the thing says. My ma could read it, but Roscius won't trust her, of course. Somehow Roscius knows this man, Marcus Lupercus, and he trusts him, so he suggested sending for him. My ma doesn't want anybody interfering. I don't understand why. We've told her Roscius will take everything, including her. She says that's just what happens with women. She quoted something from a play by Euripides."

"'Of all living creatures,'" Aurora intoned, "'we women are most miserable'...Oh, I don't remember all of it. There's something about 'Will the man we get be bad or good?' It's from the *Medea*."

"Yeah, that's it," Junianus said. "But Roscius insisted."

Which must mean he's confident about what the document says, I thought. That would be an interesting piece of papyrus to get hold of. "Have you read it?"

Junianus shook his head. "I can't read but just a little. My ma and my grandma taught me some, but it's too much work. The letters get kind of mixed up for me. Ma reads real good, almost like she's singing. I'd rather have her read to me. Especially the *Odyssey*. I love all those stories in it, like the Cyclops." He dropped his voice to a growl and turned to Aurora, raising his arms like a threatening beast. "'I'll eat Nobody last!'" She squealed and chuckled, as she had been laughing at everything he said since he joined us.

"Has your mother seen this document?" I asked.

"Roscius won't let her look at it. Just waves it in her face. He says he'll show it to the magistrate when he gets here."

I hoped the magistrate would arrive while we were still in Collis.

My uncle had enough *auctoritas* in his narrow stripe to get a look at that document. Something about this whole business didn't feel right. I turned to the interior of the mill and asked, "Where was your father… when he died?"

"They found him lying just inside the door here. They said it looked like he had climbed up there to check something in the gears. He lost his balance and hit his head beside the door when he fell. Right here." He touched a spot on the stone wall.

Someone had cleaned the spot, but the porous stone had soaked up enough of the blood that a trace was still evident. "Was that something your father would do—I mean, climb up there?"

"Yeah. This building is old. Sometimes things get jammed up. If he'd had too much to drink, he might have had trouble keeping his balance."

"Did he drink a lot?"

"Sometimes…You know, you sure do ask a lot of questions."

I lowered my head apologetically. "That's what my mother tells me. I'm sorry. I'm just curious about what might have happened."

"Why? He wasn't your pa. It's none of your business."

"You're absolutely right. But I've never been sure what happened to my own father. I was so young when he died that I don't even remember him. People have told me what they think happened, but nobody is sure. I guess that's why I always want answers."

Junianus rubbed his hand on the stone wall again. "My pa fell, hit his head, and died. That's…all there is to it. Sometimes the answer is right in front of you."

———

[*A.D. 87*]

A MAN about my age came into the dining room. "Excuse me, sirs," he said. "My stepfather tells me that the bath is warm enough now. Would you like to go there while supper is being prepared?"

"You're Junianus, aren't you?" I asked.

"Yes, sir." He gave a slight bow. "My mother said you folks were here some years ago."

"At the time your father…died," I said.

"Yes, sir. That was a dreadful time. You were very considerate of me. I do appreciate it."

"We were glad to see that Argos is still around," Aurora said. "And still sprightly."

"And it looks like he hasn't forgotten you. Which doesn't surprise me. You're hard to forget."

Aurora blushed. "How are you?"

"Well enough, thank you."

"We were sorry to hear about your sister. I still recall a talk I had with her when we were here before."

"Yes, it's very sad. She lost one child and then died birthing another baby four years ago. My wife and I have the child, with help from my mother."

"I'm glad to hear she's being cared for. Who is your wife?"

"I married Roscia."

Wait a moment, I thought. Junius and Roscius were cousins, the sons of sisters. That meant Junianus had married his cousin. Well, the imperial family does that all the time. In a town this small there must not be a lot of potential marriage partners.

"Enough chitchat," Torquatus said. "Shall we bathe? Gaius Pliny can continue this intriguing story while we soak. Perhaps he'll say something that will lead to the solution."

"But then the women won't hear the rest of it," Julia protested.

"I'm sure Aurora can fill you in," I suggested. "She knows what happened as well as I do."

The women were gathering around her as we left. Even Lucina, who was supposed to be preparing our meal, lingered in the dining room. I wondered when we would get to eat the rest of our meal and how much she actually knew ten years ago.

⸺ ⸭ ⸺

[A.D. 77]

GAIUS touched the spot on the wall that Junianus had indicated. "Yes, an answer can be right in front of you," he said. "But you have to be sure it's the right answer."

Junianus' brow wrinkled as he frowned. "What do you mean?"

"Every question can have lots of answers, but only one right answer." Gaius held up his index finger.

Junianus' face looked like what one of Socrates' students must have looked like when the old satyr started throwing definitions and questions at them. *"I don't understand."*

"Did you see your father's body?" Gaius asked.

"Yeah. Magnus fetched Roscius, and Roscius sent for Ma and me. He said we'd need to take care of him. You know, the funeral and all."

"Had anyone moved him before you got here?"

"I don't think so."

"So you saw how he was lying? The exact position?"

"Yeah."

"Can you show me?"

"What? What are you talking about?"

"Was he lying on his back? On his stomach? Was he stretched out, or curled up?"

"What difference would that make? He was dead. He wasn't taking a nap. Are you crazy?"

I had to agree with Junianus—not about Gaius being crazy, but about asking what difference it would make if his father had been lying in any particular position. But Gaius had a look on his face that I had seen a few times before, when we used to go up the Esquiline to the Gardens of Maecenas and watch people, like we were spies. We'd try to figure out what they were doing, sometimes what they were hiding. It amazed me how many people seemed to have something to hide. And nobody paid any attention to a couple of kids.

"I'm just trying to understand," Gaius said, *"what might have happened to your father. If he fell from up there, where those gears are, could he have actually fallen in such a way that he hit his head at that spot on the wall and landed in a particular position? So, describe as accurately as you can, how he was lying."*

Junianus shrugged. *"Well, he was on his left side, with one arm under him and the other one out."*

"It would help if I could see someone in that position."

Gaius was looking at me, so I lay down on the ground, arranging my stola as modestly as I could. "Like this?"

"Yeah, pretty much," Junianus said. "But a little closer to the wall, and the arm that was stretched out was pointing more down."

"Were his legs drawn up or straight?" Gaius asked.

"Sort of halfway in between," Junianus said.

I scooted closer to the wall and moved my legs and arm as he described, like a puppet responding to pulls on its strings.

"That's it," Junianus said. "Or real close."

"And where was the wound on his head?"

"Over his left ear."

Gaius knelt and put a hand on my shoulder. "Don't worry. I'm not going to bang your head against the wall."

"Thank you, my lord."

Gaius stood, walked around me, and looked up at the gears. "How big a man was your father? Tall? Heavy?"

"I guess you'd say he was normal-sized. His belly was starting to get bigger."

"From the drinking, perhaps?"

"Some men just get heavier as they get older," Junianus said. "If you want to know what he looked like, just take a look at Roscius. They look more like brothers than cousins. My pa wasn't a drunk."

"I didn't mean to suggest that," Gaius said. "Now, one more question, and it may be the hardest one. How big was the wound on the side of his head?"

I got up in time to see Junianus run his finger from beside his eye to back over his ear and up to the top of his head.

"That large?" Gaius said. "And a good bit of blood?"

Junianus nodded, unable to say anything. I knew what my first thought was, and it looked like Gaius had the same idea: that was too large a wound to have been caused by one accidental knock of his head against the wall.

I stepped in front of Gaius before he could ask his next question. "We ought to be getting back to the inn, my lord. My mother will be wondering where we are."

We left Junianus and Argos in the mill. The dog started to follow me until Junianus called him back.

"I don't think there's any hurry about us getting back," Gaius said as we crossed the road. "Why—"

"He was about to start crying," I said. "I didn't want to embarrass him."

[A.D 87]

THE bath was what one would expect in a town as small as Collis. Nondescript frescoes of geometric patterns, in need of repainting, decorated the walls. The *frigidarium* doubled as a dressing room, with a dozen niches along one wall for patrons' clothes. As we disrobed, I noticed that Torquatus bore a purplish mark on the back of his right leg, just above the knee. I must have kept my eyes on it longer than I realized.

"I was born with it," he said without turning to look at me. "Believe it or not, I was once a rather handsome boy. My mother said the gods marked me with this to keep me humble. I guess I wasn't humble enough, though, so they inflicted this face on me."

The other room of the bath combined the *tepidarium* and *caldarium*, which was just a pool at one end of the large room. Our servants waited just inside the door for their turn to bathe. We rinsed off in the warm water of the large basin in the center of the room and applied some olive oil. Torquatus settled into the pool, lowering his voice so that the rest of us had to lean forward to hear him. "So this fellow Roscius—our very own innkeeper—killed Junius and made it look like an accident. That's as plain as anything. Then why is he still walking around a free man?"

"It wasn't that simple," I said. "Roscius had an unbreakable alibi for the time when Junius died, or was killed."

"And what was that?"

"He was with Junius' wife."

Torquatus snorted. His badly healed nose made the noise especially loud. "A cheating wife is hardly a reliable witness."

"No one was cheating. Roscius and Lucina were in the kitchen at the inn, looking over supplies. In those days Lucina and her mother-in-law, Secunda, made cheese and provided bread for the inn. Several servants swore to that."

"So the two men heartily disliked one another but still did business." Torquatus scratched his belly. "I guess that's not so unusual."

I shrugged and scratched a spot on my shoulder with the *strigl.* "They had no choice. It's a small town. Junius and Lucina had the largest farm in the area."

"And Roscius was their biggest customer."

"Exactly. And Roscius and Junius were cousins. Their mothers were sisters."

One of Torquatus' eyebrows was higher than the other because of the distortion of his face. He raised the one eyebrow that he could still move, as he sipped the cup of wine he had brought with him from the inn and placed it on the edge of the pool. "Then there wasn't a strong motive for Roscius to kill Junius."

"I've been told that they hated each other as only relatives can."

"That does make the matter more problematic. But, as for business, they complemented each other, so Roscius wouldn't have been eliminating competition by killing his cousin."

"Unless," Tacitus said from the other side of the pool, "it was competition for Lucina. He did end up married to her."

"And ten years ago she would have been quite something," Torquatus said with a smirk. "She's still tempting, although I doubt any woman is worth killing for. The next one down the line will always do." He seemed to sink within himself for a moment. "None of them will have me, of course, unless there's money involved. Then they want me to take them from behind." He rubbed a hand over his face. "The sight of this doesn't heighten the romance." With a sigh he recovered his mood. "So, what about this Magnus fellow? What was so 'great' about him?"

"He was quite large, especially in his shoulders and chest. Perhaps you'll see him before we leave."

"So he could have attacked Junius for some reason—unhappiness over how he was treated in the mill, perhaps."

"We had to consider that."

"What about the money Junius owed?" Tacitus put in. "Did you find out what that piece of papyrus said?"

Before I could respond to either comment we were interrupted by Charinus, who stood over us on the edge of the pool and addressed Tacitus. "My lord, it's starting to snow. Before it gets completely dark I thought I would ride ahead and see how conditions are on the road."

"All right. That could be helpful. Do you want anyone to go with you?"

"No, my lord. It's been a long day. I don't want to tire anyone else any further. I'll be back in an hour or so."

When Charinus turned away, Torquatus said, "It must be nice to have a servant who takes some initiative. My lot won't lift a finger unless they're told exactly what to do and given some encouragement with the whip." He glared at his two servants who were standing alongside ours, waiting their turn to bathe.

Tacitus' gaze followed Charinus until he was out the door. "Sometimes I wonder if Charinus doesn't have his own aims. He's a freedman, not a slave, and I think he stays with me mainly because his mother and his woman are still part of my household."

"Then you're confident he'll come back this evening?" Torquatus said. "I wouldn't have such faith in mine." He spoke loudly enough that his servants, standing against the wall, could easily hear him. I wondered how securely the man slept at night.

Tacitus nodded. "I'm sure he will. He's a hard worker, so I try not to think too much about his motives. I know he's trying to amass enough money to buy the women's freedom. I don't imagine I'll see them again after that."

"Aren't you concerned about him going out alone tonight? Possibly being attacked?"

"He came from around here. He speaks the local language."

"Quite well," I said. "I can testify to that."

"All right then. We'll assume he can take care of himself." Torquatus emptied his wine cup and handed it to a servant to refill. "So, Gaius Pliny, tell me more."

I wished I had brought my cup of wine with me, but I went on to tell Torquatus about how I gathered information from Junianus, how Aurora had lain down to simulate the corpse, and how I had concluded that Junius most likely was not killed in an accidental fall but by someone slamming his head against the stone wall.

"Several times, you think?" Torquatus asked.

I nodded. "Assuming that the wound was as large as Junianus described it. From the blood streak on the wall, I think it had to be."

Torquatus submerged himself and came back up, wiping water from his disfigured face. "That means this was murder."

"I'm convinced it was."

"Do you have any idea who did it?"

"No, we weren't here long enough, and I couldn't convince my uncle to take us seriously. We were too young."

"'Us'?"

"Aurora was a big help to me, as she always is. She often sees things I don't see, or sees them in a different light."

Torquatus pursed his lips. "It's too bad you're only going to be here the one night. Otherwise you could reopen your investigation. I'm sure the local people would be relieved to know who killed the man. Living with a killer in your midst must be uncomfortable."

"Isn't it possible," Tacitus said, "that it was not a local person? Large numbers of people pass through here regularly. Who's to say it wasn't one of them?"

"That's a distinct possibility," Torquatus said. "And makes it that much more unlikely that the killer will ever be caught."

Tacitus laughed. "It could be any one of us who had ever been here before. That would include me."

"Fortunately it would eliminate me from suspicion," Torquatus said. "This is my first visit to this place. On my only other trip to Lugdunum I took the coast road and then turned up the Rhodanus."

"But," I objected, "what motive would some random stranger have had for killing the man? Aren't most murders committed by people who are close to the victim?"

Torquatus took another sip of wine. "I'll concede that. But you could not find enough evidence, ten years ago, to convict anyone. Is that true?"

"Yes, but I was young and inexperienced. Given the opportunity now, with what I've learned in the past few years, I think I could find a solution."

Torquatus raised his eyebrow. "Do you really?"

"Yes, but I simply don't have the time."

"So we'll never know the culprit. Pity. Still, Gaius Pliny has provided a fascinating tale. It might make for an interesting challenge. Can any of us solve it?"

I wished I could read Torquatus' facial expression. That might help me understand why he was so intrigued by this story. I know from my own experience that a murder can be solved, even if it was committed some years ago, but it would take time, time we didn't have. "It's all too far in the past, I'm afraid, and, as you say, we're only going to be here overnight."

———————— ⸭◦⸭ ————————

Our servants bathed quickly. When we returned to the inn through the snow, we sent the women over to have their turn in the bath. Whatever this place lacked in amenities, it was nice to be in a town where women could walk by themselves. There was no telling when we might have another opportunity to enjoy the luxury. They rejoined us as we were about halfway through dinner.

"It's starting to snow really heavily," Julia said as she sat next to Tacitus. The inn did not offer couches for a more civilized meal. "Travel is not going to be easy tomorrow, I expect."

"It may not be so bad," Tacitus said. "Charinus returned just before you got back from the bath. He says the road is clear, in spite of the snow. He doesn't think we'll have a problem as long as we start early and keep moving."

"I hope he's right," Julia said.

Lucina and Aemilia brought in cheese and fruit to finish our meal. Little Junilla seemed to follow her grandmother everywhere. This time another woman was with them. "This is Roscia," Lucina said to those who hadn't already seen her, "my husband's daughter. She did a lot of the cooking tonight."

"It was quite good," Julia said.

"Thank you, my lady."

"She's my aunt," the little girl said, taking Roscia's hand.

"Your family seems to be doing well," Julia said to Lucina, "in spite of your losses."

"We've kept things close," Lucina said. "Roscia is married to my son, Junianus."

I could see that Julia was tracing the family history the same way I was. Roscius and Junius were the sons of sisters, so they were cousins. That meant their children were related to one another, and now married to one another. Well, I thought, if it worked for Augustus and his family, and if Domitian could have his brother's daughter as a mistress, I guess ordinary people could follow the example. It's one way to keep property in a family.

Of course, some of those relatives in Augustus' family killed one another. I had a vague memory of Naomi telling a story from one of her Jewish holy books about one brother killing another. And Romulus killed his twin brother, Remus.

VIII

I COULDN'T TELL if the sun was up yet when I was awakened by a distant rumbling noise and a slight shaking of the bed. At first I thought it was thunder, but it was too cold, I reminded myself, for thunder, and thunder doesn't usually shake the furniture. This area is not prone to earthquakes, that I'm aware of. Aurora stirred and snuggled closer to me but did not seem to be fully awake.

I lay quietly beside her for a bit, until I had to admit I was not going to be able to get back to sleep. I managed to get up without disturbing her, slipped on a tunic, and wrapped a blanket around me. The room was cold enough that I could see my breath. Whoever was responsible for the hypocaust must be sleeping on the job. I took another blanket from the pile Lucina had provided us and laid it over Aurora to compensate for the loss of warmth from my body. When I looked through the shutters, I gasped. Snow was falling so heavily I could not see even the outline of buildings on the other side of the road, which I had been able to barely make out, even in the dark, when we went to bed last night.

My breathing quickened as I was overwhelmed by the feeling that I was back at Misenum, watching the ash pile up as Vesuvius erupted and threatened to bury everything. As far away as we had been from the volcano, the ash had fallen as quietly as this snow. My mother and I had tried to escape from our villa and travel north. Whenever we stopped for a few moments because of her frailty and sat down beside the road, using monuments or tombstones to shield us from the press of the crowd, the ash began to cover us. We had to stand frequently and shake it off. We finally decided to turn back home.

I've heard veteran soldiers say that some of their most frightening experiences remain etched in their minds for years afterwards. Hearing a certain sound or finding themselves in a certain situation can make them relive that incident as vividly as they experienced it the first time. I knew exactly how they felt. I had to shake myself now to remind myself that what I saw falling was snow, not the ash spewed out by a volcano. No matter how deep it got, it would eventually melt. It would not bury us.

But what effect would it have on our travel today? I went downstairs and found Roscius in the main room of the inn. His daughter, Roscia, was lighting lamps and putting fuel on the heating braziers. The old dog, Argos, snored on a mat in one corner.

"Good morning, sir," Roscius said. "You're up early. It's at least another hour 'til sunrise, as if we'll be able to tell when it happens."

"Will we have some heat in here by then?"

"Yes, sir. My men are working on it right now. I thought we'd use the braziers in addition to the furnace. It is frightful cold this morning."

I looked at the braziers with mistrust. Their fumes can be deadly in a closed-in room. In the days of Marius and Sulla a defeated opponent of Marius had been ordered to commit suicide. He had had fires started in braziers set up in a sealed room, sat down to read a book, and finally succumbed to the fumes. Or maybe it was a deadly boring book. At least this room was large and had shuttered windows. I could feel a draft already as the braziers and the cold air canceled one another out.

"Will we be able to tell when the sun comes up, as heavy as this snow is?"

Roscius chuckled. "You're right about that, sir. I've not seen it this bad in many a year."

Another rumble sounded closer to us.

"What's that?" I asked.

"I'm afraid it's what we call an avalanche, sir, a landslide of snow. As soon as we get some light I'll send Junianus to see what the situation is."

"Do you think it will block the road?"

"I'm afraid it very well could, sir. The pass ahead is narrow, with steep sides. Once that snow starts sliding, it doesn't stop until it has to."

"Meaning, at the bottom of the hill, where the road is."

"Exactly, sir. Right where the road is."

⸻

Tacitus, Torquatus, and other members of our party straggled downstairs during the next hour, most of them with at least one blanket wrapped around them. As promised, Roscius sent Junianus to check on the condition of the road. Lucina outfitted him with leggings, pieces of leather sewn into tubes, lined with wool. He returned in a short time, much too short a time.

"It's completely blocked," he told us, "just to the west of us. The pile of snow's twice as tall as any building in this town."

"Surely you're exaggerating," Tacitus said in despair.

"I wish I was, sir, for your sake. I know you're anxious to get on your way. But it's going to be a while before anybody leaves here in that direction."

Tacitus rolled his eyes and raised his head as though offering a prayer, although I knew it was more likely a curse.

Julia slipped her arm through his. "Should we turn back?" she asked. "We could take the coast road."

"We'd never get there in time," Tacitus said.

"I doubt you'd have much luck that way either, my lady," Junianus said. "The snow that fell overnight is nearly a foot deep and still coming."

Tacitus turned to me. "Let's ride out there and see the situation for ourselves."

"You'll need some warmer garments, sir," Lucina said. "Pardon my frankness, but you Romans prance around in your tunics and togas like it's always summer out there. Wait here a moment." She went into the back part of the inn and returned with pieces of leather like Junianus was wearing. "Put these on your legs," she said. "They tie at the top and they've got some fleece lining. You'll be nice and warm."

Tacitus and I couldn't help but laugh at one another, with Aurora and Julia joining in, as we slipped on the ridiculous-looking garments. The emperor Augustus, I've read, wrapped strips of wool around his legs in the winter when he got old, and I know our soldiers on the German frontier have taken to wearing some elements of barbarian dress, but I didn't think I would ever be reduced to it.

"Julius Caesar was ridiculed for appointing some Gauls to the Senate," I said, "when they showed up dressed like we are now."

"And no wonder," Tacitus said. "The tunic has been the costume of civilized men for centuries. I hope no one back in Rome ever sees us looking like this."

Lucina chuckled. "But aren't you warm for the first time since you got out of bed this morning?"

"All right. That I'll grant you." Tacitus rubbed his hands up and down his thighs.

Julia tugged at his leggings. "Maybe we women should try them."

"Oh, no," Tacitus said. "It's bad enough Gaius Pliny and I have to wear them. I hope the day never comes when women will be seen wearing this sort of thing. Put on another stola."

"But the cold air just comes right up—"

"Then squeeze your legs together."

Julia glared at him from beneath her half-lowered eyelids. "I might do just that tonight."

Junianus brought our horses from the stable to the front door of the inn. He and Roscius helped us mount.

"You won't have to go far at all, sirs," Junianus said. "The snow's piled up just around the second bend in the road."

"And there's no way past it?" I asked. "No side roads?"

"No, sir. There's nothing but a goat track, and it's mostly covered. There's nothing a horse or a wagon could use. I can show you, if you'd like."

"That would be helpful."

Junianus remounted the horse he'd been riding and led us to the edge of town. The snow was falling so fast that all three of us were quickly turned into white statues on horseback. "I hope we can find some *hipposandals* when we're ready to leave," I said. And then we came around a bend in the road and ran into a wall of snow several times higher than a man. It didn't look like we'd be going anywhere any time soon.

"By the gods," Tacitus muttered. "I never imagined there could be this much snow in one place. Is there *any* way around it?"

"I'm afraid not, sir," Junianus said. "The passage is narrow here and the sides are steep."

"Why did a snowslide—or whatever they call it—have to hit just now, right here? Talk about a damn coincidence!"

"It's an avalanche, sir," Junianus said slowly. "And it might not be just a coincidence."

"What are you talking about?" Tacitus snapped.

"Well, sir, when your man Charinus left last night to check on the road ahead, I followed him."

"Why did you do that?"

"I was talking to Aurora when he left, and she said she felt like there was something funny about him, with him being a Gaul. She told me about the way Gaius Pliny and his people were attacked on the road. She didn't think Charinus was fighting as hard as he could have. She just doesn't quite trust him. I told her I could follow him and see what he was up to."

The fellow really was besotted, I thought. All Aurora had to do was say the word, and he did her bidding.

"And what was he up to?" Tacitus asked.

"He rode another mile or so beyond this point, stopped, and gave a whistle. Two men came out of the woods and they talked for a few minutes."

"That hardly seems a crime," Tacitus said. "He and his mother came from somewhere around here. Maybe they were relatives of his."

"But Charinus said he was going to check the condition of the road," I pointed out, "not meet someone. I know he's one of yours, Cornelius Tacitus, but—"

"But what? I've known him since he was a boy. Are you questioning my judgment about the loyalty of someone from my own house, someone you barely know?"

I went straight to the point. "Two days ago he told me that conquered people will always try to rise up against their conquerors."

Tacitus stilled his horse and laughed. "He has said the same thing to my face, more than once."

I wished I could describe how the Gauls who attacked us—even their leader—had reacted to Charinus with what looked like awe, or at least respect. Tacitus hadn't seen that, but I suspected he would have some justification for it, too. He felt some commitment to this man, or knew something about him, that I could not fathom. I turned to Junianus. "Could you hear what they said?"

"No, sir."

"Did they do anything more than talk?"

"Before the men went back into the woods, they clasped hands with Charinus. Like this." He offered his hand to Tacitus, grasping him near the elbow.

"Again, that doesn't sound like a criminal activity," Tacitus said. "You and I have shaken hands in a similar manner, Gaius Pliny."

"But handshakes are often…commitments," I said, "agreements to do something."

"And they are often just handshakes. Now, unless you have some firm evidence that Charinus is plotting something against us, I want to get back to the inn. My legs may be warm, but my balls are freezing." He turned his horse around. We had gone about as far as we would be able to go anyway.

"What if those men caused the avalanche?"

"What are you talking about?"

"Like Junianus said, it might not be a coincidence."

"How could men cause an avalanche? Isn't it just too much snow and it starts to move?"

Junianus had nodded as I talked. "That's true, sir. But people can cause it to move. We have to be very careful if we go hunting when the snow's this deep. One wrong step and…" He waved his arm at the pile of snow in front of us.

"I'll talk to him as soon as we get back," Tacitus said.

"I don't think you should," I said. "If he knows we suspect him, that could make him more careful about whatever he's planning." I held up a hand as Tacitus started to protest. "All right, *if* he's planning anything. We don't want him to put his guard up. Junianus, can you help us keep an eye on him? I don't think he'd suspect you."

"I'd be glad to, sir."

"Gaius, I must object. I've known and trusted Charinus for years."

"But I haven't," I said to his back.

Tacitus said nothing else until we were coming back into town. Then he directed himself to Junianus. "How long will it take for this to melt?"

"Days and days," Junianus said. "If word gets to Lugdunum about the problem, the governor will probably send troops to start digging from that side, but that could take quite a while."

"And turning around and going back doesn't seem to be possible right now?"

"No, sir."

"So I just have to sit here while my brother dies."

"At least we have a roof over our heads," I said. "If we had been caught out on the road when this happened, we would have frozen to death."

Tacitus patted his leg. "Not if we were wearing these. As odd as they look and feel, they do keep you warm."

We rode back to the inn and reported what we had seen. Our entire party was now gathered in the dining room. Roscius' mother, Aemilia, and Lucina took good care of anything we needed.

"What are we going to do?" Julia asked Tacitus, anxiety rising in her voice.

"Try to stay warm." Tacitus kept his tone even.

"The servants are firing up the hypocaust," Lucina said. "Just give it a little time. Meanwhile, this is what we use." She put several bricks into the braziers. "Those will be warm in no time. Wrap them in a cloth and put them under your feet."

"It must be hard to get any work done," I said, "when you have to sit still to keep warm."

"Being up and moving around helps keep you warm," Roscius said.

"That's what we ought to be doing." He motioned to his servants to get busy at something. His daughter took charge of the crew.

Aurora and I sat down close to one another, as the rest of our party, ignoring Roscius' advice, huddled together. It was nice to have an excuse to do so. "Do avalanches happen often around here?" I asked.

Roscius shrugged. "Every now and then. They're usually higher up in the pass. I can't recall the last one that hit this close to us, and I've lived here all my life."

"I've been here even longer," Aemilia said, "and this is the first one I've seen this close to the end of the pass."

"What causes them?" I expected they would say something about angry gods.

"It's mostly the weight of the snow," Roscius said. "Or sometimes animals step in just the right place and knock something loose. Maybe a tree snaps from the weight of the snow. Once a little snow starts to move up high, everything below it is going to come down."

Tacitus' earlier questions about why *this* avalanche in *this* place had been on my mind since he posed it. "Could a person or persons cause it?"

"Well, yes, sir. Just like with an animal, if they step in exactly the right place."

"Could they cause it deliberately?" Torquatus asked.

Roscius raised his eyebrows like he'd never considered that possibility before. "I suppose so, but why would they? It's a mighty disastrous prank to play."

"What makes you ask that question?" I said to Torquatus.

"It's a possibility, isn't it? You've said one should consider *all* possibilities when looking for the answer to a question. Maybe this was just a prank that went too far."

But what if it's not a prank? I thought. What if you want to trap someone who's made you angry until you can take vengeance on them? What better way to do it?

Tacitus drew a blanket tighter around himself and Julia moved even closer to him on the bench they were sharing. "Do you just sit here and wait for it to melt?" he asked.

"No, sir. It's my job as *duovir* to get some men organized and start digging us out. We might as well wait until the snow lets up, though. And it will take time. I suggest you have a bite to eat and find some way to entertain yourselves."

"This would be an excellent time," Torquatus said, "for Gaius Pliny to continue his account of what happened ten years ago."

Roscius' brow darkened. "Well, that's all past and done, isn't it? I don't see much point in stirring up old trouble. We got enough of today's trouble, as it is."

"You were *duovir*, then, weren't you?" Torquatus asked. "What did you do about Junius' murder?"

"Murder?" Roscius sputtered. "What murder, sir? He fell and hit his head. He shouldn't have been climbing around in those gears when he'd been drinking."

Lucina stepped in front of him. "That's what you say. That's what you've said for ten years." She waved her hand in his face. "Nobody ever did a proper investigation into what happened. Gaius Pliny here tried, but you wouldn't listen to him."

Roscius turned to me with his hands raised in front of him. "With all due respect, sir, you were just a boy. Even your own uncle thought you were seeing things that weren't there."

Torquatus' eyebrow arched in its off-balance fashion. "What sort of things?"

"I'm not going to listen to this," Roscius said as he stalked out of the room. "I've got to get us dug out from under all of this snow."

"Well, I certainly *do* want to hear the story," Lucina said. She took off her apron and draped it over her shoulder, waving her daughter-in-law back to work. "May I listen in, sir?"

"Be our guest," Torquatus said. "Gaius Pliny, please go on."

I felt like a bard in a Homeric poem being told to entertain the crowd. I wondered why Torquatus was so insistent. When bards in epic poetry are urged to tell a story, it's often to reveal something about one of the characters who's hearing the tale, like Odysseus breaking into tears when he hears Demodocus sing the story of Troy. At least I didn't have to sing and accompany myself on the lyre. I could do that for a short piece—I'd even written a few—but not for an epic tale, which this was turning out to be.

⸻⸺◆⸺⸻

[A.D. 77]

BY the time Aurora and I got back to the inn from our walk around town, the dishes from the evening meal had been cleared and Lucina had brought out a *latrunculus* board. My uncle was passionate about the game and had taught me to love it as well. It was the only distraction from his work that he allowed himself. I stood behind him as he finished a game with Monica. Aurora stood behind her mother, placing a hand on her shoulder. Monica kissed her hand lightly.

"And there!" my uncle crowed, moving a piece to finish surrounding Monica's *dux*. "Game over!" He turned to me. "Gaius, take a turn. With apologies to Monica, I need some stiffer competition."

Monica pouted. "I'm sorry, darling. My head is really hurting."

"Have you taken some of your poppy syrup?"

"Yes, but it doesn't seem to be helping much this evening."

"I know you could beat me, dear, but perhaps the syrup has dulled your wits. It can do that. Clear-headed Gaius will have no such handicap. He'll attack me like a gladiator fighting for his life against an older, more experienced opponent. Won't you, son?"

He calls me "son" only once in a great while. I never know if he means it in some legal sense or just in the loose way that older men sometimes use it when talking to younger ones. I guess I'll find out when we read his will, which I hope doesn't happen any time soon.

Monica moved her chair closer to my uncle and I pulled up a seat across the table from him. Aurora stood at the end of the table, between us. She has never developed a fondness for the game. My uncle and I arranged our pieces in their starting positions.

He made his moves quickly, confidently, giving me little time to plan my strategy. When he finished me off, he looked disappointed. Monica kissed him on his cheek. "I have quite a headache," she said. "I'll see you upstairs. I assume you're going to work a while longer with Glaucon."

"Yes." He began putting the game away. "Do you need some more poppy syrup?"

"No, I have plenty. Good night, Gaius Caecilius." She motioned with her head for her daughter to follow her, but Aurora moved to stand behind me.

"I'd like to stay, Mother," she said.

"If we had been gladiators," my uncle said, "I'd have cut you to ribbons. Do you have something on your mind?"

I put the white stones I'd been using into their little bag and drew the string. "Yes, Uncle, I do. I don't understand what happened to that man, Junius."

My uncle did not stop bagging his black stones. Without looking at me, he asked, "And why is that any of your concern?"

"It's not *my* concern, so much as the...the concern of justice. If someone did something to him, they should be punished. Isn't that what our laws are all about? And aren't they as applicable here as they are in Rome?"

"Of course. That's all true. But I'm told he fell and hit his head. What does the law have to do with that?"

"Junianus saw the body. He says the wound on his head was quite large. Aurora heard him describe it." I ran my fingers over the area Junianus had described as Aurora nodded.

My uncle pointed to a chair for Aurora to sit down. He shook his head. "People do tend to exaggerate, you know, especially in stressful moments or when a loved one is involved. A mere scratch can become a blood-spewing gash when they retell the story."

"I just think—"

"Look into it all you want, Gaius. I know you and Aurora have some sort of morbid fascination with crime. I have work to do. My *Natural History* is nearly complete. The servants have finished bringing my books and writing materials out of the broken *raeda*. Glaucon and I are going to organize things tonight so I can settle down to work beginning tomorrow morning. Roscius has cleaned out a storeroom that I can use as a library. It even has shelves."

I could see I wasn't going to get any help from him. I was wondering how I could get him to show some interest in Junius' death when Auro-ra asked, "How near are you to finishing, my lord?" She had played right to his sense of pride in his work, which is considerable. It was as clever a move as if she was playing a game. She was trying to get him on our side and keep him from retreating to his books.

He leaned back in his chair, obviously pleased to have a chance to talk about the project. "I'm writing the dedicatory epistle. That's always the last touch, and the hardest. You have to sound sincere without being a sycophant."

"Are you dedicating this one to Vespasian, too, my lord?" she asked. He had dedicated his last few works to the *princeps*.

"No. He told me not to. I'm dedicating it to Titus. He'll succeed his father, and I'm afraid it may not be long before that happens. Vespasian says he doesn't feel well some days. He won't admit it to the Senate or to anyone else but Titus and me."

"Do you think a transition is...imminent?" I asked.

"No, I don't think he's going to die tomorrow, but he's almost sev-enty and says he doesn't expect to live longer than a couple of more years."

"I'm sorry to hear that." And I truly was. "For the most part he's been fair and competent, don't you think?"

My uncle nodded. "And I think Titus will be the same. Let's hope he lives long and prospers, and the empire along with him. Domitian would be...well, let's just say he's a very different man than his father and his brother. My fondest wish for you, Gaius, is that you *not* be subjected to Domitian as *princeps*." He turned his attention to Aurora. "And you, young lady, did not hear a word of that, did you?"

"A word of what, my lord?" Aurora looked him right in the eye without changing her expression.

My uncle smiled. "That's an even better answer than 'no.' You two haven't been through a transition in leadership. You were barely seven, living away from things at Laurentum, when Vespasian took power. Aurora, you had only recently arrived in Italy."

"I didn't understand anything that was going on around me, my lord," Aurora said. "Even if I had spoken Latin or Greek, all I knew was that everyone seemed as frightened as I was. Why, I didn't know."

My uncle nodded. "I don't think Gaius here grasped the situation much better than that. I put my family out at Laurentum to protect you. We had some difficult, chaotic times with the end of Augustus' line. Rome was attacked, part of it even burned. But I think all will be well now, at least for the rest of my life and much of yours." He folded his hands on the table in front of him and looked at Aurora. "Now, my dear, as for this man Junius, do you think there is anything suspicious about his death, which my nephew calls murder?"

"Like Gaius Caecilius, my lord, I have…a few questions."

"Well, we have nothing better to do for the next…however many days, so you two might as well indulge your curiosity. It'll keep you occupied, and I don't suppose it can hurt anything. You'll find people unwilling to talk to you, I'm sure. Just remind them that I'm your uncle and I'm an advisor to the *princeps*. Tell them I'm not satisfied with what I've heard about Junius' death and you're making inquiries on my behalf, since I'm somewhat incapacitated. That should get their attention." He motioned for us to help him heave himself to his feet. "Now I bid you good night."

Aurora and I stood silent until my uncle had hobbled out of sight. We heard his familiar wheezing as he called for Monica to help him climb the stairs.

"He still treats us like children." I mocked him: "'I don't suppose it can hurt anything.' By the gods, we're talking about a possible murder here!"

"But he's letting us use his name and—by implication—the name of the *princeps*. That could be a big help."

"Yes, I guess so."

"So, where do we start?

"We start with what we know."

"And what do we know?" Aurora asked.

"We know where Junius was killed, when, and how. We have a strong suspect in Roscius—"

"Who has the perfect alibi."

"That's where we ought to start digging tomorrow," I said.

"'Digging'? What do you mean?"

"I mean we'll see just how perfect that alibi is."

———◦•◦———

As I listened to Gaius, his account brought back so many memories of our first real investigation. Our first step was to find Junianus the next morning and ask him to tell us again every detail of what he saw in the mill. He was sitting with Argos beside the stream where we had first encountered him. We sat down beside him.

When he heard our questions, his impatience boiled up. "Why are you asking me about this? I already told you everything I know."

"Sometimes," Gaius said, "people can recall something they didn't think about to begin with if they go over an incident a second time. Try thinking about what you saw, but not just your father's body. I know that was a horrible sight. Right now, try to remember what was around his body."

Junianus looked confused.

"Try to imagine," I said, "that you're back in that mill. But don't look at your father's body. Look at the things around him." This was a technique Gaius and I had developed. We made ourselves look not at a particular thing but at what lay around it. One of us would close our eyes and describe what we'd seen while the other checked for accuracy. "For instance, Roscius says your father had been drinking and that made him fall. Did you see or smell any sign of that? A wineskin? Stains on his clothes, maybe? Just look around."

"I didn't see any wineskin. And the only stains I saw were blood."

"Did you see anything that was out of place, that was missing or didn't belong there?"

Junianus twisted his mouth in annoyance. "I didn't have time to take an inventory. I barely had time to see my pa before Roscius and his men started moving his body."

"Do you know of anyone who would have wanted to hurt your father?"

Junianus petted Argos before he answered. "Half the men in town want to have a go at Lucina. Most of them make no secret of it."

"How does she react to them?"

"She teases them, leads them on." He threw a rock into the water hard enough to splash on our feet. "I wish she wouldn't."

I was surprised to hear that. I hadn't taken Lucina for that sort of woman at our brief meeting. Was that one of the secrets my uncle had alluded to? "Did that make your father angry?" I asked.

"Sure, he told her to stop it, like any man would, many a time."

"Do you think those men want her badly enough to kill your father?" Gaius asked.

"When you look at most of the other women in this town, you can see why my ma is considered a prize." In spite of himself, his voice betrayed a trace of pride. "Sometimes she works in Roscius' inn, you know, cooking and serving meals. A woman flirts with men in that situation. My pa had words with some of them when they came sniffing too close around her."

"Just words?" Gaius asked.

"No. He got into some fights over her."

"Was your father a man who often got into fights?"

Junianus shrugged. "He had a temper. Nothing made him madder, though, than people whispering about his ma and Roscius' pa."

"What were they whispering?"

"He and Roscius looked alike, you know, since their mas were sisters. But some people said it was because they had the same pa as well."

Gaius persisted. "You mean people thought they were brothers?"

"Some people talk too much. And you're one of them." Junianus got up. "I have to go. C'mon, Argos."

As we watched Junianus and his dog walk away, Gaius rubbed his chin and said, "Well, talk about big secrets in a small town. I think we just hit a gold mine."

"Do you think Roscius and Junius might have known who their father was?"

"Wouldn't that explain a lot about Junius the man? He had to live with the knowledge that he was illegitimate. That says a lot about his mother."

"Wait a minute, Gaius. The elder Roscius could have forced himself on her."

"That's true. I hadn't thought about that."

I shook my finger in his face. "Men never do. They always assume the woman is guilty. Go all the way back to Lucretia and the beginnings of Rome. She was raped, but she had to kill herself to make the men in her family believe her."

Gaius raised his hands in an apology. "You're right. It's quite likely that the elder Roscius married one sister and raped or seduced the other. Our Roscius holds it over his half brother. So, in addition to drinking too much, Junius has a bad temper. Having other men pay attention to his own wife must have infuriated him."

"And maybe Lucina didn't know what had happened. She flirted with the other men around her. That would just provoke poor Junius all the more. I wonder if that was intentional on her part. I mean, did she know about who his father was? Was she really interested in those men, or was she just annoying her husband?"

Gaius tented his fingers and rested his chin on them. "That's something we'll definitely have to consider. Women do sometimes flirt with men to arouse jealousy on the part of a man they're interested in." He smiled ever so slightly. "Don't they?"

"Ovid says they should." I squirmed. He obviously had noticed the attention I was paying to Junianus, with precisely that aim in mind.

"Then I think the number of suspects just increased considerably."

"So how are we going to eliminate some?" I asked. "We can't just go around asking men if they were interested in Lucina."

"Maybe we could ask if they're willing to kill for her."

"Oh, don't be ridiculous. I thought we were taking this seriously."

"I am," Gaius said, "but this is so much more complicated than our games of following someone who looked suspicious through the streets of Rome and trying to figure out what they were doing."

"That made me feel like everybody has something to hide."

Gaius tossed a pebble into the river. "What if everybody here has something to hide? Anyone in this town could have a motive for killing Junius. Jealousy because of his wife, an argument sparked by his temper—who knows?"

I got to my feet and dusted off my gown. "And maybe it was just an accident."

"But if it was an accident, wouldn't the killer have stopped after hitting

Junius' head against the wall once? Junius could have been arguing with someone. That person pushed him hard enough to knock him against the wall. If it were you, wouldn't you stop at that point? If someone knocked him against the wall several times, that makes me think they really intended to hurt him badly."

⸻ ∘⊙∘ ⸻

[A.D. 87]

THE room was getting more comfortable as the hypocaust warmed up, but Torquatus exchanged the brick under his feet for a warmer one from the brazier. "Didn't people object to you questioning them? It's not as though you were Praetorians. You didn't have any kind of authority except what your uncle tried to give you. Why would anyone answer your questions? I don't think I would have talked to you as long as Junianus did."

I nodded. "That was a problem. Like my uncle, most people just regarded us as troublesome—or amusing—children who had to be humored because of my uncle's equestrian stripe. Being able to invoke Vespasian's name did help, though."

He sighed as the warmth penetrated into his feet. "So what was your next step?"

"We intended to talk with Lucina, but the arrival of the magistrate from Augusta Taurinorum led us in a different direction."

IX

WE WERE COMING up the bank from the stream onto the road when we saw a small group of horsemen—six armed guards wearing breastplates and three men wearing ordinary tunics—approaching from the direction of Augusta Taurinorum. They halted beside us and the soldier closest to us in the front said, "Good day, young man. We're looking for a fellow named Quintus Roscius. Do you know where we might find him?"

I pointed in the direction of the inn. "That's his inn, at the end of this first block."

With a nod of thanks the man prodded his horse with his heels and the little troop resumed their progress. Three guards rode in front of the men in tunics and the other three behind them. I took the older man in a tunic with an equestrian stripe riding in the center of the group to be the magistrate we were waiting for and the other two to be his assistants. The magistrate's thick hair was turning a distinguished gray. He was thin, and his cheeks were beginning to sink in.

Aurora and I followed them, keeping to the side of the road. Like most paved Roman roads, this one widened as it approached the town, allowing for raised pedestrian paths on either side. The paths separated people from animals and wagons and allowed people to walk without having to step around the animals' droppings or risk being run over by a driver who was in too much of a hurry (or was a maniac, like Nero's father, who deliberately ran over a child with his chariot).

124

"Sometimes I wonder," I said, "if there could ever be a type of transportation that does not rely on animals."

"It would certainly leave everything so much cleaner," Aurora said. "And we wouldn't have to listen to all the noise the animals make and whips cracking and drivers shouting."

We came to the door of the inn as the men were dismounting. The three who had been riding in the rear took the reins and stayed with the horses while the rest entered the inn. Aurora and I started to go in, but one of the guards held out a hand. "What's your business here?"

"I am Gaius Caecilius, nephew of Gaius Plinius, an advisor to the *princeps*. We're staying in this inn." The guard withdrew his hand and we went inside. Aurora found a place beside the door to sit and be inconspicuous, something she doesn't do all that well because she's so pretty.

Roscius was standing in front of the magistrate, with Lucina beside him and a younger couple off to one side. Putting together what I'd heard thus far, I guessed they were Junius' daughter, Junia, a small woman with reddish blond hair and her husband, Draco. He was short, with brown hair and long, slender features that did, in fact, suggest a dragon.

The magistrate held the document he was being asked to evaluate and was reading it, but not loudly enough for me to hear what he was saying. He stopped and looked in our direction. "Did I hear the name of Gaius Plinius mentioned?"

I stepped forward. "Yes, sir. I am his nephew, Gaius Caecilius."

"Is he here then?"

"Yes, sir. He's working on a book. I believe Roscius has given him a room for that."

Roscius nodded eagerly. "Yes. He and his scribe are in the storeroom at the end of this hallway behind me."

"I will look forward to meeting him. I'm Marcus Lupercus." Some men's names describe their appearance, as Draco's did, or their personality. Lupercus did not have the appearance of a wolf, which his name implied. Perhaps there was something voracious about his character. Or maybe the name was just something he'd inherited. Some distant ancestor had been wolfish. My uncle wasn't the second child in a family, but some ancestor of his must have been, so he was Gaius Plinius Secundus. That's who I would become when he adopted me, even though I'm an only child.

"I'm pleased to meet you, sir. May I listen to what you're reading?" Lupercus raised an eyebrow. "Of what interest is it to you?"

I decided it was time to invoke my uncle's *auctoritas*. "My uncle, who is an advisor to the *princeps*, has some questions about the death of Junius. He has asked me to look into it for him. He's deeply involved in his work, and is somewhat limited in his movements."

"I see." Lupercus pursed his lips. "I suppose there's no harm in that. The document is a typical promise of repayment of a loan." He handed me the single sheet of papyrus long enough for me to run my eyes over it, then took it back. "I was just getting to the part where it lists particulars. The loan was for three thousand *sesterces* and Junius agrees that Roscius will take all of his property if the loan isn't repaid."

"And it specifies his mill, his farm, and his servants, doesn't it?" Roscius persisted.

"Yes, it does," the magistrate assured him.

"I made him list everything individually," Roscius said, proud of how clever he'd been, "just so there couldn't be any arguments. That's why I didn't even care if they brought you in to look at it." He glared at Junia and Draco. "That daughter of his and her husband think they're so smart, but they aren't going to get anything."

"That just shows what a thief you are," Draco said.

I wanted to forestall what was surely a frequent argument. "What was the purpose of the loan?"

"Does that matter?" Lupercus asked. Annoyance spread over Roscius' face.

"No, but, as I said, my uncle is curious. That's a lot of money, especially in a small town like this, I would think. Where would he spend it?"

"He liked to gamble," Roscius snapped, "but he didn't have much luck. He was always getting into games with people who were passing through here. When he lost, he always thought he could win it back if he kept at it long enough."

Lupercus nodded ruefully. "We all know how that goes."

"So you loaned him money," I said, "knowing you were unlikely to get it back."

"I knew I'd get the property."

"And that's what you actually wanted, wasn't it?"

Roscius put a hand over his heart. "What if it was? I didn't force him to take the money. I didn't put the damn dice in his hands. I had offered to buy his property, but the stubborn fool wouldn't sell."

"He wanted to leave us something," Junia said.

"Why were you so eager to buy?" I asked.

Roscius addressed Lupercus. "What does this have to do with certifying the loan agreement? That's what you came over here to do. Do I have to answer this boy's questions?"

"Would you rather I asked them?" Lupercus said. "They seem perfectly reasonable questions to me."

"And to me," my uncle said from the doorway behind Roscius. I had seen him tottering toward us, but Roscius hadn't. He walked around Roscius and placed a hand on my shoulder to steady himself. Aurora got to her feet and took his other elbow. "Your answers might help us to understand what happened to poor Junius."

"He fell and hit his head on the wall," Roscius said, restraining himself with difficulty. He clenched his fists as tightly as his teeth.

"It's hard to determine if that's what happened," my uncle said, "without a body to examine."

"It's summer, sir, an unusually warm summer, I might add. You can't leave...the deceased lying around forever. If I'd known there was going to be so much interest in him, I might've brought some ice down from the mountains and packed him in it."

"Were you the one who organized the funeral?" my uncle asked.

"Yes, sir. His wife was too upset to do it, and his daughter and her husband don't have two coins to rub together."

I was surprised at how he could talk about Junia and Draco as if they weren't there.

"Junius and I weren't friends, but we were cousins and we knew one another all our lives, so I stepped in. Was that a bad thing?"

"No," my uncle said. "Someone had to take the responsibility. You were gracious."

"You still haven't answered my question," I said.

"Which question?" Roscius had the desperate look of a man who was completely surrounded. "You've been asking so many."

"Why were you so eager to buy Junius' property?"

"It's obvious, isn't it? He's got the only mill in town, and his farm is on one of the few flat places around here. Why wouldn't I want it?"

"Did you want it badly enough…to kill him?" I only dared ask that question because my uncle was standing next to me. My heart pounded as I formed the words.

Roscius staggered as though I had hit him. "What…kill…? That's absolute nonsense. He fell. Why can't you understand that? I wasn't anywhere near the mill when they found his body!"

"Where were you?" my uncle asked. Lupercus and the others had fallen completely quiet, becoming mere spectators in awe of what was happening in front of them.

"I was just getting out of bed. It was barely sunrise. His mill-hand, Magnus, rousted me out. He's the one that found Junius. You can ask him."

"Where would we find him?"

"Maybe at the mill. If not there, he lives out on Junius' farm."

"His parents work a piece of it," Lucina said. "They pay us a portion of the crops as rent."

My uncle patted my shoulder. "Then I think talking to Magnus would be your next step, my boy." He looked around him. "Now, what did I come out here for?…" He shrugged and twisted his mouth. "Well, I guess I don't need it. I've got to get back to work."

Lupercus made a small gesture with the hand holding the sheet of papyrus. "Oh, yes," I said. "Uncle, this is Marcus Lupercus, one of the magistrates from Augusta Taurinorum. This is my uncle, Gaius Plinius."

"It is an honor to meet you, sir." The "wolf-man" extended his hand, which my uncle shook.

Aurora and I left them talking as we set out for Junius' farm. My uncle was leaning toward the room where he and Glaucon were working. He has little patience with anyone who draws him away from his books. Glaucon waited in the hallway to help him make his way back to work.

"Then he had to spoil it all by calling me 'my boy,'" Gaius groused as we walked back to town. "I didn't feel like a boy. I don't feel like a boy. I interrogated Roscius as well as anybody could have in court, don't you think?"

"Definitely," I said. "It was amazing to watch. You could see that Lupercus was impressed, too. I thought Roscius was going to confess right there."

Gaius really did have a knack for the courts. It would still be three years before he tried his first case, opposing Regulus and defeating him, thus insuring that the enmity between his family and Regulus would last at least one more generation. But his ability was easy to see even then.

"He wasn't going to confess," Gaius said, "unless he was a complete fool."

"What makes you say that?"

"He didn't do it."

I stopped and took his arm. "Didn't do it? What are you talking about?"

Gaius ran a hand through his hair, as though he was exasperated by talking to someone who couldn't see the obvious. "Didn't you see how he reacted when I asked him if he wanted Junius' property badly enough to kill him?"

"Yes. He seemed stunned."

"Exactly. It was the first time the possibility of Junius being murdered and not just dying in an accident had even entered his mind."

That seemed to me to overstate the case. I had been deeply impressed, however, by the way Gaius had handled his questioning of Roscius. For the first time, I think, I realized that we in fact weren't children anymore. We still had a couple of years to go before we would legally be adults, but we weren't children. My approbation, as sincere as it could be, didn't seem to make Gaius feel any better, though.

"And Uncle had to go and spoil it all by calling me 'boy.'" He spat out that last word.

I wanted to turn his attention to something else. "Don't you think that document points to Roscius as having the most reason to kill Junius?"

"No, just the opposite."

"What—"

"Since he does have the most reason, he would never kill Junius. Everybody would suspect him at once."

"But we've heard that they argued a lot. Arguments can get out of hand."

"Junius was killed sometime during the night. Why would Roscius go to the mill to argue with him? Why was Junius there at that time? It doesn't make sense. That whole 'loan' business doesn't make sense. Why lend money to a habitual gambler who's not even very good at it. Or very lucky, as the case may be."

"Like he said, he knew he could eventually get the land and the mill, and that's what he wanted."

"And who was he gambling with? This is a very small town."

"With a lot of people passing through it, staying at Roscius' inn."

"That's a big part of the problem. Whoever killed him could be someone who was here for a day or two and is now miles away, never to be seen again."

We had been out to Junius' farm to talk to Magnus, but we didn't find him there. He was chasing goats up in the hills, one of the servants informed us. The day was quite warm, and we were starting to sweat. I'd expected cooler weather up here in the mountains. It had taken us about a quarter of an hour to walk out here, and now we faced the same amount of time going back. At least it was a lovely walk, or it would have been if Gaius hadn't been in such a dark mood. He couldn't even appreciate that the area had so many plants we'd never seen before. This far up in the mountains, things grow that don't thrive lower down. Some of the most interesting parts of his uncle's Natural History are about plants and how they can be used to treat various ailments, like my mother's poppy syrup.

We came to a pond that we had passed on our way out to the farm. "Could we stop and put our feet in the water?" I said. "I'm really hot, and *we don't have anything urgent to do." I thought the break might improve Gaius' mood as well.*

"Sure," he said with no particular enthusiasm.

We sat down on the edge of the pond, which had a rocky shelf hanging over it, about twenty feet above us. A waterfall cascaded from the ledge. We slipped off our sandals and hiked our garments up a bit.

"Watch out," Gaius said. "I see your knee."

That was a line from Ovid that we used to laugh about—how daring it was for a woman's knee to be exposed. We had swum together nude and bathed together in all innocence when we were children. When we were ten, Gaius' mother insisted that we stop. That was the last time we'd seen one another unclothed.

The water in the pond was cold, as all the water around here seemed to be, coming from snow and ice up in the mountains, but this pond had full exposure to the sun and wasn't very deep, so it wasn't cold enough to take one's breath away, just cool enough to be refreshing on a hot day. I was so hot I couldn't resist a sudden impulse. I stood up, walked around to the other side of the pond, removed my stola, and stepped under the waterfall. Then I entered the pool, stooping down until the water came up to my shoulders. I heard Gaius gasp, but I couldn't bring myself to look directly at him. I didn't want him to see how red my face was. The warmth of the day wasn't the only reason I had done this.

I was aware of Gaius getting into the water and turned to face him. He had also stooped down. I splashed a little water on him and squealed when he retaliated. We looked at one another and I wasn't sure what was going to happen next. I didn't know what was he was doing when he yelled, "Look out!" and lunged at me. We fell to one side and went under the water as a large boulder splashed into the pool. If Gaius hadn't grabbed me, it would have landed right on top of us.

We came up in one another's arms, spluttering and wiping water off our faces. I turned to look in the direction Gaius was pointing. All I could see were a few loose pebbles dislodged by the movement of the boulder and falling beside the waterfall like rain into the pool.

"That was deliberate," Gaius said.

I shivered, more from fear than from the cold. "We'll never catch him."

"Maybe not," Gaius said, "but I want to take a look."

"Is that a good idea? Whoever did it could still be up there."

"I don't care."

Gaius boosted himself out of the pool. Something told me to avert my eyes, but I couldn't. Before he pulled on his tunic, I could see that he was developing a wiry physique. He would probably never be particularly tall or muscular. He picked up a broken branch that was large enough to be a weapon, and I followed him as quickly as I could.

Not even bothering to put on our sandals, Aurora and I scrambled up the hill to the ledge overlooking the pool, but, of course, whoever had pushed the boulder down on us was nowhere to be seen. The ground was covered with small stones, which meant there were no footprints or other traces to be found. The only clue we could find to what had happened was a thick branch poised over a small rock.

"Someone used that as a lever," I said.

We looked around the small level area, keeping an eye on the slope above us, in case the person who had tried to kill us made another effort at it. From the ledge we could see across Junius' farm and down into the valley beyond it. In spite of today's heat, the fields were lush and green, watered by the snow melting above us.

"If someone hadn't just tried to kill us," Aurora said, "I would enjoy looking at this scenery. It's spectacular."

With the immediate danger past us, the only scenery I had in my mind was the sight of Aurora removing her stola. I tried to block it out. I did not want to be a master who took advantage of his female slaves. I needed to think about something else.

"Who on earth could have done this?" I said. "Was somebody following us?"

Aurora took my arm to steady herself and brushed dirt off the soles of her feet. "I didn't see anyone, but I wasn't paying that much attention. Who knew we were coming out here?"

"We don't know who might have overheard what we were saying when we talked to Lupercus."

"Does somebody think we know something?"

"Maybe they want to make sure we *don't* know something. Or don't learn anything."

"The servants said Magnus was out in the field with the goats. He could have been anywhere, including up here." Aurora looked around, as though she might spot the missing man. "Do you think he could have pushed that boulder over on us?"

I picked up a pebble and dropped it into the pond. It was fascinating to watch it plunge from this height. "You've seen Magnus. He's as big as his name. For that matter, with this lever, just about anybody could have done it, even Draco. But the question is, why would he—or anybody else—do it? This looks like another 'accident' that wasn't really an accident."

"Do you think," Aurora asked, "Draco would have the strength to smash Junius' head into the wall?"

"I'm sure he would. But, again, why?"

As I surveyed the area I noticed a cluster of white, star-like flowers growing among the rocks. I picked one and gave it to Aurora, who put it in her brown hair. That and her olive skin, so unfashionable among Roman women, made the flower stand out.

"Beautiful," I said.

"Thank you, my lord." She lowered her head and touched the flower.

"I meant you, but the flower's pretty, too." I don't know where I found the courage to say that.

She reached up and touched my cheek.

"Somebody could still be watching us," I said.

"Do you really care? I don't see that dog anywhere around."

I pulled her to me and kissed her, as I had longed to do for some time. Her response was warm and lingering. I kept my arms around her, and she laid her head on my shoulder. I didn't really know what to say at this point. The best I could do was "We should be getting back into town."

When we reached Collis, the first greeting we got was from Argos.

When we arrived in town and passed the latrina, *I saw Junia entering the building. "I'm going to stop in here," I told Gaius. "I'll see you at the inn."*

"Do you want me to come in with you?"

"No. This might be a chance for some serious girl talk, if there's no one else in there." I gave Gaius a gentle push toward the inn and turned into the latrina. *"Take the dog with you."*

Like any public facility in a Roman town, this one contained a number of seats. The walls were painted with old-fashioned geometric patterns in subdued colors, probably done at the same time and by the same artist as the inn and now needing updating. The floor tiles depicted the four seasons. Windows placed high in the walls and fitted with translucent pieces of mica let in light while preserving privacy, though I sometimes chuckle at the idea of "privacy" in a Roman latrine. People of all ages, all classes, and both genders use them at the same time. The long, loose garments that both men and women wear make it possible to cover ourselves as we sit down. The latrines, as much as the Forum, are the center of social life in a large Roman town. Fortunately, in a small town like Collis, there were no poets, musicians, or sausage sellers vying for the attention of patrons.

When I entered, I saw, as I hoped, Junia by herself, occupying a seat in one corner. I picked up a stick with a sponge on the end out of a bowl by the door and took the seat that put me at a right angle to her. That would make it easier to talk, and I was glad to have a few unexpected, undisturbed moments with her.

For her age, Junia was a small girl with reddish blond hair that most Roman women would kill for and wide blue eyes that gave her a sweet, childlike appearance. Seeing her on the street, I would not have taken her for someone's wife. We greeted one another as I sat down. She moved her stick with a sponge on the end of it to give me more room.

"Where did you get the flower?" she asked when I was settled. Her tone seemed accusatory and immediately put me on my guard. I'd heard earlier that she and her husband were quite poor. Sometimes free people who are in the lowest class resent the servants of the wealthy, who dress better and, in general, live better than they do.

"Oh, I'd almost forgotten it." I raised my hand to the flower.

"In case you want to know, it's called stella alpina, *the Alpine star. It*

only grows up here in the mountains. We give a bloom to someone we feel committed to."

She had thrown me off balance. "I see. My lord Gaius Caecilius noticed it and gave it to me. We'd never seen one before and thought it was... beautiful."

"Do you always call him 'my lord so-and-so'?" She sneered.

"Yes, of course. That's what I'm supposed to call him."

She folded her hands in her lap. "He's handsome. Have you ever coupled with him?"

I drew back until I was leaning against the wall. "No! By the gods, why would you ask that?"

"Because you're clearly in love with him, and he with you. It shows every time you look at one another. And now the flower."

I straightened my stola, just to have something to do with my hands. "I think you're reading too much into our expressions. We didn't know anything about this commitment idea you're talking about. It's just a pretty flower. We've been friends since we were children." And if it hadn't been for a boulder crashing down on us, we might have become more a short while ago.

"Would you refuse him if he wanted to couple?" Before I could do more than cringe, she said, "At least you would be with someone you want, not with a slimy weasel like the man my father forced me to marry."

As a slave I couldn't object to a free woman talking to me this way, but Junia was taking advantage of her status and this situation. We were not just two girls having an intimate conversation—a too-intimate conversation. She was a bitter young woman taking her anger out on me. If she lived in a big house in Rome, she would know never to let her guard down like this. Like a conniving slave, I decided to see if I could turn her carelessness to my advantage. "I don't think Gaius Caecilius would force himself on me," I said.

She persisted. "That's not what I asked. Would he have to force himself?"

"Whom did you want to marry?" I asked quickly.

"Magnus. He would never have to force himself on me. And he wants me. But Papa wouldn't hear of it."

All I could think of was that Magnus would crush her. The conversation wasn't going where I wanted it to. As I would do if I were riding an unruly *horse, I needed to change direction, abruptly and quickly. I lowered my head in a gesture appropriate for a servant. "I'm sorry for your father's death."*

Her sneer relaxed, but only for an instant. "Thank you. I've heard that you and your lord so-and-so have said it might not have been an accident. Why?"

Gaius says we shouldn't tell people what we suspect if they are part of an investigation, but I knew of no reason to think Junia had anything to do with her father's death. "The way your brother described the wound on his head, it made us think he must have hit the wall more than once."

She gasped. "So you mean somebody killed him?"

"We suspect so."

"But who—"

"We don't know yet. Do you know if he had been arguing with anyone lately?"

"Draco, my husband, says Leonix, the servant who works with them in the mill, had no respect for my father. They often had words."

"We've been told that Junius had a bad temper."

Junia drew her shoulders back. "Who told you that?"

"Your brother."

Junia gave a sharp, harsh laugh as her haughty demeanor returned. "You can't believe anything that idiot says, especially about my father."

"Was there a problem between them?"

"When the man doesn't want to lift a hand to work around the farm, what can my father do?"

I couldn't help but notice that she was saying "my father," not "our father." I said, "It sounds like there might have been a problem between you and your brother as well."

We heard the voices of two men coming through the outer door of the latrina. Junia finished what she needed to do, used her sponge, and stood up, shaking her stola to let it fall into place around her. "What goes on in my family is none of your business. You can tell that to your lord so-and-so. I'm sorry I said as much as I did."

And so the natural order was restored.

X

[A.D. 87]

O F COURSE," I said, "I was not privy to Aurora's conversation with Junia, but she gave me the gist of it as soon as she got back to the inn. We decided we needed to talk to Magnus."

"You two certainly were a couple of young snoops," Torquatus said with a laugh. He loosened the blanket he had wrapped around himself. The room was finally getting warm, even though the snow was still falling at an amazing rate. It must have been the fourth hour by now, but the gloom outside made it feel like very early morning.

"They still are snoops," Tacitus put in. "The worst sort. They've even infected me, I'm afraid."

"Maybe you should try writing history," Torquatus said. "Lots of unsolved mysteries in the past. For instance, did Claudius really just get some bad mushrooms by accident? Did Nero poison Britannicus or kill his mother?" He lowered his voice. "Did Domitian kill Titus?"

"And there are lots of people who don't want those mysteries solved." Tacitus raised his wine cup. I was relieved that he changed the subject. "I'll stick to writing speeches, thank you. They're much safer."

"As we soon found out," I said.

Torquatus sat up, his interest piqued. "You mean someone tried to harm you again? Dropping a boulder on you wasn't enough?"

"Apparently someone was determined to finish the job and was watching every move we made."

[*A.D. 77*]

WITH Argos trotting between us, we found Magnus alone in the mill. Since Junius was dead, Magnus and the slave Leonix had to take on extra shares of the work. They not only ground grain; they sharpened tools as well. The waterwheel that turned the grindstone could be attached to a belt that kept a whetstone spinning.

Magnus was sharpening an axe when we approached him. The noise obscured our steps until we were right on him. I made certain to come up to him from the front so as not to startle him too badly. After all, he was a large man with a sharp implement in his hands. Aurora stayed a few steps behind me. I had asked her to survey the mill in as much detail as she could while I talked to Magnus and tried to distract him. Argos sat down beside her.

"Good afternoon," I said. "Are you Magnus?" Junianus had identified him to me, but I didn't know how else to start the conversation.

The behemoth pulled the axe away from the whetstone and rested it on one of his broad shoulders, ready for use. "Are you so stupid you need to ask?"

He seemed to be the brute that his name implied. Aurora had told me that Junia wanted to couple with him. What attraction she found in him, I couldn't imagine. He hadn't shaved or bathed in several days. Dust and chaff from the grain was embedded in his hair, which badly needed cutting and washing. But most of all he was large. Not just *magnus*, but *maximus*. I guess he was right to chide me for asking who he was.

"My name is Messenio," he said. "People call me Magnus for the obvious reason. Who are you and what do you want?" He spoke slowly and carefully, like a man who is not particularly intelligent and not entirely comfortable with language.

"My name is Gaius Caecilius. My uncle, Gaius Plinius, is an advisor to the *princeps*. I'm helping him inquire into the death of Junius."

"Helping your uncle or the *princeps*? What interest does either of them have in this little armpit of the Alps?"

"We all want to see that justice is done." I hoped that was a vague enough answer. It seemed to satisfy—at least mollify—Magnus. Or maybe he was having trouble understanding the implications of the words. I hurried ahead before he could ask any more questions. "I believe Junius was the man you worked for?"

"Yes, he was."

He was not going to volunteer any information. "You found his body, didn't you?"

He lowered the axe and ran a thumb along its edge, reminding me how sharp it was. "Yeah."

"Could you tell what happened to him?"

"He fell and hit his head against the wall over there. I'm sure you know that, so what is there to 'inquire' about?"

"Did you notice anything out of the ordinary?"

"Yeah, he was dead. That's as out of the ordinary as you can get, isn't it? Ordinarily people aren't dead."

Argos moved up next to me. His closeness bolstered my courage. I wasn't going to let Magnus' sarcasm throw me off track. "I mean, did you see anything out of place? Had anything been taken?"

"Look around. There's nothing in here worth taking. Maybe the grindstone and this whetstone, but who can lift them? I couldn't even manage that. It would take several men my size."

But he could push a boulder off a cliff. "Did Junius have any sort of cash box? Where did he keep his money when people paid him?"

"On those rare occasions he put it in a bag, on a cord that he tied around his waist, along with his keys." Magnus spat, not right at my feet but in my direction. "And it never did look very heavy."

Aurora and I exchanged a glance. Junianus had mentioned his father's keys, but this was the first we'd heard of any money.

"People didn't pay him?"

"Sometimes they were slow, but they paid if I went and...talked to them."

"Was that money bag still on him when—"

"Look, I don't know what you damn kids are up to, but I've got work to do. You need to get out from under my feet." He shifted the axe in his hands and turned his back to us, letting me know he wasn't going to pay any more attention to us. Aurora took advantage of the opportunity to peer into a couple of the darker corners of the mill.

"Could I ask one more question?" I said.

"I'll bet I can't stop you, can I?" he replied over his shoulder. He did not demonstrate the usual sort of deference plebeians show toward the higher classes. Maybe it was because he looked down on us, quite literally, or because I wasn't old enough to be wearing the equestrian stripe that I would lay claim to in a few years.

"I would just like to take a closer look at the gears."

Magnus' head jerked around toward me. "What for?"

"Junianus says people think his father fell from up there."

"As far as I know, that's what happened. Why do you want to look at the gears? You could get hurt, too." He took a step toward us. "Both of you, get out of here. You're poking your noses into places where you got no business." He waved his arm, like he was shooing away a couple of pesky animals.

When a man that size moves toward you, especially when he's carrying a weapon, you can't help but step back. It's an instinct, no matter how brave you consider yourself. I didn't think he would actually attack us in the middle of the day in a place where someone could easily see what was happening, but I didn't want to put Aurora in any danger. Even Argos withdrew. I pushed Aurora toward the door, keeping close behind her. I stopped long enough to turn and ask, "Do you know why Roscius and Junius disliked one another so much?"

The giant snorted. "They were like slaves chained together and forced to work. In a town this small they couldn't get away from one another. That's what they really needed to do, just get away from one another."

"But why?"

"You'd have to ask Junius about that. Oh, wait, he's dead, isn't he. I guess you'll never know. Now get out of here. Don't let me catch you nosing around here again."

Once we were out of the mill, Aurora said, "You're going to go back in there and look at those gears, aren't you?"

"He definitely didn't want me to. That's all the reason I need. And he called us 'kids,' in case the first reason wasn't enough. He said not to let him catch us, so it will have to be at a time when he's not there."

"So, tonight?"

I nodded.

I COULD hear my uncle snoring in the room next to mine. Finally I heard the sound I was waiting for—Aurora's knock on my door. We use a signal—two quick knocks followed by three slower ones.

"I was beginning to worry," I said as I opened the door.

"Sorry. Mother's head was hurting. I had to sit with her until she could get to sleep."

"That seems to be happening more and more often," I said.

Aurora came into my room and I closed the door behind her. "Yes. I'm really worried about her," she said. "Her poppy syrup helps her get to sleep eventually, but I don't think it's curing anything. And she's using more and more of it."

"There's probably not a doctor around here, but when we get to Lugdunum, or when we get back to Rome, I'm sure my uncle will see that she gets the care she needs." I took her hand and squeezed it. She returned the gesture and added a quick kiss on my cheek.

"I know he will, and I love him for taking care of her, but it'll be a long time before we even get to Lugdunum, let alone back to Rome."

"Would you rather stay with your mother tonight? I can do this by myself."

Aurora shook her head. "There's nothing I can do for her. At least she's asleep. I guess that's the best thing right now. Keeping busy will help me. I know I couldn't get to sleep if I was worrying about you *and* her. Let's go."

[A.D. 87]

AS Gaius reached this part of his story, I had to leave the room. I was overcome by the sadness raised by the memory of my mother's illness and death.

Once our raeda had been repaired, we went on to the elder Pliny's new

*estate in Gaul. My mother seemed to be recovering. She was having fewer
headaches and was in a good mood. She always did enjoy traveling, and
the scenery in the Alps was spectacular, so unlike anything we'd ever seen in
North Africa or even Italy. The Apennine Mountains that run down the
center of Italy like a spine are impressive, but they're not the Alps.*

*We arrived safely in Lugdunum. Mother and I were sitting in the
garden of the house there one afternoon when she gasped, put her hands to
her head, and slid off the bench onto the ground. Before I could touch her,
she was dead.*

*When Gaius inherited his uncle's estate two years later, one of his first
acts was to sell the villa in Lugdunum. He said he knew I would never want
to visit there again, even though I had never told him that.*

[A.D. 77]

WE left the inn as quietly as we could. Aurora was wearing one of her
darker colored gowns. I didn't have anything darker to change into, so
my white tunic made me uncomfortably visible. Our trip to the mill
took only a couple of moments, and the only living creature we saw
was Argos sniffing his way through an alley. As soon as he saw Aurora,
he trotted over to us. There was no one else in sight. Unlike Rome or
any other big city, a small town like Collis isn't plagued by drunkards
and troublemakers in the streets after dark. It's a common saying that
anyone who ventures out in Rome after dark without first making out
his will is a fool.

"I wonder where Junianus is," Aurora said as she scratched Argos'
head.

"Maybe he has a girlfriend."

She made a face at me.

The door to the mill opened outward, toward the street, as doors
in most Roman buildings do. It was closed and barred but not locked.
"I guess Magnus meant it," I said, "when he told us there was nothing
worth stealing in here."

With Argos between us, we entered and closed the door behind us.
I found a flint next to the lamp tree and lit two of the lamps hanging

on it. I can see better in the dark or in low light than most people, but in an unfamiliar place I wanted the security of a lamp. "There are no windows, so I don't think anybody will see us."

"We do need a bit of light," Aurora said, "for those of us who aren't owls."

The mill was quiet. The waterwheel had a gear and a belt that could be disengaged when the grindstone and whetstone weren't in use, leaving the wheel turning idly outside. Chaff and straw littered the floor.

"They ought to sweep up in here once in a while," Aurora said.

She can be a bit fussy about things like that. I left one lamp hanging on the tree and took the other one as I began to climb up to where the axle of the waterwheel came through the outer wall of the mill. The gears themselves provided a kind of ladder.

"Please be careful," Aurora pleaded. "That looks really dangerous and you've only got one free hand."

"I don't want to climb it in the dark," I said, trying to mask how unsure of my footing I actually was. The gears were solid, but they were wet and slick from the water that leaked in. "I don't think someone as big as Magnus could even get up here. Draco might, but not Magnus."

"Do you see anything that would make it worthwhile to climb up there?"

I balanced the lamp on one of the gears, leaving one hand free. I ran that hand in the narrow space between the gear and the wall. It seemed to me that would be the most likely place for someone to hide something.

"No…wait, there is something back here."

Aurora started to climb the gears. "What is it?"

"It's a box. I've got it. Don't come up. I'm coming down."

Our attention was completely focused on what we'd found until we heard the door creak. We turned our heads to see the door of the mill opening slightly. A hand reached in and toppled the lamp tree. Oil from six broken lamps spilled over the floor. The chaff and other unswept mess blazed up at once. Aurora screamed and we ran for the door. It was closed and the bar that secured it had been dropped into place.

[A.D. 87]

"AND now I need to relieve myself," I said, "and get something to drink. Telling a story like this does work up a thirst."

Torquatus let out a groan. "You're locked in a burning building with no windows! You obviously got out because you're standing right here. But how?"

"All in good time," I said. "As you noted, we did get out. That does lessen the drama. I'll return shortly."

As I left the room, Torquatus turned to Aurora. "Don't make us wait, dear girl. You tell the story just as well as Gaius Pliny, and you're much prettier to look at."

[A.D. 77]

WHILE *my lord Gaius Pliny and I were looking for something that would help us break down the door before the flames got too high, Argos barked and ran toward the back of the mill. He turned back, barked again, then ran to the wall. We watched in amazement as Argos flattened himself on his belly and squirmed under the wall. We grabbed a couple of the tools that Magnus had been sharpening and ran to the spot where Argos had disappeared. The hole he had made gave us a start. We dug like the flames behind us were the Furies coming after us and within moments had made a hole large enough for a person to scrape through.*

"I'm assuming you mean a small person," Torquatus said, patting his belly.

"Well, not Magnus perhaps, but large enough for us at age fifteen."

Then, clanging our tools together and with Argos barking, we quickly woke most of the town and had the fire extinguished before any serious damage was done. The wood in the mill was old and hard and there was plenty of water at hand.

"How did the dog know the opening was there?" Julia asked.

"Apparently he made it. The grain in the mill attracted all kinds of small creatures. Argos went in, mostly at night, and helped himself."

"And what about the box?" Torquatus asked. "Was it worth risking your lives and nearly burning the place down?"

"Ah, yes," Gaius said as he re-entered the room, "the box. We'll get to that."

Once we got back to the inn and everyone had settled down, my uncle took us into the room where he and Glaucon were working. As a storage room, it already had shelves, so it wasn't hard to turn it into a small library, with a few hastily scavenged chairs and a table. He pushed aside the scrolls and scraps of papyrus that littered the table and told us to sit down.

"You two rascals came close to getting yourselves burned alive," he said. "And I've already heard people whispering that you set the fire."

"What! That's ridiculous."

"Oh, they think it was accidental, but you did light a couple of lamps in a place strewn with straw and chaff. You weren't being very careful."

"The person who set the fire, my lord, was the one who knocked over the lamp tree," Aurora said. "Whoever it was must have been familiar with the mill. They knew right where the lamp tree was."

My uncle sighed. "My dear, in a town this small, everyone has had dealings with the mill at one time or another. They've had something ground or an implement sharpened. People merely walking past the place would have seen the lamp tree. It's right by the door."

It was hard to argue with his logic.

"So what were you doing in there?"

"I wanted to see if there was anything hidden that might help us find out who killed Junius," I said.

"Did you find anything?"

I set the box in the middle of the table. It was quite plain, serviceable rather than decorative, made from unvarnished wood. From side to side it was about the size of the span of my hand and from front to back the same. Its height was the same as my four fingers held up beside it. "This was hidden up high, behind the gears."

"What's in it?" my uncle asked.

"It's locked. I haven't had a chance to open it. A couple of things do rattle."

He shook the box gently. "Three or four items, I would say. Get me that lead rule."

I guess because Aurora is accustomed to having people tell her what to do, she got up before I could move and retrieved the lead rule that Glaucon uses to make sure the lines of writing on a page of papyrus are straight. She handed it to my uncle and took her seat again.

"Hold the box, Gaius," he said.

"Junianus may have the key to this lock. He said he knew what all of his father's keys went to, except for a small one."

My uncle screwed up his mouth. "And he may not have it. Do you want to want until tomorrow morning to find out?"

"Well, I suppose not." I wasn't sure we had the right to break into someone else's treasure box or whatever this was, but my uncle looked determined. An equestrian stripe gives one a certain audacity.

"Hold it tightly." He placed one end of the lead rule against the lock and smacked the other end with his palm. The small lock was no match for the hard metal.

"Now," my uncle said, "let's see what we've got." He removed the broken lock, opened the lid of the box, and emptied the contents onto the table. "Curious combination of things."

What he spread out on the table was a silver slave's bracelet that someone had cut, a small wooden box, and a set of dice made from animal bones. I couldn't resist the impulse to roll the four dice. The Venus throw—a total of fourteen—came up.

"Very first time! That's some luck," Aurora said. She picked up the dice, shook them, and threw them. "Look at that!" The Venus throw had come up again.

Scooping up the dice, my uncle rubbed each one carefully between his thumb and forefinger and held them up close to his face. "They've been doctored," he said. "You'll get the Venus throw every time." He threw the dice and there it was.

"So you'll always win," Aurora said.

"Until someone gets suspicious," my uncle said. "Which shouldn't take long. You would have to keep these concealed and manage to switch them for any other dice that were being used in the game."

"How would you do that?" I asked.

"I suspect you would use this." He picked up the other item, a rectangular, tube-like box, and turned it over a couple of times. "It's called a *fritillus*. You put the dice in here, shake them, and throw them out."

"How does that make it possible for you to cheat?"

"I'm not quite sure, but it has to be the key."

"May I see it?" I asked. My uncle gave me the box, which fit comfortably into a person's hand. I turned it over and over, with Aurora leaning into my shoulder.

"There has to be an element of deception and distraction involved," my uncle said. "You know how a magician can get you to look over there while he's doing something over here that he doesn't want you to see? That's the key."

"How about this?" I asked. I had found a panel on one side that slipped down when pressure was applied.

My uncle took the box. "I think you've found it, my boy!"

There was that damn "boy" again. Aurora patted my knee under the table, where my uncle couldn't see her hand.

"How would that enable you to cheat?" Aurora asked.

"Well, you would have to have two sets of dice—the one that was being used in the game, and your 'special' set, which you keep in this box."

"Wouldn't the two sets would have to look very much alike?" Aurora asked.

"Definitely. You would have to show one set, let the others in the game throw them a few times to be sure they were honest, and then the game would begin." He turned his back to us. "I'm going to put the rigged dice in here. We'll have to imagine there's another set of dice in the part of the box with the open end. You hold the *fritillus* so that your hand covers the open end and you shake it. I imagine you would put your other hand on the box as well, like this, as some gamblers do. As you make your throw, you slide this panel down."

When he did what he was describing, the four dice tumbled out, and there it was—the Venus throw. When we turned our eyes back to him, he was holding the *fritillus* up as though everything was normal. He smiled at us. "You were so caught up in watching the dice that you paid no attention to what I was doing. I made sure to throw them a little farther, and your eyes followed them. As I said, deception and distraction."

"What if someone asked to use your *fritillus?*" Aurora asked.

"Oh, you would never let anyone else use it, or even touch it. Gamblers have their superstitions, you know. Each one would have his own box."

"Would they all be cheating?" I asked.

My uncle chuckled, a sort of growling noise because of his breathing problems. "There's a good possibility of that."

"Surely somebody would notice what you were doing."

"Not necessarily. It would take practice, but a skillful gambler could learn to do it. He would save these rigged dice until there was a lot at stake. He would use them once, then scoop them up and replace them in the *fritillus* and roll again but let the set of dice in the other end—the honest set—come out. He wouldn't care if he lost that roll."

"That all sounds so complicated," Aurora said.

"Now and then you'll run into somebody who's gotten quite good at it. You would never want to play a 'friendly game' with them, though."

"Roscius said that Junius gambled a lot, but without much luck."

My uncle rubbed the dice together between his fingers. "Maybe he took these from someone who had cheated him. Or he bought them or made them and hoped to use them. I guess we'll never know." He put the dice back in the *fritillus* and set it aside.

"What about this?" Aurora asked, picking up the slave bracelet. She has never been required to wear such a thing. None of our slaves wear one or are marked in any way. My uncle says it's a sign of arrogance to have your name stamped on your slaves like you do on your pottery or your bricks. He would never brand a slave, as the cruelest owners sometimes do.

Aurora turned the bracelet around. It was thick and from top to bottom it was the size of two of a person's fingers, a considerable amount of silver. The owner's seal had been impressed into the metal. Aurora read the inscription on it. "It says 'Lucina, slave of—'"

"Lucina?" I grabbed the bracelet from Aurora's hand. "That's Junius' wife!"

My uncle took the bracelet from me and read it. "So it would seem. 'Lucina' isn't exactly a common name. I don't recognize the master's name. 'Tiberius Pomponius' sounds like a name from the provinces."

"Nobody has said anything about Lucina being a slave," I said. "She acts and talks like a free woman."

"Maybe she is, my lord," Aurora said. "Maybe she was emancipated at some point and this bracelet was cut off."

"Then why was it hidden where it was? We need to ask her about it." My uncle held up a hand. "No, Gaius, I don't think you do."

"But what if she's a slave pretending to be free? That's against the law. You've always taught me that laws have to apply to everyone."

My uncle nodded slowly and put the bracelet back on the table. "There are indeed severe penalties for that. But we're not magistrates. It's not our job to make such inquiries. She probably has her emancipation document tucked away somewhere."

"Then why keep this?" I held up the bracelet. "Why not melt it down? There's enough silver in it to be worth something."

"People sometimes keep things that remind them of some part of their past that they're thankful to be done with, to remind themselves not to make the same mistake again. I still have a ring that my wife gave me. You've never seen it, and you never will, but I've kept it."

"This wasn't kept where Lucina could see it. It's more like she *didn't* want to see it."

"Or didn't want anyone else to see it, my lord," Aurora said softly.

I wasn't ready to concede the argument. "It could also mean that Junius was concealing a runaway slave for who knows how long."

"You're absolutely right," my uncle said. "That is against the law. The penalty is, in fact, death. But how are you going to inflict that penalty on a dead man?"

I picked up the bracelet and ran my fingers over the lettering, including Pomponius' seal. "I don't know, but this raises questions that need to be answered. They may even have something to do with Junius' murder." I held the bracelet up to my uncle. "Look. This is a nice piece of work. I think it came from a wealthy household. Lucina is obviously well educated. She reads Homer to her son. She's not some kitchen drudge. There's something out of place here."

"I agree," my uncle said. "I'll ask Glaucon if he has ever run across the name Tiberius Pomponius in his research for me, but I don't think we should go beyond that for now."

"If you ask her about this," Aurora said, "she'll know we've found it. That would put her on alert. It's better if she doesn't suspect anything right now."

"The girl's entirely right," my uncle said, using an affectionate form of the word that really meant "little girl."

I could see that Aurora didn't like being called that, any more than I liked being called "boy." I wished my uncle would acknowledge that we were growing up. I would have to show him that we were.

———————

[A.D. 87]

"I'VE known you for only a couple of days," Torquatus said, "but I would bet that you decided to talk to Lucina in order to show your uncle you were right."

"You would lose," I said. "I didn't talk to her."

"But I did," Aurora said. All eyes turned toward her.

Torquatus looked around. "Is she here? Perhaps she could tell us that part of the story from her own perspective."

"There's nothing to tell," I said. "She showed Aurora her letter of manumission, with her owner's seal on it."

Torquatus looked utterly confused, if I wasn't misreading the distortion on his face. "She had such a document? I would never have thought—"

"Yes," I said. "She showed it to Aurora, so we gave her the bracelet. I'm sure it was melted down and made into something else long ago."

"Into this actually," Lucina said. We hadn't realized she had come back into the room. She pointed to her necklace. "As anyone around here can tell you, I haven't taken this off in years. It reminds me of that part of my life without revealing it to everyone."

It wasn't a beautiful necklace, just a round, flat piece on a leather strap. She must have melted the necklace down in the kitchen and fashioned it into a piece of jewelry as best she could by herself. She couldn't have taken it to a silversmith, not without raising a lot of questions. She and Aurora exchanged a smile. I resisted the urge to smile, too. Other than the two of them, I was the only person in the room who knew what it meant. The sight of their smiles and the necklace took me back to one of the most frightening times Aurora and I had ever shared. I could see that she was reliving it, too.

XI

[A.D. 77]

W*HERE HAVE YOU BEEN?"* Gaius blurted as he answered my knock on his door that night. *"I can't find Lucina's bracelet."* The box he had discovered in the mill was sitting on the table beside his bed, with the dice and the fritillus beside it.

"I took it," I admitted.

"What? Why? How?"

"You haven't asked 'when' yet, so I'll save you the trouble and answer all your questions at once."

"You'd damn well better," he said.

"Please don't be angry with me. You'll have every right to be, but please don't be."

I took both of his hands in mine. He would definitely have every right to punish me, I knew, but I had done what I felt was the right thing to do—the only thing I could do. It was the first time in my life I had deliberately done something I knew would be against his wishes and against the law. I didn't think he would turn me over to the magistrates, but he might break off our relationship, and that would be even worse.

We sat down on the bed and I took a deep breath.

"Well?" he said.

"Please don't interrupt." I knew it was pointless to ask that. Gaius always interrupts because he wants to know more than you're telling. "Remember when we finished talking, you and your uncle went to the latrina." Someone always has to help the old man get from one place to another. "You asked me to hold the box."

"Yes. But I didn't ask you take anything out of it."

I put my hand over his mouth and rushed ahead. "I took the bracelet and hung it from the strap that our Tyche ring is on. You took the box back and were helping your uncle to his room. I told you I would see you in a little while. Here I am."

"All right. So where is the bracelet?" He held out his hand.

"I don't have it anymore."

His face registered lack of comprehension. "Did you lose it?"

"No...I gave it to Lucina."

His look turned to utter shock. "You did what?"

"Gaius, please. I can tell this more quickly and more easily if you'll just let me talk."

"Go ahead. I don't know what to say."

I looked down at my hands, twisting them in my lap. "I went into the kitchen. I found Lucina there, preparing bread for tomorrow. I asked her if there was someplace private where we could talk. I guess she saw I had something serious to say, so she led me into the supply room.

She asked me what I wanted and I showed her the bracelet. She staggered back against the shelves. "Where did you get that?"

"Gaius found it in a box in Junius' mill."

"By the gods, so that's where it's been all these years. Practically next door."

"We also found some dice—"

"And the fritillus?"

"Yes."

"Then you know my story."

"I don't think I know all of it, or enough of it. You were a slave. Legally you still are, I guess."

"And I could be put to death if I were returned to my owner." She pointed to the seal on the bracelet "Is that what you're going to do?"

"I'm not going to do anything. Right now I just want to know how all of this came to be."

A wineskin hung near Lucina's shoulder. She took it off its hook, found a cup, and poured some. "Forgive me for not offering you any," she said. "I need it a great deal more than you do."

There was no water to mix with the wine, but I don't think she would have used it if it had been available. She drained the cup, refilled it, and sat down on a stool, the only place in the small room for anyone to sit.

"Yes," she said, "I was a slave in the house of Tiberius Pomponius in Mediolanum, as you've read. It was a wealthy household. You can see how much silver he put into that bracelet. It's heavy enough to be uncomfortable to wear. It not only told everyone who and what I was; it advertised how rich he was."

"Were you born there?"

"Yes, I was. Life there wasn't so bad, I guess most people would say. I ate well, dressed well, and I was educated. Unlike a lot of people, Pomponius felt a slave who could read and write was more useful, even a credit to him, not a threat. But when I was fourteen he...he tied me down and raped me." She choked up and tears formed in her eyes.

"Is that how he usually treated his slaves?"

"I had heard stories in the house about what he did to the pretty female ones. I thought I was safe because I was still a child. I had barely started my monthlies." She gulped down more wine. "Not long after that a few of the women—not including me, I swear it—drowned him in his bath. They escaped and I went with them. We split up. I got as far as Augusta Taurinorum. I kept myself alive by working in inns and doing whatever odd jobs I could find. I slept in doorways and alleys, wherever I could find other lost people sleeping. I hope you never sink that low. Even if it means you have to be a slave, I hope you always have a roof over your head and enough to eat."

All I could do was nod. My tears were too close.

"The baths were where I met a man named Quintus Decius," she said. "He and some men were always throwing dice over in a corner. The other men would come and go. They would lose a little money, get disgusted, and leave. Others would replace them. Decius seemed to have pretty good luck. He told me he would pay me if I would walk around where they were play-ing, letting my legs show or bending over and letting them see my breasts."

I nodded. "My lord Gaius Pliny told us how gamblers who cheat use things or people to distract the men they're cheating."

"I was a considerable distraction, if I'm not being too boastful."

"No, you're not, not at all. How did you disguise the fact that you were a slave?" I held up the bracelet. "This thing is pretty obvious."

"I managed to get it off. Even with some olive oil, it scraped and hurt for a while, but I knew I had to get it out of sight."

"Why did you keep it?"

"You can see how much silver there is. I figured if I could melt it down, it could keep me going for a while. But I couldn't just go to a silversmith and ask him to do it. I wore it on a strap around my neck, thinking I would find a chance. When I moved in with Decius, though, he took it and I couldn't get it back. He told me I was his slave from then on."

I knelt in front of her. "That must have been a hopeless feeling."

"No more than what any slave feels, I suspect. You must feel it."

"Gaius and his uncle are very good to my mother and me."

She gave a short, harsh laugh. "I hope you can still say the same five years from now. Decius was good to me, though. The oddest thing about him was that he didn't want anything to do with sex."

I raised my eyebrows. "That is odd for any man."

"He never tried to couple with me and pushed me away whenever I acted like I wanted him to. I wouldn't have objected. He was a gorgeous man. The only time he would let me touch him at all, though, was when he would wake up in the night, crying and moaning from a bad dream. I would hold him until he settled down. In those moments he would cuddle up to me like a child."

"That certainly is peculiar."

"Anyway, one day Junius came into the baths and joined the game. He lost some money, but he came back the next day, and the next. Finally he took Decius outside and talked to him. I didn't understand what was going on, but I could see that Junius was angry. I depended on Decius' money and, I'll confess, I cared about him, so I followed and listened from where they couldn't see me."

"Was he accusing Decius of cheating?"

Lucina nodded. "He had ignored me and concentrated on how Decius used his fritillus. He even took the box from Decius and showed him what he had seen. He knew that Decius signaled me by touching his ear when he was about to make the Venus throw. Decius couldn't deny any of it. That's *exactly what he was doing—what we were doing. He said he wasn't going to be blackmailed for the rest of his life. Junius told him there would be only one payment. He wanted half the money Decius had won that night, the dice, the fritillus…and me. He had seen that distracting the other men was a key part of the scheme."*

"How did Decius react?"

"At first he refused. He said he saw no reason to agree to such a ridiculous demand. Junius told him the other three men they were playing with would slit his throat the minute they found out what he was doing. And he would help them. He ordered Decius to go back in there, lose back the rest of what he'd won, and then never show his pretty face around here again, or they would rearrange it for him."

"'Pretty face?' That's a curious thing to say about a man. Was Decius a handsome man?"

"Handsome? What comes to your mind when you hear 'Adonis'? You could probably say he was the prettiest man you'll ever see. Junius wasn't wrong about that. With long hair and some makeup, he could have passed for a nice-looking woman, if you could disguise that lump in his throat that all men have." She touched the spot on her own throat.

I'd never known a man I would describe as "pretty." Gaius was handsome, at least handsome enough, but nowhere near pretty. But I made myself focus on the topic at hand. "So Junius must have realized you were a slave."

Lucina nodded. "And I was. Not Decius' slave, but a slave—a runaway at that—so I couldn't protest. Decius handed Junius what he'd asked for and removed the cord around his neck. That was where he kept my bracelet. 'You'll need this to keep her in line,' he said. He went back in, did what Junius had told him to do, and that was the last I saw of him. He never even said good-bye. Junius told the other men the game was over. He took me back to his room. He told me he would treat me as his wife but he would always keep the bracelet where I couldn't find it. I was trapped, just as surely as if he had bought me in the market."

She drank more wine. "So, that's the story, except that Junius never did become particularly clever with the fritillus. He was just too clumsy. He never was good with his hands. The mill was a good place for him. The grindstone did the work. He never let me forget that he was my master, not really my husband. To make it worse, he was as clumsy with me as he was with the dice. I guess you're too young to understand what it means to say a man is clumsy with a woman. Has Gaius Caecilius taken you yet?"

I blushed deeply as I shook my head.

"But you want him to, don't you?" She chuckled. "All in good time, dear. I just hope, for your sake, that he's more adept with his hands than Junius was, no matter what he was doing with them. I had to practically dance naked and let the men paw at me to provide enough distraction when he was throwing the dice. We lived in Augusta Taurinorum for a few more years. That's where Junianus was born. Then Junius' father died, so we came back to Collis to take over the farm and the mill. Junia was born here."

She took another long drink of wine. "Now that you know all this, what are you going to do? The law says you have to turn me in."

It did not take me any time to make a decision. "Come with me."

"Where are we going?"

I led her to the little library room where we had talked with your uncle.

"Should we be in here?" she asked, crossing her arms over her chest as if to protect herself. "What are you going to do?"

"This won't take long." I found a clean sheet of papyrus, some ink, some wax, and a sharp reed pen. Glaucon always sharpens a few at the end of the day so he'll be ready for the next day's work. Gaius' uncle likes to start work immediately in the morning. I wrote a short manumission document, recalling the wording as best I could from ones I'd seen your uncle write. I softened the wax with the lamp I was carrying, dropped it onto the papyrus, and pressed the seal on Lucina's bracelet into the wax. Then I gave her the bracelet.

Gaius gasped as I finished the story. "Do you realize what you've done?"

"Yes, I've freed her. It must be the first time in the history of Rome that one slave freed another." I paused. "Well, at least since the days of Spartacus."

"And remember what happened to him. Don't you see that you've put yourself and your owner—that's me—in peril of our lives?"

"Meaning no disrespect, Gaius, but I would do it again right now, with you watching if I had to." I stood up and stepped away from the bed, *squaring my shoulders. "That poor woman has suffered more than anyone ever should. She's never hurt anyone—"*

"How do you know that?" Gaius grasped the sides of his head as though he might need some of my mother's poppy syrup. "Just because she said she didn't kill her master doesn't mean it's the truth. And she's a runaway. That's a crime in itself. By the gods, Aurora! You've gotten us into serious trouble."

He leaned his face right into mine, but I would not back down. "Only if someone finds out," I said. "Everyone in town has assumed for years that she's free. Junius knew the truth, but he's dead."

"And she might have killed him!"

"Why would she have waited so long, if that's what she intended to do? Now she has a document that says she's free, if anybody cares to ask. Only three people know it's a forgery. Lucina's certainly not going to tell anyone. I'm not. Are you?"

[*A.D. 87*]

NO, I didn't tell anyone. I had carried the secret for ten years now. I never expected to see Lucina again, and I didn't think it would make much difference to anyone in Collis to know her true legal status.

That was a lie, of course, I reminded myself. Revealing that she was a runaway slave would have meant she would have been arrested and probably thrown into the arena, perhaps even crucified, as captured runaways often are, as Spartacus and thousands of his followers were. It is the most agonizing, protracted death we can inflict on anyone, and we want to impress that on the people we fear the most. Her children would have been reduced to the status of slaves. "Justice has been served," we would smugly say, but would anything else have been accomplished, except to subject a number of people to misery and despair? The law should strive for a higher purpose than that, shouldn't it? But misery and despair are often its ultimate effects.

I watched Lucina, assisted by Aemilia and little Junilla, tending to the members of our party as we tried to convince ourselves we were actually feeling warmer. I wondered if she had enough pairs of those fleece-lined leggings to go around. Perhaps we could share them. But, once someone put them on and got warm, they weren't likely to be willing to take them off. Perhaps we could each have one leg and alternate between left and right. Seneca urges us to be thoughtful in our treatment of one another, but in reality we all put our own interests and welfare above anyone else's, like animals at a feed trough.

Lucina was offering encouragement to each one of us. She touched a shoulder here, patted a knee there. It would be interesting to know how old she was. From what I knew of her life and the ages of her children, she must be around forty, and yet she looked the same as she did when I first saw her, ten years ago. My mother, and her servant Naomi, certainly do not look the same as they did a decade ago. Why do some people retain their youthful appearance while others show their age in every way, from wrinkled skin to stooped shoulders to gray hair to faltering voices? Why do we think such features give a man character but make a woman less attractive?

Pygmalion's ivory statue that was turned into a living woman— would she have shown the effects of age? Statues, left to themselves, don't age. The marble bust of my father that my mother keeps in a niche outside her room has not changed, except for the darker spot created where her hand brushes his cheek each time she passes it. Would Pygmalion's girl have been grateful to him, and to Venus, for that gift of life? Was he a good husband, retaining his affection for her even in old age? They had a child or two, as I recalled the story. Giving birth usually changes a woman's appearance, and not for the better.

Torquatus, too, seemed focused on Lucina, following her movements with his good eye. I turned my attention to the man. Even after being around him for a few days, I still could not imagine what sort of beating he had endured to be left that mangled. I've seen masks used in the theater that weren't as ugly as he was. They say that when Aristophanes' play The Clouds was presented, with an actor portraying Socrates as the main character, the old philosopher stood up and turned around so the audience could see that he was indeed as ugly as the masked character representing him on the stage. Still, I don't think a mask could be as deformed as Torquatus' face. An actor would

have difficulty projecting his voice through something that misshapen.
Torquatus had enough trouble speaking through his own mouth. I've
read of men who ended their lives after suffering far less.

As Torquatus followed Lucina's movements and I fixed my gaze on
him, our eyes met. Before I could look away he said, "Still can't believe
how ugly I am, eh, Gaius Pliny? Did your nurse frighten you with stories about something like me when you were a child?" He laughed in a
way that scared me more than his appearance. "Most adults are gracious
enough to look away after their first horrified glimpse."

"I am sorry, Lucius Torquatus—"

"Let me give you a quick lesson in civility, young man." Torquatus
stood and straightened his clothes.

Before I realized what he meant, he lunged at me. Grabbing the
neck of my tunic, he slammed me up against the wall. I tried to pull
his hands off me, but the strength of his grip surprised me. I could see
Aurora and Tacitus both moving to help me. Standing over me, Torquatus had the advantage of leverage, but he had made a mistake men
sometimes make in a fight when their emotions get the better of them:
he had exposed his most vulnerable area. His legs were straddling mine.
I regard it as unmanly to do so, but I brought one of my knees up to his
crotch, with considerable force. He crumpled on top of me as Tacitus
grabbed his shoulders and pulled him back, throwing him to the floor.

As Torquatus writhed, his tunic worked its way up his legs. Lucina knelt beside him. I thought she was going to offer him some help,
but she appeared to be just straightening his tunic. He offered some
resistance. She drew away when the back of his right leg became clearly
visible. Her face registered shock.

XII

WOULD YOU HELP ME get him up to his room, Aurora? I
don't think he'll be walking by himself for a while."

I was surprised when Lucina asked me to assist her. I glanced at Gaius,
touching the spot where I hide my knife to assure him. He barely perceptibly
nodded his approval.

Torquatus couldn't stand up straight, so I took one of his arms and Lucina held the other. We had to climb one set of stairs off the dining room. His
door was to the right at the top. It was the nicest room in the inn, Roscius
had boasted, and the walls of the stairway were better decorated than any
others in the building.

Torquatus groaned as we deposited him in a chair beside the bed, rather
heavily I thought, for a man who was already in pain. "Damn him!" he
said. "He's not going to get away with this."

"Shut up," Lucina snapped.

"How dare you?" Torquatus said between groans.

"Shut up, Quintus Decius, you bastard!" Lucina hissed.

I gasped when she slapped him.

Torquatus rubbed his cheek and lowered his head but made no effort to
retaliate. "Your choice of epithets is most appropriate, my dear," he finally
mumbled. "It's good to see you again, too."

"I don't want to hear that," Lucina said. "What I want to hear from
you is the truth."

"'The truth'? I've heard of that before. Not sure I would recognize it,
though."

161

"Don't play games with me." Lucina stood over Torquatus, hands on her hips.

I stepped back to the door. "Is everything all right?" I asked. "Do you want me to leave?"

"No, I most definitely want you to hear this," Lucina said. "I want a witness, and I know I can trust you."

I didn't have time to point out that a slave's testimony is worthless unless the slave has been tortured.

Torquatus' shoulders slumped like a man admitting defeat. "With what little piece of 'the truth' shall I start?"

"By telling me who you are."

"I guess you do deserve that." He clapped his hands on his knees but still did not sit up entirely straight. "I am Lucius Nonius Torquatus. That is the name under which I was born. Men bearing the same name—brothers and cousins of mine—have held high offices, including the consulship. No such honors have come my way. My father despised me because I bore a strong resemblance to one of his stable hands. My mother never admitted to such a dalliance, but Father divorced her and did not insist on keeping me. He had two other sons whom he believed to be his."

Under Roman law children belong to the father unless he waives that right. Few men do, especially when the child is a son. If this man's father had not kept him after a divorce, he must have had strong suspicions about his paternity.

"How old were you when this happened?" Lucina asked.

"I was seven. After the divorce my mother and I went to her family, but they were not eager to have us either. They hoped for favors from the man they considered my father, so we made our way down to Baiae, where no one asks questions about such trivial matters as paternity."

I have only heard of Baiae, on the Bay of Naples. I gather it isn't the sort of place Gaius would appreciate. In one of his moralizing epistles Seneca called it a city "unacquainted with good morals." Naomi hasn't been there, either, but she compares it to some towns in the Jewish holy books called Sodom and Gomorrah.

"In Baiae," Torquatus went on, "we had to survive on whatever talents nature had blessed us with. For Mother that meant using her good looks in *seduction. As laughable as it seems now, I had inherited her fine features— or maybe they came from the stable hand—so for me it meant submitting to pederasts, beginning when I was eight years old, at my mother's insistence. The first time it happened, she held me across her lap, covering my mouth with her hand."* Torquatus took a breath to steady himself.

I put my own hand to my mouth. He was explaining so much, including Lucina's story of his aversion to coupling. How could a person suffer what Torquatus had endured and not hate the world and himself? How could a woman do such a thing to her own child?

"You'll get no sympathy from me," Lucina said, "no matter how much you embroider your story."

"I'm not looking for sympathy." Torquatus spat out the word. "You wanted to know my story. I'm telling it. For both my mother and me, all we had to do was spread our legs or open our mouths. We even shared some of the same customers, often at the same time in the same bed."

I couldn't believe what I was hearing. Roman men are supposed to look with disdain upon "Greek" behaviors in the bedroom. The Bay of Naples— that whole part of Italy—was more Greek than Roman, but this...?

Torquatus took a deep breath and went on. "Time was the enemy of both my mother and me. Being a successful whore requires that a woman maintain her looks, and no woman can remain twenty-five forever, although you, dear Lucina, have come as close to doing that as any woman I've ever known." He reached out to her, but she stepped back.

"And pederasts don't want a boy as big as they are showing his hairy ass in front of them. Little boys, no matter how pretty they are—and I was a real beauty—inevitably do sprout hairy asses, you know. It doesn't matter how often their mothers shave them."

The horror of what I was hearing caused me to tremble and wrap my arms over my chest.

"Within a few years I had to turn to petty thievery to keep myself alive. My mother and I rented two rooms on an upper floor of an insula, but I spent most of my time on the streets. Her clients became baser and baser, and so did what they required her to do.

"One night she was with a man who, she knew, would treat her roughly. He had done so before, but she was getting desperate and was willing to submit to a beating. She asked me to be at home when this man came around because she was so afraid of him. That night, from the other room I heard the noises I expected to hear, but then my mother cried out and everything got still.

"The man who was with her called for me to come in there. When I entered the room, I saw him standing over my mother. She was lying on the bed, alive but unable to move. The man was in a panic. He had broken her neck. 'What are we going to do?' he cried.

"He was several years younger than me, and I started to tell him that we weren't going to do anything. It was his problem. But I saw how this situation could be turned to my advantage. That's how I looked at every situation I found myself in. I took out my knife and stabbed my mother in the heart."

Lucina and I both gasped. "You killed your own mother?" I cried.

"It was surprisingly easy," Torquatus said with no show of emotion. "All I had to do was recall that first time, bent over her lap. I clamped my hand over her mouth and—"

"Why would you do that?" Lucina asked. "I know you. You're not a monster."

"I did it to show someone very powerful what I was capable of, what I was willing to do."

"But who could be that powerful?"

"Who do you think? And don't speak your answer out loud."

Lucina glanced at me. I wasn't sure she knew who he was talking about, but I did. It had to be Domitian. Stories circulated around Rome about his "bed-wrestling" with prostitutes.

"When did this happen?" I asked.

"Vespasian had been emperor for only a couple of years. Titus had just destroyed Jerusalem."

That would place it shortly after I arrived in Gaius' house. "That's why you're carrying that pass, isn't it?" I said.

Torquatus put a finger to his lips. "Careful, careful. No names, please. I did find myself with a powerful friend. He commandeered a cart and that night we took my mother's body to one of the lakes around Baiae, tied a rock around her neck, and dumped her."

"But wouldn't somebody miss her?" Lucina asked. "Or want to know *who she was when they found her?"*

"In Baiae people like my mother and I disappear practically every day. That night this man and I reached an uneasy truce, like two men who recognize one another as soul mates or—less delicately—who have each other by the balls. I know he will protect me because of what I know about him. He knows he can depend on me to do certain unsavory tasks that he does not want traced back to his official entourage."

"You mean the Praetorians?" I said and saw the light dawn in Lucina's eyes.

"I said no such thing," Torquatus protested, holding up a hand. "And you'd best be more careful about what you say. I am well compensated, and that allows me to engage in my favorite pastime—I would even say my passion—throwing the dice." He shook his hand as though about to make a throw.

"Especially when the Venus throw will come up any time you like," I said.

"Ah, so you found them."

"Yes, the box and the dice."

"And the lovely Lucina's slave bracelet? I suspect Junius kept them all in the same spot. He had no more imagination than that. Where was it, by the way?"

"In the mill," Lucina said before I could stop her. At least she hadn't told him the exact spot. I was surprised that he asked. What difference did it make where it had been?

"And how did you come to be 'emancipated'?"

Lucina stepped toward Torquatus, causing him to draw back. "You don't need to know that. But I do need to know how you became Quintus Decius."

———≈◦◦≈———

"Do you think it's all right for Aurora to go up there?" Tacitus asked as we watched the two women assist Torquatus up the stairs. "That man could take out his anger against you on her, you know."

"If he lays a hand on her, I suspect he'll lose it." On my thigh I patted the spot where Aurora carried her knife.

Tacitus nodded and sat back down. "So what are we going to do now? Just sit here and wait for my brother to die?"

"You've got to keep your hopes up," I said. "As long as we can't do anything else, I want to try to understand what caused this avalanche. Let's go out and take another look." Tacitus' face showed his lack of enthusiasm for that prospect. "It's what my uncle would have done."

"At the risk of sounding unkind, isn't that what got him killed?"

"I don't think this is as dangerous as sailing toward an erupting volcano. The avalanche is over. I just want to see if we can find any evidence of how it started."

"You mean, did someone start it deliberately, like Junianus suggested?"

"Exactly. And I want him to go with us. He'll know what signs to look for."

We each wrapped another cloak around ourselves, pulled up our fleece-lined leggings, and set out for the mill. Roscius told us that's where Junianus was most likely to be. Even with more snow falling, we were reasonably comfortable, except for our feet. There didn't seem to be any way to keep them dry and warm. Old Argos, on his way back in after relieving himself, turned and walked with us.

We found Junianus sharpening a knife. When I told him what we wanted to do and asked him to accompany us, he said, "Moving around in the snow when it's this deep can be tricky, sir. And you'll have to walk to get there. The snow's so deep now, horses will sink in it, especially with a rider on them."

"How do you people manage?" I asked. "You can't just sit here all winter."

"No, sir, we don't. We use these." He stepped into the back of the mill and returned with three pairs of what could best be described as wooden sandals. The soles were longer and wider than a man's feet. Leather straps ran through holes drilled around the edges. Junianus sat down on a stool beside the whetstone, fastened the contraptions to his feet, and stood up.

"*Hipposandals* for humans," Tacitus said.

"They give you more of a surface on the snow," Junianus said. "You can't ride when you're wearing them, but they keep you from sinking into the snow when you're on foot. See, if you take a board and turn it sideways, it'll go right down in the water. Lay it flat on the water, and it'll stay up."

Tacitus and I were soon shod in the other two pairs. We had to proceed slowly as we left the mill and walked toward the western end of town where the avalanche had blocked the road. The wooden sandals forced us to lift our feet and made us as clumsy as children learning to walk. Even as experienced as he was, Junianus did little better. Argos seemed to find it easier to trot in the snow on his four legs than we did to walk in it on our two.

"What exactly do you expect to find, sir?" Junianus asked.

"If someone was up there, I hope to find footprints or some trace of a camp."

Junianus shook his head. "We've had enough snow already today, sir, to cover up any marks they might've left. That's why I don't understand why you want to go to all this trouble."

"It's called his damnable curiosity," Tacitus said. "It gets him into all sorts of trouble."

"I like to understand the causes of things," I said in my own defense. "It's what my uncle taught me."

Holding on to trees that were buried almost to their tops, we struggled to climb the side of the hill where the snow had settled. Argos seemed to want to make a game of it, walking close to me, then trotting ahead, then coming back to get patted or scratched. Although he was Junianus' dog, he stayed beside me more than with his master.

I couldn't imagine how long it would take Roscius and a crew to clear a passage or how we would get over the snow if they weren't able to clear it. I could envision us sitting here for a month. But I didn't want to say anything that might discourage Tacitus.

"I don't see how we're going to get out of here in less than a month," Tacitus said glumly.

"Around here things can change quickly, sir," Junianus said. "The sun could be shining tomorrow."

"It'll take a couple of suns to melt this stuff." Tacitus swiped his arm through the snow, which was above our knees, even with the sandals we were wearing. Without them, it probably would have been chest high.

As if to prove his point, a shift in the direction of the wind blew the snow right in our faces. When I wiped my eyes, I looked up ahead of us. "Is that someone walking up there, to our right?"

"I believe there are two people," Tacitus said.

"What are they doing?" The two figures appeared to be stamping hard, as though they were marching. Then we heard the rumble.

"Run, sirs!" Junianus cried. "As fast as you can! This way, to the side!"

I had turned around and taken only a few stumbling steps when a wall of snow hit me from behind, knocked me on my face, and rolled over me.

Torquatus leaned back and sighed. The pain in his groin must have been subsiding. "Oh, yes, Quintus Decius," he said. "Well, I was gambling in Mediolanum. It was twelve years ago. I was having a run of bad luck against a man of that name, an older fellow. Someone accused him of cheating. I stepped in to keep him from getting beaten. How's that for a touch of irony? We became friends. He told me he usually had someone working with him in a game, to distract people."

"I'll bet he preferred a pretty young woman," Lucina said. "That was your choice. You must have learned it from him."

"Actually he did, but he thought an Adonis like me could fill the bill. I had learned how to appeal to men as well as any woman. I was more of a novelty than a woman. Men like novelty. Decius and I formed a partnership and took a small house in Mediolanum. During the games I kept up a chatter and did whatever I could to divert attention when he was about to make a Venus throw. He would scratch his nose as a signal." Torquatus showed us the motion. "But it takes some dexterity to manage the fritillus. Decius' hands were beginning to stiffen as he got older. When he was almost caught again, I realized he was more of a liability than an asset. So, when he died—"

"You mean when you killed him, don't you?" I said.

"Well, yes, if you want to be legalistic about it. When I killed him, I took his signet ring and his fritillus and moved to Augusta Taurinorum. Having a second name can be useful at times."

"How did your... powerful friend keep in touch with you?" I asked.

"He has an unseen army of people like me, with an entire chain of command. I'm no more than a...centurion in those ranks. I get my orders from one individual, a man in Mediolanum. He is the only one who needs to know about my two names."

"Marcus Regulus must hold high rank in that army," I said.

Torquatus snorted derisively. "That blowhard? He thinks he's ferocious, but he's like the sons of noblemen who hold a tribuneship for a year. No one takes him seriously. His money is the only reason he has any influence with Domitian."

That certainly wasn't the impression Gaius had of him.

"I've told Aurora the rest of the story from that point," Lucina said. "About how you used me and left without any remorse."

"Why, Lucina, you almost sound like you missed me." Torquatus gave his best twisted smile. "Do you love me?" He puckered his misshapen mouth as though he would kiss her. "I did not leave willingly, if you'll recall. You hadn't been able to distract Junius, and he caught on to what I was doing with the dice. You have to take some of the blame."

Lucina blushed. "No, I don't, damn you." She punched him on the shoulder, but it was more a gesture of affection than anger. "And I never did love you."

Something about the look on her face and her gestures suggested otherwise to me.

"Well, as you can see, my darling, I have paid dearly for my misdeeds. After that bastard Junius took my dice and you, I couldn't find a replacement for either. Pretty slaves can be found easily enough, but nobody brags about having a set of weighted dice for sale. You have to know someone who knows someone or, like Junius, you have to steal them. I tried making my own, but I could never get them honed without it looking like they'd been tampered with."

"You didn't try to get them back from Junius?" I asked. "That surprises me. You've admitted that you kill people without any remorse."

"And I would not have hesitated to kill Junius."

"So you're saying you killed him in his mill?"

"No. Don't put words in my mouth. I certainly had good reason. He

took everything from me: Lucina, the dice, and a large sum of money. But
before I could do anything about it I was given an assignment—"

"By a powerful person?"

"Exactly. That took me to Massilia. One night I was in a game with
some men there. They suspected what I was trying to do with my inferior
dice and inflicted this on me." He waved his hand over his face. "People
don't want to throw with me anymore, once word gets around about this
monster with the Gorgon's face who cheats at dice. By the time I recovered
and could get back to Augusta Taurinorum, Junius and Lucina were gone."

I was covered with snow, as though I was underwater, face down. My
arms and hands were out in front of me because I had instinctively
tried to break my fall. Frantically I scraped at the snow, gasping to
breathe. Snow seems so light, even fluffy, when it's falling, but, when it
settled, the weight was like the ash coming from Vesuvius. I could hear
vague noises above me. Or maybe below me. When you're completely
covered, you lose all sense of up or down.

Then I realized that what I heard was a voice, calling me. I could
feel the snow shifting around me. I braced myself for the avalanche
to continue. Instead I became aware of a wet touch on my leg. The
weight of the snow began to lighten. In a short time a hand grabbed
my shoulder and pulled me up.

"Thank the gods!" I cried, embracing Tacitus as he helped me stand
up. I took deep breaths, gulping air like a man saved from drowning.

"No, thank old Argos here," Tacitus said. "We had no idea where
you were, but he found you. You must really stink, for him to be able
to track you under this stuff."

The dog circled me, looking up as though wanting reassurance that
I was in fact all right. I reached down and scratched his head. "You are
going to get a fine meal tonight, my friend."

"We'd best get back," Junianus said, "before anything else happens."

"Why weren't you two covered?"

"The slide was very narrow." Junianus made a V-shape with his
hands. "We were off to the side. You were right in the path."

"As though someone was aiming at you," Tacitus said.

I began to shiver, partly from cold and partly from the realization of how close I had come to being buried alive. I don't think of myself as fearing death. It's simply the end; there is nothing after that. What I do fear is being confined in a narrow space or covered so that I'm unable to move or breathe. I've had a couple of experiences in tunnels or small caves that still make it difficult for me to breathe when I think about them.

"We need to get back to the inn before we freeze to death," Tacitus said.

"Did you see who did it?" I asked.

Junianus shook his head. "It looked like there were two men up higher there, but it was hard to make them out."

"They were wearing Gallic clothing," Tacitus said. "One of them was much bigger than the other, a very large man."

"There are a lot of big Gauls, sir."

XIII

I WAS IN THE DINING ROOM of the inn, beginning to feel that I might survive. Julia and her woman Alkippe were wrapping blankets around me and putting warm bricks at my feet. Alkippe was making certain she was closer to me than Julia could get. I felt better as my shivering had subsided. When Aurora came into the room by herself, I said, "Where's Lucina?"

"She's still talking to Torquatus. It seems they have a lot of catching up to do. I'll explain later. Are you all right?"

"Yes, thanks to Argos."

Tacitus petted the dog. "He deserves some special treatment. He actually saved Gaius' life. He dug him out of an avalanche."

Aurora hugged the dog and then sat down, inserting herself between Alkippe and me. "Why don't you take him into the kitchen?" she said to Alkippe.

"I'm not your servant," Alkippe snapped.

"But you are mine," Julia said. "Take the dog into the kitchen and get him something to eat."

"Yes, my lady." Alkippe's words were as icy as the snow outside. I could see the question in Argos' eyes as he looked up at Aurora but then followed Alkippe out to the kitchen.

"That will, no doubt, be reported to Sophronia when we all get to the estate," Julia said. "And from there to Livia."

"By the time the story gets to Livia," Aurora said, "Sophronia will probably be the one who dug Gaius out of the snow."

172

"With her bare hands," Julia said with a laugh.

"What did you mean about Lucina and Torquatus catching up?" I asked.

The three of us listened, almost open-mouthed, while Aurora recounted what Torquatus had revealed about himself and his past.

"Did he say anything that made you think he might have killed Junius?" I asked when she finished.

"That's a hard question to answer. He might have wanted revenge— maybe even wanted his dice back—but with his face so disfigured, surely somebody would have noticed him if he'd come through here. Nobody who's seen him this time remembers seeing him before."

━━━━◦❖◦━━━━

All we could do was watch the snow continue to pile up. Early in the afternoon Gaius and I went up to our room. He was still shaken by his experience in the small avalanche that had buried him. He slept fitfully while I watched over him. He was awake and we were about ready to go back downstairs when we heard a knock on the door. I opened it to find Lucina standing there.

"I hope I'm not disturbing you," she said.

"Not at all. What can we do for you?"

"May I come in?"

"I'm sorry. Certainly, come on in."

I motioned to the only chair in the room and sat on the bed beside Gaius. We looked at Lucina expectantly.

"Torquatus and I have had a long talk," she said. "We've decided that we're going to leave here as soon as the road is open." She held up a hand. "Don't worry, we're not going to impose on you. We'll make our own way, probably toward Genua. It will mean leaving my family, I know, but they have one another. Torquatus has no one. I've never loved Roscius; he considers me his property."

"Did you love Junius?" I asked.

"No, because he took me from the man I did love and still do love. I love Torquatus and want to be with him."

"That's a brave move," Gaius said. "Frankly, with his face—"

"I know. We hope to find a small piece of land and live to ourselves. He has money."

"I wish you well," Gaius said.

Lucina took a deep breath. "Because of what you two have done for me, I want to tell you some things that may help you understand what has gone on here in the past."

"Such as who killed Junius?" Gaius asked.

Lucina cocked her head. "You still think I did it, don't you?"

"I can't seem to prove that anyone else did."

"I don't think I can help you there. What I can tell you is how we got into this situation. As someone from outside, I've done my own probing and listening and begun to understand some of it. It's not a pretty story."

"Murder never is," Gaius said.

"There's more than just murder involved, sir. It has all the trappings of a Greek tragedy."

We listened like the audience in a theater as Lucina told us how the twin sisters, Aemilia and Secunda, had married the elder Roscius and the elder Junius, respectively. But Roscius had raped Secunda, "just to see if he could tell the difference in the dark." She bore a son and raised him as Junius', keeping her secret until the elder Roscius died, sixteen years later. As misfortune would have it, the younger Roscius overheard his aunt and his mother talking about it. He became aware that the younger Junius was his half brother, and he never let him forget it.

"But this gives Junius motive to kill Roscius, not the other way around," Gaius said when she finished. "Because of that so-called loan document they had signed, Roscius was the last person who would have wanted to kill Junius. He would be under suspicion immediately."

"I don't know what to make of this," Lucina said. "I've been under suspicion for killing my husband for years. It's one reason I'm eager to leave and start a new life. All I know is that I did not kill Junius, but I believe the history of the two men is involved in some way. I don't think anyone else would tell you this, so I wanted you to know before I leave."

———◈———

Roscius and his crew returned to the inn late in the day. Lucina and Roscia bustled around, getting them food and extra blankets.

"How much progress have you made?" Tacitus asked.

"I think we've lost ground, sir," Roscius said. "As fast as the snow is falling, we can't keep up with it. I've never seen anything quite like it. And it sounds like there's been another avalanche farther into the pass."

Tacitus slapped the wall beside his table in frustration. "Damn it! We're going to be stuck here until summer! By the time I get to Lugdunum I won't see anything but Lucius' tombstone." He refilled his wine cup, drained it in a gulp, and refilled it again. Julia put her hand on his arm, as if to slow him down, but he shook her off.

I didn't know what to do for Tacitus. It seemed the best I could offer at the moment was companionship. Julia seemed to sense that she should stay away. She went upstairs. Tacitus and I sat silently, eating a bit while he drank a lot. Aurora sat near us on a bench against the wall. She supplied us with wine, which I noticed was getting increasingly weaker as the evening wore on. I nodded my approval.

Finally Charinus approached us. "My lord, may I make a suggestion?"

Tacitus raised his bleary eyes and waved his hand to signal his permission.

"I think it would be possible, my lord, for a handful of us to work our way around the avalanche."

Tacitus sat up. "How do you propose to do that?"

"There is a trail near here that my people have used for generations. We could pick it up on the other side of Lucina's farm. Perhaps you and I and a couple of others, on horseback, could take that route. It would be slow going at first, but once we're around this blockade we could pick up the road through the pass and be on our way."

"Why haven't you said something about this before now?" Tacitus asked.

"It will be a difficult trip, my lord. I thought it would be better—and safer—to wait and see if we were going to be able to get over what's in front of us. It looks like we won't be able to for some time, though."

"How do you know this trail?"

"My mother and I used it when we traveled with our tribe, my lord."

"But you were a child then. That was twenty years ago."

"I became very familiar with the trail, my lord. In this part of the world things don't change much in that amount of time."

"How is this going to help us?" Tacitus said. "It's bound to be more difficult traveling. How can it be any faster?"

Charinus picked up a partially burned stick from one of the braziers and began to draw on the table. "The Roman road from Augusta Taurinorum to Lugdunum makes a big loop north, like this, to follow the pass that goes through Collis. This trail, though, will take us completely away from the Roman road." He drew a straighter, shorter line on the table.

"And away from any possibility of help if something goes wrong," Aurora said.

Charinus' mouth twisted in resentment at her interruption. "It will let us get moving without waiting until that mountain of snow can be moved, and who knows how long that will take? This will be faster. I thought speed was what my lord Tacitus was primarily concerned about."

"It will also mean that we have to go on horseback," I said, "with no wagons. That means carrying limited supplies and sleeping out of doors."

Charinus nodded. "It does, my lord. There are a couple of caves we can use, so we won't be out in the open at night. We'll even be able to light a fire. As you say, we will have to go on horseback."

"I'll go," I said.

"I couldn't ask you to do that," Tacitus said.

"You didn't ask me to come all this way, but I did. What's a few more miles in the snow?"

"It will be difficult few miles, my lord," Charinus said, "but I think the three of us"—he pointed to Tacitus, me, and himself—"will have to make the trip alone. The rest of the party can come along when the avalanche has been cleared."

"I know Julia won't like that," Tacitus said, "but she'll just have to accept it."

"Well, I don't like the idea of leaving Aurora here," I said. "If

Orgetorix's spies—and I know he has at least one here—make him aware that she's here without much protection, he will attack. I think that was his reason for triggering the avalanche in the first place, with whatever help he had. He wanted to trap us here."

"There will still be several of your men here, my lord, and the towns-people," Charinus said, ignoring my accusatory tone.

"Without leadership I'm not sure how much of a defense they would provide," I said. "Half the townspeople are related to the Gauls." I clapped my hands on my knees. "I would prefer to take Aurora with us. She can fight as well as a man, if need be."

"I've seen how brave she is, my lord," Charinus said, "but this will be an arduous trip." He turned to Aurora. "You may well be a hindrance, and I'm sure you don't want that."

Aurora squared her shoulders. "If you could do it when you were ten, I'm sure I can manage it."

Charinus shook his head and raised his hands as if to forestall further discussion. "Don't say I didn't try to talk you out of it."

"Orgetorix is going to be looking for me specifically," Aurora said, "because I killed his son. If I'm with Julia and the others, I'll be endangering them. With you three armed men, off the main road, I'll be less likely to draw attention. We have a better chance of slipping past them."

"That makes sense," Tacitus said. "I think we should take her with us."

"All I can do, my lord," Charinus said, "is offer advice. I don't think Aurora should be riding with us, but I'll guide you along the trail, whatever your decision is. I know the important thing is to get to your brother as quickly as possible."

"Let's plan on leaving at dawn then," Tacitus said.

"Yes, my lord. I'll gather some supplies that we can carry with us."

"I'll do the same for us," Aurora said.

As soon as both of them were out of sight, I turned to Tacitus. "You've had a lot to drink. Are you thinking clearly? Can you really trust him?"

"With my life." Tacitus slurred his words a bit. "Just like you trust Aurora, and for much the same reason."

"What does that mean?"

Tacitus belched and put a hand on my shoulder. "Think about it, my friend. Charinus and I grew up together on my father's estate, from the time we were ten. We coupled for the first time when we were thirteen. He's kept our secret for all these years. How can I not trust him?"

"Does Julia know what has gone on between you?"

"She does. I told her. She doesn't approve, of course, but all she asks is that Charinus live on the estate in Gaul. She doesn't travel with me when I go up there. I get to spend a little time with him on those occasions." He leaned back against the wall. "So, yes, I've coupled with one of my slaves. You, of all people, Gaius, have no right to criticize me for that. I did not force myself on him, any more than you did on Aurora."

"How do you know—"

"I know *you*. For Charinus and me it just happened one afternoon long before we were old enough to shave our beards. We went for a swim on a hot day. I don't love him in the sense that you love Aurora. I don't ache to be married to him, as you do to her, but I enjoy being with him. You've known since we became friends in Syria that I can feel the sort of attraction to another man that those old Greeks felt and admired. And yet I love my wife very much, just as you love Aurora. I hope we will stay together, have a family."

"How can you live—"

"Gaius, you have no idea how torn I am, how torn I have been for all these years."

———◦•◦———

I wasn't sure I was ready to leave Collis again without learning who had killed Junius. The man's death meant nothing to me personally, but confronting a puzzle that I couldn't solve frustrated me. Since I couldn't sleep, I went downstairs to see if I could find something to eat or drink. That sometimes helps me get to sleep. I found some bread, dried fruit, and a cup of wine in the kitchen. On my way I noticed Torquatus sitting at a table in the dining room with writing materials in front of him. A brazier burned low next to the table.

"Would I disturb you if I sat here?" I asked.

"You already have, so please." He pointed to another chair. "I hear you're leaving in the morning," he said, laying down his pen.

"Yes. Charinus has offered to show us a trail that will take us around the avalanche." I sat down at the table across from him.

"That sounds risky."

I tore off a piece of bread. "It is, but Tacitus is desperate to get to his brother."

"Ah, fraternal affection. Very commendable. Sorry I've never known it, though I have two men who can be called my brothers, if you don't inquire too closely into our paternity."

"As an only child myself, I can't say that I have experienced it either. Tacitus is as close to a brother as I'm ever likely to get." I held out the bread and he took a piece.

"So you have to leave again, without solving Junius' murder. Again. Pity."

"Are you offering to confess?"

Torquatus made that snorting noise that passed for a laugh from him. "From what I've heard, you have plenty of suspects, all with good motives." He got up and put another piece of wood on the brazier.

"Have you been investigating? Perhaps we should compare notes."

He sat back down and picked up a pen but did not resume writing. "In a sense I have. Not as thoroughly as you, I'm sure, but Lucina has told me a lot about this little cesspool as we've been catching up. Some things you may not even know."

I didn't think he could know what Lucina had told Aurora and me. I looked forward to comparing his version of events with hers.

"For suspects," he said, "you could start with Roscius."

"Well, he's the most obvious. Too obvious. He and Junius fought one another for years. Then they signed that loan agreement, and the fighting stopped. It was like a treaty to end a war."

"There was no loan."

"The document said there was. I saw it."

"I've seen it, too. Lucina still has it. Alongside her 'emancipation' certificate, which looks very real, by the way. The loan document really was a treaty. You're quite right about that. It put an end to a civil war, years of fighting between two brothers. Well, half brothers."

"Brothers? I thought they were cousins." I decided to play dumb.

"Yes, their mothers are twin sisters. But"—he paused as dramatically as I would in a speech in court—"Lucina learned some years ago that Roscius' father had married one of the twins, Aemilia, and raped the other. He wanted to see if he could tell the difference in the dark, he said."

"How would she 'learn' something like that?"

"When the elder Roscius died, Lucina found Secunda and Aemilia weeping. She thought it was grief, but Secunda, her mother-in-law, told her the whole story. She said she'd had to keep it secret for years. Unfortunately the younger Roscius overheard them talking about it. He was sixteen. After that he lorded it over Junius. 'I'm the son, you're a bastard.' That sort of thing. Lucina says he agreed to stop doing that if Junius would sign the document. There had been an uneasy truce between them for a year or so before Junius' death."

"So Roscius had every reason to want Junius dead, but he was the most obvious suspect. If anything happened to Junius, everyone would look at Roscius."

Torquatus nodded. "Unless they were looking at Magnus. He had every reason to hate Junius, too. He wanted to marry Junia, but her father wouldn't approve. For years Junius put the big ox down as stupid while he was benefiting from his work in the mill."

"Yet Junia wanted to marry Magnus. She told Aurora that ten years ago."

"Well, *de gustibus* and so on, as the philosophers say."

I washed down a dried plum with some wine. "So Junia might be another suspect, although we can't talk to her since she's dead. Would she have killed her own father because he opposed the marriage to Magnus? He did find her a suitable husband."

"A suitable husband who had sufficient reason to kill Junius once he realized he and Junia weren't going to inherit anything. He must have married Junia expecting at least some inheritance. Lucina says his family has nothing. Once he realized that they would become little more than Roscius' servants, he could have gotten into an argument with Junius, which could have escalated into physical violence."

"'Could have' isn't proof. Draco is a small man." I held up my hand to estimate his stature. "I doubt he could have inflicted the kind of injuries Junius suffered. The same goes for Junia. I saw her with my own eyes. She was even smaller, and a woman."

"Your Aurora is a reminder that women should not be immediately dismissed when looking for a culprit in a crime."

"I suppose that's true."

"I know it is. One of the villains who attacked me was a woman. She landed her kicks as effectively as either of the men."

"So we have several people who might have wanted Junius dead. We also know he gambled. Someone could have been angry at losing money."

"Funny how people react to losing money."

"Do they react the same way to losing a *fritillus* and crooked dice?"

"Are you suggesting I killed Junius? I wasn't anywhere near Collis when it happened."

"Where were you?"

"To tell you that I would have to admit to killing someone else in another place. As I'm sure Aurora has told you, I've been doing that sort of work for Domitian for some time. You're still in a quandary because all of these people we've mentioned have alibis, though, don't they?"

"There is one person who doesn't."

"Oh, who is that?"

"Lucina."

Torquatus sat back, as though absorbing a blow. "I understood she was with Roscius the whole evening. Servants saw them working together."

"That's true, as far as it goes. It just doesn't go far enough. I've been told that there was a point in the evening when Lucina left to use the *latrina*. She was gone long enough to kill Junius." Actually, no one had told me any such thing, but I was so desperate to find an answer that I was willing to use a hunter's technique of beating the bushes and seeing what might run out of hiding.

"But why would she have done that?"

"Oh, she had more, and better, motives than anyone else we've been talking about. He had taken her away from the one man she ever loved. That would be you, Quintus Decius."

"Why would she love me?"

"Her previous owner had raped her. Junius treated her little better than a slave. As Quintus Decius you treated her well, and you needed her. Roscius wanted her, so he provided an alibi. I think I should turn her over to the magistrates in Augusta Taurinorum. They will get the truth out of her. People do tend to remember things differently—more keenly perhaps—when faced with the prospect of death in the arena. If Lucina's emancipation proves not to be legitimate, as you suspect, she could face crucifixion as a runaway slave who killed a free person. As you well know, Domitian is always looking for victims for the arena."

"You can't let them do that to her!"

"It's not up to me. The law is the law. Look at how the case would be laid out in court. We don't know the exact time of the murder. We do know that Lucina claims that she went to the latrine at one point, but no one saw her there, so her alibi does have that large hole in it. Roscius, I think, was covering up for her because he wanted to marry her. They had to get Junius out of the way for that to happen. Roscius hated Junius, in spite of that so-called loan document they had signed. He would probably supply testimony against her, once he realizes that he could face charges as well."

"She couldn't have killed him, Gaius Pliny."

"Why not?"

"Because I did."

"There's no proof of that."

"I just admitted it. Isn't that proof enough?"

"Not necessarily. You weren't even in Collis when Junius was murdered."

"Oh, but I was. I had developed a profound hatred for the man, as you can imagine. He had taken the woman I loved from me, and my best means of earning a living. Because he had taken my dice, I was beaten up one night when I was caught cheating. I blamed Junius for everything that was wrong with my life. I found out where Lucina was and came here in that summer ten years ago."

"No one saw you."

"I developed a talent for hiding. Given the kind of work Domitian wanted me to do and this mockery of a face, I had to become practically invisible as I moved around."

"You claim to be an imperial assassin. What proof do you have of that?"

"I can give you a list of the people I've killed. My first assignment from him was to murder Gaius Licinius Mucianus."

I knew that name. My uncle had consulted some of his writings while working on his own books. I had met the man once. "Mucianus died about the time Titus became *princeps*, didn't he? That was quite a while after you claim to have begun...working for Domitian."

"Yes. He was my first assignment, but not the first person I killed. You would have been too young to remember that Domitian tried to make himself master of Rome when Vitellius died in the summer of that awful year after Nero's death." He shook his head. "Galba, Otho, and Vitellius all claiming to be emperor within a few months before Vespasian restored order. Even stories about Nero coming back to life."

"I was only seven. My uncle had sent me and his household away from Rome because everything was so chaotic."

"He was wise. Mucianus arrived in Rome the day after Vitellius' death and assumed command on behalf of Vespasian. Domitian was young and had hated Mucianus for years. He thought Mucianus had robbed him of his chance to be *princeps*. For a long time he tried to pretend that he had handed the power over to his father. He ordered me to kill Mucianus any time I had the chance. But the man was highly placed and well protected. It took me a long time to get to him. I brought down a number of others in the meantime. I can give you a list."

"That might be a dangerous list to have."

"To Domitian, yes. To someone else it could be...powerful. So, we are at an impasse. I admit that I killed Junius, but you're not ready to believe me. Yet you can't prove that I didn't do it."

"I wonder if you're just trying to protect Lucina."

He laughed. "As I told you, Gaius Pliny, the next woman down the line will always do. What if I told you something that I could know only if I did kill him?"

I knew that he was just trying to protect Lucina. Whether he could admit it or not, he loved her. But what if she didn't kill Junius? Did he know for certain? Did he love her enough to put his life on the line if he wasn't sure?

"All right, convince me."

"You saw the spot where he died, didn't you?"

I nodded.

"His head had been slammed against the wall several times, on the left side. He was lying on the ground like this, if I remember correctly." He pushed chairs aside and lay down, arranging himself almost as Junius had been. "How would I know that if I hadn't seen him?"

"I know it and I didn't see him. Junianus described the position of his body to me and to Aurora. I don't know how many other people he told, or how many people they told."

"You have wanted to solve this case for ten years. I just handed you the solution. Why won't you accept it?"

"Because it was his left arm, not his right, that was extended like that."

XIV

AURORA AND I came downstairs the next morning to hear Lucina calling for Torquatus. She accosted us as soon as we came into the dining room. Junianus and Roscia were there, looking somewhat bewildered. Little Junilla clung to her aunt's gown.

"Have you seen Torquatus this morning?"

"No," I said. "It's rather early. We're only up because we're riding with Charinus."

"But he's not in his room. And his servants don't know where he is." She waved an arm toward Torquatus' two servants, who were sitting at a table near a brazier. Lucina must have rousted them out.

"Do you know where your master is?" I asked them.

"No, my lord, but last night he told us to give you this as soon as we saw you this morning, to make sure you didn't leave without getting it." One of them handed me the leather bag Torquatus had been carrying for the entire trip. He had sealed it with an emblem of Venus.

Lucina gasped when she saw it. "That was Quintus Decius' seal."

I opened the bag and removed several pieces of papyrus. They were not the documents I would have thought Torquatus had been carrying. "These are addressed to me," I said. "Do you know what he did with other documents he had been carrying?"

One man pointed to a brazier in another corner of the room. "There are some pieces of papyrus in there. I think he burned whatever was in the bag."

Aurora poked at the charred scraps of papyrus. "I can't tell what they were."

"Well, let's see what he's left us instead." I pulled out several pieces of papyrus. The first was addressed to me and gave me the two servants at the table. "Do with them as you see fit," it said. "They are decent men, even if they're not the hardest workers I've ever known. All of my other assets in this bag are now yours."

I put the document in front of the men. "Can you read?"

"I can, my lord." One of them picked up the document, his eyes widening as he read it to his comrade. They both looked up at me. "What would you have us do, my lord?" the first man said.

"For now just sit there," I said. "I'll make some decisions later."

Next I pulled out Torquatus' imperial pass. Finding that in there let me know right away what his plan was. I turned to Lucina. "Did he take a horse or any provisions?"

"No." She twisted her hands in front of her. "He's gone, isn't he?"

"It looks that way."

Roscius entered the room with a good deal of noise, causing little Junilla to cower even farther behind her grandmother. "Where is the rascal? He makes me oust people with his damn imperial pass. If he's gone, I don't have to worry about that pass, do I? We'll settle up then." He looked directly at me.

"Not so fast," I said. I showed him the imperial pass and Torquatus' letter. "It seems this is now mine, so nothing has changed." Roscius' face fell.

"This one is for you," I said to Lucina as I drew out the next sheet, folded and sealed. She took a seat in one corner and opened the letter. She read silently, moving her lips but not making any sound. She could not have read more than a few lines before her tears began to flow.

Roscius snatched it away from her. "Some love letter, is it?"

"You can't read, so how are you to know?"

"Well, you're not going to read it either." He was about to toss it into one of the braziers, but I grabbed his wrist and took the letter away from him.

"It's hers." I gave the document back to Lucina.

Roscius stomped out of the dining room.

Lucina looked up from the letter, her face in anguish. "Somebody's got to go look for him. Please."

"We can't," I said. I held up the last piece of papyrus. "There's no point. This is his confession to the murder of Junius."

Lucina gasped. "But he didn't—"

"He has confessed to it in writing. The case is finally closed. Tacitus and I are about to set out on the trail with Charinus. We don't have time to look for Torquatus. There's no way to know even which direction he went. I suspect he would have taken a route that allowed him to get as far from Collis as he could before leaving the road and going into the woods."

"But how far can he go without the pass and a horse?"

"I don't think he intends to go far, just far enough that no one can find him."

Junianus put a hand on his sobbing mother's shoulder. "I'll take a horse and look for him."

The snow eased up as we got our horses out of the stable. With the wind settling, we could actually see several paces in front of us. Charinus led the way, with Tacitus close behind him. Aurora and I took advantage of the trampled snow that their horses provided for us. We were all clad in Lucina's wool-lined leggings and extra layers of tunics and cloaks, and travelers' hats. We carried two weapons each. I had even decided to flout the law and let Aurora carry a sword.

"This is at least bearable," I said after we had been riding for an hour or so. "Not pleasant, but bearable." I touched the Tyche ring under my tunic in the hope that we would meet nothing more unbearable.

"We're dressed adequately, and we seem to be making good progress," she said. "I can't tell how Charinus can pick out a trail, though."

"He seems to be watching for boulders. We've turned slightly as we've passed a couple of large ones."

"That's the only thing he *could* see under all this damn snow."

"We're going uphill, aren't we?"

"I think so. That's what I would expect. We're riding *over* the mountains rather than taking a pass through them."

For the most part we rode in silence. There was nothing to talk about except snow, and the wind began to pick up, making it difficult for us to hear one another when we did speak. Charinus suggested we keep quiet in case anyone was trying to track us. Around midday we shared some bread, cheese, and sausage while we rode. Tacitus didn't want to stop even long enough to get off our horses to eat. I did insist that he let us stop to relieve ourselves. A man might be able to do that on horseback, but not a woman.

At one point I called to Charinus, "Isn't this a cave we're passing?"

"Yes," he said over his shoulder, "but it's early yet and that cave's too small for the horses. We wouldn't even be able to stand up in it."

At long last Charinus pointed up ahead and said, "There's a cave up there. It's large enough that we can bring the horses in. And we can have a fire."

"Do you have any idea what time it is?" I asked.

"It's hard to tell because of the clouds, isn't it?" Tacitus said. "It does seem to be getting a little darker. I don't know if the sun is setting or the clouds are getting thicker."

"The sun sets early," Charinus said, "because of the mountains. Away from here it's probably only late afternoon, but we need to stop. It's a considerable distance to the next usable cave, and we can't risk traveling in the dark."

Much to my relief, this cave was large enough for the horses to stand. I did not feel confined, as I usually do in small spaces. A large part of what we were carrying was grain for the horses. Charinus promised that, once we were over the mountains, they could graze, but we had to keep up their stamina until then. Aurora scooped out a place to serve as a manger and looked after the horses at the rear of the cave. The one that Charinus had been riding was particularly restless, but Aurora soothed him with her touch and her words.

Meanwhile Tacitus, Charinus, and I gathered some wood and started a fire—no easy task with the wood as damp as it was. Finally Tacitus and Charinus sat on one side of the fire with a blanket wrapped around them. Aurora and I copied them on the other side. With the fire, the blanket, the leggings, and the warmth of our bodies, we were soon reasonably comfortable.

As we finished eating Aurora looked right at Charinus and asked, "Do you still think I'm an impediment on this trip?"

"Not at all," he replied. "You've done all we could have asked of you. I'm not sure I could have gotten that horse settled down the way you did."

We arranged for taking turns on watch and tried to get some sleep.

The next day passed in a blur. When we reached another cave I could hardly move enough to get off my horse. People who don't ride don't realize how difficult it is. The cold weather also caused my entire body to tighten up. We did the same routine, hardly speaking. While we were eating, Charinus brought out a vial from his pack.

"This is an elixir that my people use to relieve sore muscles." He made a gesture to pour some in my wine, but I put a hand over my cup.

"How do I know what's in that?"

Tacitus glared at me and held his cup so Charinus could put his elixir into it. I couldn't do anything but let him add some to my wine.

"You'll get a good night's sleep," he assured us. He poured less in Aurora's cup. "A woman won't need as much."

"What about you?" she asked.

"I'm more accustomed to this type of work, from living on my lord's estate. Pardon my saying it, but you folks live in a big house in the city. Your bodies aren't used to such hard labor. This will help, I promise you."

———⊰◦⊱———

I was awakened by someone shaking me. Charinus was telling me to get up. The fire had burned down to almost nothing.

"What?" I forced my eyes open and tried to turn to Gaius, but Charinus pulled me away.

"Get up," he said. "We've got to get moving." He jerked me to my feet. Before I realized what he was doing, he tied my hands behind my back with a leather strap and pulled it tight.

My eyes were open now, mostly from fear. "What—"

"Shut up and move."

I looked down at Gaius and Tacitus. "Are they dead? Gaius! Tacitus! Wake up!"

"They're not dead. They'll sleep for quite a while yet, but they're not dead."

"You drugged us. That stuff you put in our wine—"

"Yes, I gave them something to make them sleep soundly. I gave you less because I need for you to be able to walk and ride a horse."

"Why? Where are we going?"

"All I'll say is that Orgetorix is going to be very happy to see you. Now come on! You're wasting time."

He grabbed me by my arm and pulled me out of the cave. I was dizzy and couldn't get my legs to do what I wanted them to do. What I most wanted was to kick him, but when I tried to draw one leg back, I fell. Instead of helping me up, Charinus went back into the cave and returned with a piece of rope. He looped it over my neck and dragged me over to a tree.

"If I have to," he snarled, "I'll tie you to a horse and drag you the whole way. Get up!"

He tied the other end of the rope to the tree. While I struggled to get to my feet he went back in the cave and brought out two of the horses, which he tied to another tree.

"What are you going to do with Gaius Pliny and Tacitus?" I jerked my head toward the cave.

"They're going to have a nice, long sleep. I just want to delay them. I'm not a monster. I'm not going to kill them. I'm leaving them the horses. I know this terrain, while they don't. They'll never catch up with us. Even if, by some stroke of luck they do, it will be too late for you. That's all I need."

"But they could die."

"Yes, they could, and I would be deeply saddened by that. In spite of everything, I love Tacitus very much. They could find their way out of here, though. They're resourceful men." He went into the cave again. I saw him bend over, kiss Tacitus on the forehead, and lay another blanket over him. He put more wood on the fire.

He came back to me, untied the rope from the tree, and pulled me toward one of the horses. "We need to get going."

I tried to resist, but the drug still weakened me. "You and your people started the avalanche that blocked the pass in the first place, didn't you? Then you tricked me into coming with you."

"Yes, we started the avalanche. It's not hard to do. In a way I suppose I did trick you, but that was easy, too. All I had to do was tell you not to come. When you tell a woman not to do something, that becomes the very thing she thinks she has to do."

"You lying son of—"

Charinus clamped his hand over my mouth. "Do you want me to kill you right now?"

I bit his hand. He slapped me hard. "You can't kill me. Then you couldn't let Orgetorix have the satisfaction of watching me die. That's what this is all about, isn't it? You've seen your chance to ingratiate yourself, to become…what? Some sort of high priest?"

"My father was the high priest. That's what I told them when they attacked us on the road. The Romans killed him. I'm just going to reclaim my rightful place and my name. I am Ambiorix. I don't ever want to hear that slave name 'Charinus' again." He shoved me against one of the horses.

"And you'll do this by sacrificing me?"

"That's what I promised Orgetorix. That's why they haven't attacked us. They wanted to be sure you couldn't get away. They've just been watching and getting things ready. It will be a glorious sight, and you'll have the best view of all."

I tried to suppress the panic rising in my gut. "I've read about what you do in Caesar's book—the wicker frame, burning people alive. It's horrible, barbaric."

"You Romans have slaughtered and enslaved thousands of my people, so don't talk to me about who's barbaric. Wearing a damn stripe on your tunic doesn't make you civilized. Now you need to shut up." He cut a piece off my stola, jammed it into my mouth, and tied another leather strap around my head to hold the gag in place. "If you won't let me seat you on the horse, I'll lay you over him and tie you. You know how uncomfortable that would be for a long ride."

I fought him as much as I could while he tried to get me onto one of *the horses. Knowing that he was determined to keep me alive gave me an advantage. I hoped that, if I could delay him long enough, Gaius or Tacitus might wake up. But he was too strong for me and I found myself astride a horse. He ran the rope that was around my neck around the horse's neck and tied it. Then he tied a rope from one of my ankles to the other, under the horse's belly. When he had tied my feet he lifted my stola and found my knife. "I've seen what you can do with this," he said as he removed it and tucked it into his belt.*

He mounted the other horse and untied the one I was riding so he could lead it. "We're going to have a long day, but we should be where we need to be by the end of it. You're right, I do have to get you there alive, but Orgetorix won't care how battered or bloody you are." He grabbed my hair and jerked my head back. "Do you understand me?" When I did not react, he slapped me. "Do you understand me?"

"Sir, you need to wake up," I heard someone saying in my ear. It certainly wasn't Aurora's sweet voice. What was going on? I felt around me, groping for Aurora but feeling only hard ground. My hand hit a person, and I sat up slowly, with my head spinning. When I could open my eyes and focus, I realized I was looking into Junianus' face. He stood back, and I saw Argos behind him.

"What's happening…?"

"I think you've been sleeping for a while, sir," Junianus said. He put wood on the remains of the fire and struck a flint.

On the other side of me Tacitus began to stir. "Gaius, what's going on?"

"Your loyal Charinus drugged us," I said. As my head began to clear I looked around the cave and noticed that two horses were gone. "And now he's taken Aurora."

"Taken her where?"

"I'm sure they're headed straight to Orgetorix." I got to my feet, bracing myself against a wall of the cave and taking a deep breath. "If any harm comes to her, I will kill Charinus, I swear it, regardless of how you feel about him."

Tacitus put his hands to his head. "No, I reserve that privilege for myself. He's betrayed me."

"Let's go. We've got to find them." I tried to walk, but sank to my knees.

"With all respect, sirs," Junianus said, "neither of you looks like you're fit to walk across this cave, much less a mountain. You'd die in the dark and the snow."

"Dark?" Tacitus said, peering toward the opening of the cave. "What time of day is it?"

"It's going on nightfall, sir."

Tacitus' brow wrinkled in disbelief. "We've been asleep for a night and an entire day?"

"I think so, sir. This is the third day since you left Collis."

I sat down and pulled a blanket around me as I realized how cold I was. The fire was just beginning to blaze up. "How did you find us?"

"Magnus mentioned the trail that the Gauls use on the other side of my ma's farm. I started there. Argos found a couple of spots where you'd relieved yourselves and the cave where you stayed one night."

"That dog is remarkable." I scratched the animal's head, which he laid on my leg.

"I think he's in love with your girl Aurora. He's been sniffing for her all over this cave."

"She seems to have that effect on animals."

"And others," Junianus said, lowering his head. "Let's get you something to eat, sirs. Just have a seat and I'll pull it together." He rummaged through our packs and his and found enough for a meal that we ate in silence, huddled around the fire.

Tacitus finally asked. "Do you have any idea where Charinus might be going?"

Junianus nodded vigorously. "There's a spot just after the trail comes down on the other side of the mountains where the Gauls used to gather for their rituals. Magnus would tell us stories about it that he'd heard from older ones in his tribe. They'd build a big wicker frame—a thing like a statue, I guess—and put prisoners in it. Then they'd set it on fire. The way he told it, it was right scary."

"That's in Caesar's *Commentaries*," I said. "He could have picked it up from there."

Tacitus nodded. "Every schoolboy has read it. His account is so vivid. I never quite believed they would do something that barbaric, though. Caesar didn't mind exaggerating now and then. It made him look more important."

"Oh, it's no exaggeration, sir," Junianus said. "Not from what Magnus said. They haven't done it for a time. You Romans won't allow it. But anybody around here knows where they did it. Magnus swore it's true. This spot is in a valley up in the hills, away from Roman settlements, where you're not likely to see it until it's too late."

"That's where we'll be headed," I said, "as soon as we finish eating."

"But, sir—"

"We've already lost an entire day. My eyes are better in low light than most men's. With all this snow on the ground, it never really gets dark. Charinus won't be expecting us to follow him. He might keep a slower pace. He might even stop to rest."

"And we've got the dog to help us," Tacitus said. "We're certainly not going to get any sleep tonight."

"What are you going to do if you catch him?" Junianus asked.

I looked at where we had stacked our packs last night—or whenever we came in here. "He took our swords, didn't he?"

Junianus nodded. "I do have one, sir, but only one, and a small knife." He handed the weapons to Tacitus and me.

"Why did you come after us?" Tacitus asked.

"Aurora was so sure Charinus was up to something. The more I thought about it, I decided to trust her instinct."

Tacitus did not look up from the fire. "Don't say it, Gaius. Just don't say a word, please."

"I wasn't going—"

"I'm sorry I was such a fool. He said he loved me, and I wanted him to love me."

XV

THE TRIP BY NIGHT proved to be easier than I had dared to hope. The snow had stopped and Charinus and Aurora had left a trail that was easy to follow with Argos' help. As the sun came up I wondered aloud if we should go down the mountain and pick up the road through the pass. "Surely by now we're past the spot that the avalanche was blocking. That's what Charinus suggested we should do."

"But, sir," Junianus said, "Charinus was just saying that to draw you in. He shows no sign of going down to pick up the main road. That comes out a good distance from the place where the Gauls do their rituals. That's where he's going. If we stay on this trail we'll come out right on top of them."

"Oh, sure," Tacitus said, "the three of us with a sword and a knife against how many of them?"

"There may not be as many as you'd think, sir," Junianus assured him. "Most of the Gauls are pretty well satisfied with the way things are. It's just a small band of troublemakers that wants to stir things up. They're the ones that live up in the hills, away from the towns."

"There are malcontents in every province," I said. "We saw that in Nero's last days. Spain, Germany, Judaea—they all rose up against us."

Tacitus nodded. "The ones who want to cling to 'the old ways.'"

"They need to accept that things change."

"That's easier to accept when they change in your favor."

We rode in silence until Tacitus said, "We're going downhill now, aren't we?"

"Yes, we are," I said. "It must be late morning. Listen. Up ahead. Do you hear voices?"

Argos' ears stood up.

"Hurry!" I said.

———————◦◦◦———————

It was midday when Charinus and I came out of the woods. We were still up on the side of the mountain, so I could see a crowd of Gauls. A few were stationed here and there on the hillside as lookouts. They immediately raised a cry. I guessed there were fewer than fifty people down in the valley. They must have been there for a few days, to judge from the tents and huts clustered around a kind of square. A pen for their horses had been thrown up at one end of the encampment.

Orgetorix was easy to spot, standing on a speaker's platform. He wore a robe with a fur collar and a helmet adorned with feathers. Raising a spear, he pointed at us. The throng around him looked up and cheered. They clearly had been expecting Charinus.

And me.

My stomach churned when I saw the wicker frame they'd constructed, like the frame used to support a huge statue, say Athena in the Parthenon or the Colossus in front of the Amphitheatre in Rome. It was lying on its side in an open area apart from the temporary dwellings they had erected. Charinus dismounted and handed the reins of his horse to one of the lookouts while he guided mine down the side of the hill. The snow was still deep on the hill, but it got shallower as we descended. By the time we reached flat ground it was only ankle-deep. The Gauls and their animals had walked over it enough to make it disappear from where they had set up camp. The mud that resulted wasn't much of an improvement.

Orgetorix approached us and greeted Charinus with an embrace. He shouted Charinus' Gaulish name, and the crowd echoed it. "Ambiorix!" That much I could understand.

A majestic woman, wearing regalia that marked her as a priestess, emerged from one of the huts carrying an elaborate robe of deep blue cloth with designs worked into it with silver thread. Orgetorix beamed as he draped the robe on Charinus' shoulders and the crowd erupted again. The men added to the din by beating their swords on their shields. Several young girls brought in six sheep, which Charinus and the priestess sacrificed on an altar set up in the middle of the encampment. Charinus and Orgetorix then took turns haranguing the crowd, working them into a frenzy.

Orgetorix came over to where Charinus had tied the horse I was riding. He took the reins and led the horse through the crowd. Men, women, and children spat on me and yelled what I assumed were insults and threats. Then he untied the ropes holding me on the animal and pulled me off. Putting his face into mine, he let out a stream of words that I suspected were as foul as his breath. I couldn't understand the tirade, but the anger behind it was unmistakable.

Charinus translated for me. "He says he is greatly pleased that his son's blood will be avenged. He gives thanks to our gods."

Orgetorix took the gag out of my mouth, grabbed my hair and pulled my head back, still snarling at me.

"He wants to hear you cry and beg," Charinus said. "And you soon will."

I spat in the chieftain's face. "I won't give you the satisfaction."

As Orgetorix wiped his face, Charinus hit me, this time with his fist, right on my jaw. "That's what they always say. We'll see how you feel when the flames are licking at your feet."

"You've been in contact with these people all along, haven't you?" I said.

Charinus grabbed the rope that was still dangling around my neck and jerked me to my knees. With my hands tied behind me and unable to catch myself, I almost fell flat. He stopped me by bringing his knee up to my face. I could feel blood starting to flow from my nose. The Gauls closest to me let out a ululating howl when they saw it.

"Of course I've been in contact with them. Every step of the way. Like any Roman man, Tacitus is easy to fool. Suck his dick a few times and he trusts you with anything. That must be how you keep Gaius Pliny on your string." His face contorted in rage. "This is our land! The damn Romans think they can go anywhere and ride roughshod over anybody. You come from a conquered people. I'm surprised you don't understand. You ought to be rising up with us, instead of playing the whore to your master."

I licked the blood that was trickling into my mouth. "Haven't you heard of the Punic Wars? We tried again and again to stand up against Rome.

All that resistance got us was the complete destruction of our cities and our civilization, the deaths of tens of thousands of people." He tightened the rope around my neck until I could hardly breathe. "You won't come out of it any better," I gasped.

Orgetorix said something to Charinus, who produced my knife from his belt and handed it to the chieftain. He held it to my throat, applying so much pressure I was afraid he had changed his mind and was going to kill me with his own hand. Instead, he said something and tied a piece of leather to the handle, then looped it around my neck and let the knife dangle between my breasts.

"He would enjoy using your knife—the very weapon that killed his son—to kill you," Charinus said, "but he'll be satisfied to know it will perish with you, cleansed by the flames."

He called to two other men, who held me while he stripped off my stola. They smeared blood from the sacrificed sheep on my face and chest. Then they dragged me over to the large structure that was lying on the ground. They swung open a door to a section at the top and forced me in, like a bird being imprisoned in a large cage. No matter how much I fought and kicked, they managed to tie my hands and ankles to the framework. Then they tied the door shut. I was facing forward, with my legs spread and my hands raised to the level of my shoulders. The woman who was decked out as a priestess, muttering some incantation, spread olive oil over my body to make sure I burned faster.

"You're receiving a great honor," Charinus said, proudly drawing his priestly robe around himself. "Usually we sacrifice several prisoners at the same time, but you're the only one today. This frame isn't as tall as we like to build them. All eyes will be on you, though, and the flames will get to you that much faster."

At first I was lying down, but then they lifted the framework and tied it to posts placed upright in the ground so that, when it was standing, I was at the top, at the height of a two-story building. Looking down, I could see women piling wood around the base of the thing. Behind them stood men holding torches. Others took out bows and arrows and began shooting in my direction.

"They're not trying to kill you!" Charinus called, cupping his hands

*around his mouth. "We want you to be alive when the flames get to you,
but a few wounds will shed some of your blood, as you shed the blood of
the man you killed."*

*Most of the arrows hit the framework near me, but I still flinched. I
saw the first torch drop onto the wood piled around the base of the frame
and heard the fire start to crackle. The crowd cheered, like the crowds in the
Amphitheatre when a gladiator first draws blood.*

*Then one of the arrows stuck in the wooden framework so close to my
right hand that it drew a trickle of blood. Before the arrow became dislodged
I was able to saw through enough of the rope holding me that I could break it
with a sharp tug. With that free hand I grabbed my knife, which Orgetorix
had so obligingly hung around my neck, and cut myself free. Free to do what?
I didn't care. At least being free was better than not being free.*

*I could feel the heat from the fire. Orgetorix yelled something, and more
Gauls began shooting, this time clearly aiming at me. Most of the arrows
struck the framework, which actually formed a kind of defense for me, but
one got me in the thigh. It stung more than I would have expected from
an arrow wound. I tried to pull it out, but it broke, leaving the point in
me. I kept climbing around the framework, even as tight as it was, so they
wouldn't have a stationary target. They scrambled to surround the cage
and shot at me from all angles. I felt the framework begin to sway as the
fire consumed the lowest level. I realized the flames wouldn't have to reach
me. Before long the whole thing would collapse and I would plunge into
the fire. My heart pounded and I screamed. I was not going to let myself
die this way!*

"By the gods!" Tacitus muttered as we came to the edge of the woods
and looked down on the scene in the valley, with Argos hunched down
between us. I was too horrified to say anything. Aurora, with an arrow
sticking out of her thigh and with blood smeared all over her, was
clinging to the tall framework that was slowly being consumed by the
fire at its base. There weren't more than fifty Gauls in the camp. Fewer
than half, I guessed, were men. Some of them were shooting more
arrows at Aurora.

Tacitus put a finger to his lips and pointed with his other hand to the half dozen men on the hillside below us. Whether they were lookouts—careless ones at that—or had just climbed up here to get a better view, they were completely enthralled by the ghastly sight and oblivious to us, as were the Gauls down in the valley.

Junianus signaled to us to follow him to a higher spot off to our left. "The snow's the only weapon we have," he whispered, "but it may be our best one. Do what I do."

He began jogging back and forth, stomping as hard as he could. Tacitus and I followed his example. In no time I could feel the snow begin to slide and hear it groaning and cracking. Junianus jumped aside. Tacitus and I did so as well. The noise grew louder as the snow knocked over the lookouts and crashed into the Gauls below us. I was stunned by the speed and force with which it hit. The little bit we dislodged carried more before it. Flimsy huts shattered and disappeared. I hadn't realized how much of an impact the snow could have, even though I'd been struck and buried by it a few days before.

The fire at the base of the framework was quickly extinguished, and the framework fell over on its side, well away from where the fire had been burning. Aurora wrapped her arms and legs around pieces of it, like branches of a falling tree, and rode it to the ground. Only a few of the Gauls were left standing. Tacitus, Junianus, and I scrambled down the side of the hill, stopping only to grab swords and shields from the three dazed lookouts who had not been buried. We stained the snow with their blood.

"Much better odds!" Tacitus cried. "Remember, if Charinus is still alive, he's mine."

Most of the Gauls had been knocked down by the avalanche. A few were able to get to their feet but were in no condition to resist. We made quick work of them. The priestess had armed herself. Junianus was the first to reach her. She drew blood on his left shoulder, but he parried her next blow with his shield and dispatched her. Somewhere in the confusion Aurora was calling my name. Good old Argos seemed to be struggling, but he ran as fast as the snow would let him toward her voice.

Orgetorix was also back on his feet and moving in that direction. The avalanche had knocked his helmet off and he was mud-soaked, so he looked less intimidating, but he had his sword and was letting out blood-curdling screams. Aurora could not get out of her cage. She was still trying to cut the thick rope that tied the door shut when Orgetorix got to her. He couldn't open the door either, so he was stabbing at her. She was able to avoid his sword and wounded his wrist with her knife. He howled with rage.

By then Argos had covered the ground and jumped on Orgetorix. The Gaul threw him off, but Argos nipped at his heels and dashed in between his feet. Orgetorix turned his attention from Aurora to the dog.

That diversion gave me time to reach the framework and attack Orgetorix. He was much bigger than me and battle-tested, but I had a four-legged ally. Argos leaped up and bit the back of the Gaul's leg, above his leather shin guards. I used my shield to push Orgetorix up against the framework. From inside it Aurora grabbed his long hair, pulled his head back, and slit his throat. The chieftain suffered the same "ignominious" end as his son: death at the hands of a woman—a naked slave woman at that. His lifeless bulk slumped to the ground.

When the other Gauls saw that Orgetorix and the priestess had fallen, they set up a mournful howling, like the wolves I sometimes hear at night when I'm at Comum. Some of them dropped their weapons and knelt in surrender at Junianus' feet. As I shoved Orgetorix's body aside and began cutting the rope that held the door of Aurora's prison shut, I saw two other men still standing: Tacitus and Charinus.

The field of battle fell silent as the two of them circled one another, swords at the ready, the way gladiators in the arena look for an opponent's weak point. When Charinus stopped, I thought he was going to attack, but he just said, "Cornelius Tacitus, in spite of everything I don't want to kill you or make you kill me." Before Tacitus could react, Charinus thrust his sword into his own midsection, upward toward his heart, and fell to the ground. Tacitus knelt beside him, not even trying to conceal his tears.

I had cut the ropes holding the door of Aurora's prison and taken her in my arms, ignoring the mess smeared all over her.

"Oh, Gaius, Gaius! I was so afraid," she sobbed. "When you came out of the woods, I thought I was having a delusion."

"It's all right," I said. "You're safe now. Let's look at this wound."

I laid her down on the ground. She had been hit by an arrow in the upper part of her right leg. From my uncle's notebooks I knew that a wound in the leg, if it's in just the right place, can lead to excessive bleeding, enough to kill a person. Fortunately, Aurora was hit in a part of her leg that did not produce a lot of blood loss, but she was feverish. The place where the arrow had hit her was reddening.

"Gaius, I feel hot," she said.

"Just lie still. You were frightened and you were working hard. You'll feel better if you can just be calm."

One of the Gaulish women brought a garment to cover Aurora. She gently removed the arrowhead, and began to suck on the spot where it had hit, pausing to spit blood now and then.

I pulled her back. "What are you doing?"

In broken Latin she said something about poison. Once Aurora had broken free, Orgetorix had given the order for the men to dip their arrows in poison to kill her. "I hope I have got it out." She bandaged the wound. "She should rest, so poison does not move faster in her." She waved her hands up and down over Aurora's body.

"Too late for that," Aurora said with a grimace. "Even if I had known I'd been poisoned, I couldn't just stand still and give them an easy target. There wasn't much room, but I had to keep moving and dodging."

I helped her sit with her back against a tree. Now I was torn. Should I stay with her or go help Tacitus and Junianus? Was she going to die?

"I'll be all right," she said. The pain evident on her face made a mockery of that hope.

I looked in Tacitus' direction. He and Junianus were outnumbered but seemed to be in control. The priestess lay dead at their feet. The Gauls seemed to have lost their will to fight along with their leaders. "I need to help Tacitus and Junianus corral the rest of the Gauls," I said.

"I'll be fine. Really. Go." Before I turned away Argos crawled into her lap. "Oh, you dear, sweet dog," Aurora crooned. "You helped save my life." Argos let out a long sigh, closed his eyes, and lay still. Aurora petted him and looked up at me with tears in her eyes. "He's dead, Gaius. That was his last breath. He's dead."

I reached out to stroke the dog's head. "'No beast in the forest could get away from him, once he was on its trail.' That's what Homer said when Argos recognized Odysseus and died. He found you in spite of everything."

"We'll let that be his epitaph." Aurora wiped her tears and raised a hand to bring Junianus over.

I stood and turned when I heard men's voices coming up the valley toward us. At first I thought we were going to be attacked by more Gauls. Then I realized I was hearing Latin. Tacitus came over to stand beside me as Roman soldiers rounded the last turn in the gravel road and came into view. "May the gods be thanked!" he muttered, and I couldn't even disagree with him.

———————⊙⊙⊙———————

A centurion named Laternus commanded the unit of soldiers. They had been sent, he told us, to clear the road through the pass but had heard of something going on among the Gauls up here and had decided to investigate.

"Looks like we got here a bit late," he said, "but I see you've got the situation in hand."

"All that remains," I said, "is to decide what to do with the rest of them. There are only a few men and a couple of dozen women and children left."

"You want my advice, sir? Let's just kill them all. Sounds harsh, I know, but that's what they would do to us. Burn us alive in that contraption." He waved a hand toward the framework, now smoldering. "Killing them is the simplest solution. You gents can look the other way. We'll surround them, and it'll just take a few minutes."

"What? That's why they hate us," I said. "Surely there's some other option."

"Such as what, sir?"

"Gaius Pliny and I defeated them," Tacitus said. "Doesn't that give us the right to claim them as slaves?"

"Well, sir," Laternus said, "I don't know if that's really how it goes."

"That's what Caesar did when he conquered Gaul. Defeated people are part of the loot that belongs to the winner. It's always been that way."

"With all respect, sir, you're not Caesar. That was a long time ago."

Tightening his grip on his sword but not raising it, Tacitus stood between the Gauls and the soldiers. "I will *not* let you slaughter these people until we know the legalities of it."

"You're outnumbered, sir," Laternus said.

"Are you going to kill a Roman citizen, too, in order to get at them? That's what you'll have to do."

"Well, no, sir..."

"Look, if I'm wrong, you can always kill them later. If you kill them now and it turns out that I'm right, what can you do? You can't bring them back to life. The blame will be on your head."

Laternus scratched his chin. "You're right about that, sir. But what are you going to do with this lot until we get it all sorted out?"

"I'll...I'll take them to my estate. It's just outside Lugdunum."

I knew Tacitus was acting in large part out of guilt about Charinus, but I shared his sympathy for the wretched Gauls, huddled outside the ruins of their huts, most of them crying. They had lost sons, brothers, and husbands and had no idea what was going to happen to them. The mothers clutched their children. The Trojans before the walls of their burning city could not have looked any more pathetic.

"How do you plan to move them, sir?" Laternus asked. "I just see three of you—"

"Perhaps you could let me have a few of your men," Tacitus said.

"Or perhaps not," Laternus said.

I drew out the imperial pass that Torquatus had left with me and shoved it under Laternus' nose. "Do you know what this is, Centurion?"

His eyes trailed over the page and he mumbled as he read. "Yes, sir."

"It means I can have whatever resources I need, and it applies to anyone who is traveling with me, or anyone I'm traveling with. Correct?"

"Yes, sir," he said slowly, already suspecting this was going to cost him something. "I guess that's what it says."

"You guess? Did you did read it? Can you read?"

"Yes, sir. Of course I can."

"And you recognize the seal at the bottom?"

"Yes, sir. It's the emperor's seal."

I pointed back and forth between Tacitus and myself. "We're traveling together. We need a few of your troops to accompany us to Tacitus' estate, as well as food, blankets, and any other supplies we may require. We'll send them back to your headquarters in Lugdunum when we're finished with them. Is that understood?"

He sighed. "Yes, sir."

"Then pick out the men who will accompany us so we can get started. Six should do, shouldn't they, Cornelius Tacitus?" Tacitus nodded.

I signaled to the woman who had bandaged Aurora's leg and explained to her, slowly and in the most basic terms, what was happening. I assured her they were not going to be killed or given to the soldiers or sold as slaves— at least not right away. She understood enough of what I said to communicate with the others. They perked up and began to pack what belongings they could salvage from the snow while Laternus pointed to six men from the rear ranks of his unit and drew them out.

"Men from the rear?" Tacitus said.

"You asked for six men," Laternus countered. "That thing doesn't say I have to give you my *best* six men."

XVI

I NEVER ANTICIPATED how glad I would be to see the hills of Rome rising in front of us. I regret every minute I have to spend in the place, but, looked at from this distance in the afternoon sun, it took on a sort of mystic glow. We had gotten to Tacitus' estate to find his brother recovering from his illness but still weak. As always, he thought he had seen Tacitus just yesterday. We rested there and gave Julia and the others of our party time to catch up with us. The estate is quite lovely, with vineyards that excel those on any of my estates.

Then I sent a messenger to inform my mother that I was going straight back to Rome, not to Comum, and asked her to return to the city as well. For all I knew she was already there. It had been two months since I left Comum, and she doesn't particularly like the place anymore because of recent events connected with it. We left Tacitus and Julia in Gaul with plans to see them when they returned to Rome in September.

"Joshua will be so big we won't recognize him," Aurora said.

Joshua was all she had talked about since we left the inn where we'd stayed overnight, our last stop on the road. I had to admit the topic was wearing on my nerves. "You can't miss him. He's the only child of that age in the house, you know."

She rolled her eyes at me. "Well, he won't recognize me. He'll think Naomi or one of the other women is his mother."

"Please remember that you're not his mother. I don't mean to be unkind, but you're not."

"I know, I know. I can't help it. I feel like I'm his mother."

She winced as the *raeda* in which she was riding hit a rough place in the road. The spot where the poisoned arrow had pierced her leg was still puffy and red. She was no longer suffering from a fever, but she was not yet able to ride a horse, and she limped when she walked. A doctor in Genua had told us what type of poison he suspected the Gauls had used. It would be a matter of just letting the substance work its way out of her body, he said.

The woman who sucked out most of the poison had saved Aurora's life—and suffered some ill effects herself when she swallowed some of the stuff. Today she was riding in the *raeda* beside Aurora. All of her family had been killed, so she did not want to remain in Gaul. Tacitus and I had offered to let her come to Rome as a member of my household. She spoke enough Latin to understand that she was a slave, a captive of war. What I did not know until we'd been on the road for several days was that she was the sister of the priestess.

We arrived at my house in time for dinner. I had sent a rider on ahead when we got to the Milvian Bridge, so the household was expecting us. What pleased me most was to see that my mother had not, as far as I could tell, gotten any sicker or weaker than she had been when I left.

<hr />

On the morning after our arrival my mother found me in the garden and handed me a single sheet of papyrus, rolled up and sealed, with my name written on the outside.

"This arrived while we were still at Comum. A man named Junianus brought it from Collis Niveosus. I thought it might be better to let you settle in before giving it to you."

"Did he say how everyone there was doing?"

"Quite well, I gather. Your visit seems to have been little short of earth-shattering, though."

"Let's just say we answered some questions that had been hanging over everyone's heads for a long time. That can make people uncomfortable until they get used to living with those answers."

"That's why some things are best left alone." She turned away from me and left the garden.

I sat on the bench in my favorite corner of the garden, next to the bust of my uncle. Before I opened the letter I thought about my mother's parting comment. It wasn't the first time she had expressed such an opinion. What my uncle had said on our first visit to Collis, ten years earlier, about big secrets in a small town had proved entirely true. Would the people there be better off if no one knew who had killed Junius? Or that the elder Roscius had raped his wife's twin sister? Or that Junius and the younger Roscius were half brothers because of that rape?

"There you are," Aurora said, emerging from the front part of the house with Joshua in her arms, where he seemed to have been from the moment we had arrived yesterday. He showed no signs of having forgotten who Aurora was. The boy had taken his first steps while we were away. Aurora seemed unwilling to let him grow up even that much. She sat down beside me, keeping him in her lap. "What's that?"

"Junianus brought it to Comum. My mother brought it back here with her."

"Are you going to open it?"

"Of course. I was just reflecting on all that had happened up there."

"Whatever the letter says is probably old news by now, but you might as well open it."

I broke the seal and unfolded the papyrus. Aurora leaned closer to me as I read:

Q. Roscius to G. Plinius Secundus, greetings.

My dear sir, I am writing to let you know that we found the body of L. Nonius Torquatus yesterday, in the woods about two miles south of town, once the worst of the snow had melted. From the looks of it, he froze to death. Granted, it is not unheard of for people to get lost in the woods and to die in that fashion around here, so you might ask if we can be certain it was Torquatus. Given the grotesque disfiguration of his face and the patch over his eye, it could not be anyone else. I know your penchant for inves-

tigating unusual deaths, so I will inform you that he was wearing
only one tunic. His body bore no wounds or injuries. He was
sitting with his back against a tree, so he had not fallen. It seems
clear to me that he left Collis on foot with the intention of letting
himself freeze to death. I would rule his death a suicide, a most
difficult form of suicide. Lucina insisted that he be given a decent
funeral. I complied with her request.

I and my household send you our greetings and best wishes.
Dictated to my daughter, Roscia, on the eighth day before the
Kalends of May, in the sixth year of Domitian Caesar. I affix my
seal here.

"That's not much of a surprise, is it?" Aurora said.

I shook my head. "When Torquatus gave me his imperial pass, I knew he wasn't planning to travel far. I thought he might choose a more traditional form of suicide, but he was a tormented man, one who hated himself profoundly."

"If everything he told Lucina and me was true—even if only a portion of it was true—he had suffered more than most men would ever be able to endure. I guess the method of death he chose was his way of punishing himself."

Joshua began to fret and try to get down. "I think he wants to walk," Aurora said. "He loves to walk." She got up and followed the boy as he tottered across the garden. The soreness in her leg made it difficult for her to keep up with him. She is greatly concerned about him falling into the *piscina* and drowning. I promised her I would put up a fence around it.

Before I joined them I reread the letter. I hoped the oblivion—the nothingness—of death had brought Torquatus the consolation he'd never been able to find in life. Confession or no confession, suicide or no suicide, I still wasn't convinced he had killed Junius. He knew that his life was, to all intents and purposes, over. Domitian would eventually find him and kill him, probably by some means more horrible than freezing to death. By confessing and then taking his life he could at least save Lucina.

But did she actually kill Junius? There were several other people who had equally strong motives for killing him and alibis that were just as weak. I felt like the young men in the first book of Plato's *Republic* who have to admit that, in spite of all their effort, they cannot find a satisfactory definition of Justice. They face an *aporia*, a state of uncertainty. Socrates spends the rest of the dialogue resolving that uncertainty and showing them there is a definition—an absolute value—of Justice.

Perhaps I've been deceiving myself by thinking I'm enough of a Socrates to find justice in every situation that confronts me.

GLOSSARY OF TERMS

Also see glossaries in previous books in this series.

amicitia "Friendship"; the semi-legal status accorded to an aristocrat's inner circle of friends. It created an obligation for men to assist one another.

auctoritas The concept of "authority" or prestige, very important to upper-class Romans.

Augusta Taurinorum The Roman name of Turin, Italy. The full name would be Colonia Julia Augusta Taurinorum, a colony named after the emperor Augustus and the people known as the Taurini.

Cynics A philosophical group that developed in the late fourth century B.C. They professed to take Socrates' teachings to their radical conclusions, despising social norms and wealth. They lived in the streets. Their greatest proponent, Diogenes, lived in a wine vat in a corner of the Agora in Athens. He was known as "Socrates gone mad." The Cynics showed their disdain for social niceties by copulating in temples or performing bathroom functions in public. During the 1960s hippies were often compared to them.

distances and speed of travel The Romans did not have saddles or stirrups, so horseback riding wasn't easy. Cavalrymen, with armor, could make up to sixty miles a day on horseback, though. For people who weren't in such a hurry and were traveling lighter, forty miles would not be a difficult day's trip. In *Ep.* 2.17 Pliny says he could get from Rome to his villa at Laurentum, a distance of seventeen miles, in an afternoon with no extra effort. That works out to about forty miles in a day.

The journey that I imagine in this book would be a long one, taking a couple of months from start to finish. In the first century A.D., a trip from Rome to London would have taken at least a month. Until the invention of trains in the 1840s that trip would still have taken about a month. Trains created what we call a "paradigm shift," a complete, mind-boggling change in the way something is done. Travel in Europe did not become any easier or faster until the advent of trains.

It's all a matter of what you're accustomed to. Before jet travel, it took five days to cross the Atlantic on an ocean liner. By the 1950s a plane could cover it in half a day. Now it's only a few hours. The Roman traveler did have the advantage of not crossing international borders and being able to use one currency all along the way. It has taken Europe only a couple of millennia to get anywhere near that situation again.

duovir Towns across the Roman Empire were governed in various ways. Many in the west had a shared mayor's office, held by two men, the *duoviri.*

fritillus Cf. "Venus throw," below.

Gallia Lugdunensis By Pliny's day the Romans had divided Gaul into several small provinces. Gallia Lugdunensis was the north-central part of the territory. Its capital city was Lugdunum (Lyon, France).

Gaul The Romans envisioned Italy as beginning where the peninsula joined the mainland of Europe, roughly at the Po River. Between the river and the Alps was Cisalpine Gaul. The Gaul that was divided into three parts, according to Julius Caesar, was Transalpine Gaul, modern France.

Directional and geographical names in the ancient world were highly ethnocentric. The Romans looked at the world as having Rome at the center. Mile markers on major highways noted the distance from Rome. For the Greeks, Delphi was the *omphalos* ("navel") of the world. "North" and "South" weren't as important as the direction in which rivers flowed. A Roman province could be "Upper" or "Lower" depending on which part of a river passed through it, and the Upper part would appear on our maps as south of the Lower part, just as Upper Egypt is in the south because the Nile flows from south to north.

Genua The Roman name for Genoa.

hecatomb A sacrifice of one hundred oxen or cattle at one time. That's a very expensive proposition, of course, so the term is sometimes used of any large number of animals being sacrificed, not necessarily a hundred.

hipposandal A kind of metal cleat that could be strapped onto a horse's hoof to improve traction. The Romans did sometimes use horseshoes.

hypocaust Romans heated buildings by raising the floors on piles of tiles and circulating warm air through the resulting channels. Ducts were extended into the walls. Such systems were normally used in public buildings, such as baths or inns, and occasionally in the private homes of wealthy individuals. They required a furnace, a fuel supply, and servants to tend the furnace. All of those constituted a huge expense and did heavy environmental damage.

latrina Roman toilets, whether in a house or in a public facility, were unisex. Since men and women both wore long, loose garments, it was possible to sit down, cover oneself, and do whatever was necessary, while chatting with one's neighbor, who could be of the same or the other gender. Poets, musicians, sausage sellers, and other vendors would be strolling around the venue. As you entered, you would pick up a stick with a sponge on the end from a bowl. Your seat would have an opening in the front, where you would insert the stick and use the sponge to clean up. You would then rinse the sponge in a channel of water running in the floor in front of your seat. As you exited, you would return the stick and sponge to the bowl, to be "disinfected" by water and vinegar and to be used by the next person.

latrunculus A board game, a mixture of chess and Othello. The objective was to surround the opponent's primary piece, the *dux* (leader). *Latrunculus* boards are scratched into the steps of public buildings in the Forum, so people could pass the time while waiting on court cases or other public business.

libertus/a Word for a freed slave, masculine or feminine.

Lugdunum The Roman name of Lyon.

Massilia The Roman name of Marseille, originally a Greek town.

Mediolanum The Roman name of Milan.

mounting stone Since the Romans did not have saddles or stirrups, they got on their horses by standing on stones placed wherever they were likely to be mounting or by having another person help them. Plutarch (*G. Gracchus* 7) says that Gaius Gracchus (120s B.C.), as part of his road-building program, placed stones "at smaller intervals from one another on both sides of the road, in order that riders might be able to mount their horses from them and have no need of assistance."

Nemausus Modern Nîmes, in southern France.

Padus River Latin name for the Po, the large river that flows from west to east across northern Italy. The Romans sometimes referred to the part of what we call Italy between the Po and the Alps as Transpadane Gaul ("Gaul across the Po").

raeda A four-wheeled wagon. It could be enclosed, with a place in front for a driver, or it could have open sides, with curtains or perhaps with panels that could be closed in bad weather.

Rhodanus Latin name for the Rhône River.

snowshoes Footwear for getting around in the snow goes back at least four thousand years. Wooden sandals of the type described in this book have been found in wintry areas of northern Europe.

strigl Curved metal scraper used in Greco-Roman baths.

Tironian notation A system of shorthand devised by Cicero's scribe, Tiro. It consisted of several thousand symbols but enabled a scribe who had mastered it to write almost as fast as someone could dictate.

tonsor A barber. Roman men were clean-shaven from about 200 B.C. until Hadrian became emperor in A.D. 117. He wore a beard, perhaps to conceal a skin rash, so beards were the fashion until Constantine's time, in the early fourth century. Most upper-class men of Pliny's day had a servant who specialized in shaving others in the household. Lower-class men went to public barbers, who plied their trade on street corners. They had razors very similar to our old-fashioned straight razors, as well as ones that looked like brass knuckles with a blade attached. The iron or bronze blades dulled quickly.

Venus throw The Romans gambled with four rectangular dice, called *tali,* usually made from an animal's knuckle bones. The player could throw the dice from his hand or from a small box, called a *fritillus.* The dice were numbered I, III, IV, and VI. The Venus throw was the highest roll. Each *talus* landed on a different side, creating a score of 14. The lowest throw was the Vulture (all ones), also called the Dog throw.

ABOUT THE AUTHOR

Albert Bell is a college history professor, novelist, and weekend gardener who lives in Michigan. He and his wife have four adult children and two grandsons. In addition to his Roman mysteries, Bell has written contemporary mysteries, middle-grade novels, and nonfiction. His books have won several awards. Visit him at https://albertbell.wixsite.com/writer and www.pliny-mysteries.com

More Traditional Mysteries from Perseverance Press
For the New Golden Age

K.K. Beck
WORKPLACE SERIES
Tipping the Valet
ISBN 978-1-56474-563-7

Albert A. Bell, Jr.
PLINY THE YOUNGER SERIES
Death in the Ashes
ISBN 978-1-56474-532-3

The Eyes of Aurora
ISBN 978-1-56474-549-1

Fortune's Fool
ISBN 978-1-56474-587-3

The Gods Help Those
ISBN 978-1-56474-608-5

Hiding from the Past
ISBN 978-1-56474-610-8

Taffy Cannon
ROXANNE PRESCOTT SERIES
Guns and Roses
Agatha and Macavity awards nominee, Best Novel
ISBN 978-1-880284-34-6

Blood Matters
ISBN 978-1-880284-86-5

Open Season on Lawyers
ISBN 978-1-880284-51-3

Paradise Lost
ISBN 978-1-880284-80-3

Laura Crum
GAIL MCCARTHY SERIES
Moonblind
ISBN 978-1-880284-90-2

Chasing Cans
ISBN 978-1-880284-94-0

Going, Gone
ISBN 978-1-880284-98-8

Barnstorming
ISBN 978-1-56474-508-8

Jeanne M. Dams
HILDA JOHANSSON SERIES
Crimson Snow
ISBN 978-1-880284-79-7

Indigo Christmas
ISBN 978-1-880284-95-7

Murder in Burnt Orange
ISBN 978-1-56474-503-3

Janet Dawson
JERI HOWARD SERIES
Bit Player
Golden Nugget Award nominee
ISBN 978-1-56474-494-4

Cold Trail
ISBN 978-1-56474-555-2

Water Signs
ISBN 978-1-56474-586-6

The Devil Close Behind
ISBN 978-1-56474-606-1

What You Wish For
ISBN 978-1-56474-518-7

TRAIN SERIES
Death Rides the Zephyr
ISBN 978-1-56474-530-9

Death Deals a Hand
ISBN 978-1-56474-569-9

The Ghost in Roomette Four
ISBN 978-1-56474-598-9

Death above the Line (forthcoming)
ISBN 978-1-56474-618-4

Kathy Lynn Emerson
LADY APPLETON SERIES
Face Down Below the Banqueting House
ISBN 978-1-880284-71-1

Face Down Beside St. Anne's Well
ISBN 978-1-880284-82-7

Face Down O'er the Border
ISBN 978-1-880284-91-9

Margaret Grace
MINIATURE SERIES
Mix-up in Miniature
ISBN 978-1-56474-510-1

Madness in Miniature
ISBN 978-1-56474-543-9

Manhattan in Miniature
ISBN 978-1-56474-562-0

Matrimony in Miniature
ISBN 978-1-56474-575-0

Tony Hays
Shakespeare No More
ISBN 978-1-56474-566-8

Wendy Hornsby
MAGGIE MACGOWEN SERIES
In the Guise of Mercy
ISBN 978-1-56474-482-1
The Paramour's Daughter
ISBN 978-1-56474-496-8
The Hanging
ISBN 978-1-56474-526-2
The Color of Light
ISBN 978-1-56474-542-2
Disturbing the Dark
ISBN 978-1-56474-576-7
Number 7, Rue Jacob
ISBN 978-1-56474-599-6
A Bouquet of Rue
ISBN 978-1-56474-607-8

Janet LaPierre
PORT SILVA SERIES
Baby Mine
ISBN 978-1-880284-32-2
Keepers
Shamus Award nominee, Best Paperback Original
ISBN 978-1-880284-44-5
Death Duties
ISBN 978-1-880284-74-2
Family Business
ISBN 978-1-880284-85-8
Run a Crooked Mile
ISBN 978-1-880284-88-9

Lev Raphael
NICK HOFFMAN SERIES
Tropic of Murder
ISBN 978-1-880284-68-1
Hot Rocks
ISBN 978-1-880284-83-4
State University of Murder
ISBN 978-1-56474-609-2
Department of Death (forthcoming)
ISBN 978-1-56474-619-1

Lora Roberts
BRIDGET MONTROSE SERIES
Another Fine Mess
ISBN 978-1-880284-54-4

SHERLOCK HOLMES SERIES
The Affair of the Incognito Tenant
ISBN 978-1-880284-67-4

Rebecca Rothenberg
BOTANICAL SERIES
The Tumbleweed Murders
(completed by Taffy Cannon)
ISBN 978-1-880284-43-8

Sheila Simonson
LATOUCHE COUNTY SERIES
Buffalo Bill's Defunct
WILLA Award, Best Softcover Fiction
ISBN 978-1-880284-96-4
An Old Chaos
ISBN 978-1-880284-99-5
Beyond Confusion
ISBN 978-1-56474-519-4
Call Down the Hawk
ISBN 978-1-56474-597-2

Lea Wait
SHADOWS ANTIQUES SERIES
Shadows of a Down East Summer
ISBN 978-1-56474-497-5
Shadows on a Cape Cod Wedding
ISBN 1-978-56474-531-6
Shadows on a Maine Christmas
ISBN 978-1-56474-531-6
Shadows on a Morning in Maine
ISBN 978-1-56474-577-4

Eric Wright
JOE BARLEY SERIES
The Kidnapping of Rosie Dawn
Barry Award, Best Paperback Original. Edgar, Ellis, and Anthony awards nominee
ISBN 978-1-880284-40-7

Nancy Means Wright
MARY WOLLSTONECRAFT SERIES
Midnight Fires
ISBN 978-1-56474-488-3
The Nightmare
ISBN 978-1-56474-509-5

REFERENCE/MYSTERY WRITING

Kathy Lynn Emerson
How To Write Killer Historical Mysteries: The Art and Adventure of Sleuthing Through the Past
Agatha Award, Best Nonfiction. Anthony and Macavity awards nominee
ISBN 978-1-880284-92-6

Carolyn Wheat
How To Write Killer Fiction: The Funhouse of Mystery & the Roller Coaster of Suspense
ISBN 978-1-880284-62-9

**Available from your local bookstore
or from Perseverance Press/John Daniel & Company
(800) 662–8351 or www.danielpublishing.com/perseverance**